VINCENT CHRISTOPHER

MOUNT HIDEAWAY
Mysteries

BREAKING AND ENTERING

FREILING

PUBLISHING

Published by Freiling Publishing, a division of Freiling Agency, LLC.

P.O. Box 1264,
Warrenton, VA 20188

www.FreilingPublishing.com

ISBN 978-1-950948-54-3

Printed in the United States of America

TABLE OF CONTENTS

---— CHAPTER 1 ——

A QUIET ENTRANCE

Bethany

"Remember. First, nobody gets hurt. Second, nobody gets caught!"

The words were probably unnecessary, but Bethany Shanholtz whispered them all the same. Her crew nodded, signaling they'd heard. The four teenagers were all crouched in the bushes outside the cast-iron gate that led to the back-garden entrance to the old limestone house.

There had been a thunderstorm earlier that evening, like most August nights in the Shenandoah Valley. The ground was damp, and the air smelled steamy. Bethany studied the ground they needed to traverse. They wouldn't leave any footprints as long as they stayed on grass or gravel, and out of the mud.

The house was supposed to be vacant, but Bethany wasn't one to take anything for granted. Her dad had taught her that you should always treat a gun as if it were loaded, even if you thought it was empty.

What was it he'd said? "Empty guns can be deadly."

Empty gun. Empty house. The concept still applied. Use caution. Keep your crew safe.

Her crew.

She sized up each member of the team as they took a final check before entry.

Amy Bradford hovered at Bethany's left shoulder. Calm, cool, and collected, she was ready for the job, probably more so than Bethany herself. Bethany hid a smile. She knew she could always count on Amy. Scary-smart and fiercely loyal, she made for a perfect partner in crime.

Bethany took a deep breath and tried to mirror her friend.

Right. She had this.

Bethany supposed Amy's calm had something to do with how she was the oldest of the group. Not that she looked it. Amy Bradford's delicate features and small frame gave her a childlike look, which, among other things, tended to make people underestimate her. That was something Bethany had learned not to do… ever. All the same, Bethany always felt better having Amy around.

Rose though…

Her gaze shifted to the dark-haired girl who hung back behind the rest of the group. Restless and impatient, she wasn't good at waiting. Much as she hated to admit it, Bethany knew Rose could be a bit of a wildcard.

I'm probably not being fair. Rose was just…Rose. With different skills and talents than the rest. God made each of them unique, a fact Bethany had to remind herself of often. Looking at the world differently didn't make Rose any more right or wrong in her approach. She was just…Rose.

Right now, Rose was hovering on the balls of her feet, ready for action but just as likely to head home than to carry out the mission. Rose was tough, athletic, and was really brilliant with computers and electronics. She also had a strong attention to detail, a quality that Bethany appreciated because she knew it wasn't one of her strengths. Of course, Rose's tendency to get lost in the details slowed them down sometimes, but sometimes that too could be beneficial. Bethany didn't like getting slowed down, but she knew it was important to have all the bases covered. Rose picked up what Bethany was just as likely to miss.

Besides, Rose and Jamie were like family.

Jamie.

This was no time for distractions. Bethany was supposed to have her mind on the house. She was supposed to be counting, waiting out the five minutes she'd set for them to make sure the house was empty before they proceeded.

Definitely not the time to be mooning about over some boy.

Still…

Bethany's eyes turned to Rose's younger brother Jamie, who was the same age as herself. Strong. Courageous. What wasn't to like? That he was willing to get mixed up in a situation like this said a lot for his character. There was no way he was going to let his sister or his…well…he wasn't about to let his sister get in over her head.

He stood to her right, close enough that she could feel the warmth of him there without looking. The very fact he was there left her feeling safe. Stronger, as though his own strength somehow lent itself to her. He reached out, giving her hand a squeeze, letting her know he was there, that he had her back.

And he did. With his mechanical aptitude, he could build or fix or disarm just about anything. They'd need that tonight.

He was also charming and likable… really likable. If they were caught, she was counting on him to talk their way out of this. Seriously, that blonde hair, blue eyes just screamed, 'I am trustworthy.'

Distracting.

Bethany bit back a moan. She was going to get them all killed if she didn't shape up.

Okay, stop! No more distractions. I've got this.

Bethany collected herself and refocused on the job at hand. Where was she? Oh yes. The countdown.

Five minutes had come and gone. The house lay still and dark, as though waiting for them.

"Rose and Jamie, how does the perimeter look?" Bethany whispered.

Jamie craned his neck to see clearly around the tree they'd bunched behind to the road just beyond the hedge. "All clear. Nobody in sight."

"From the maps we made earlier, I'm sure we've avoided the cameras," Rose added, and Bethany nodded.

"If we hadn't, they'd be on us by now. Anything else?"

Rose shook her head. "So far, I'm not detecting any other alarms or traps." Rose waved her iPad, where she had a map of the property laid out in excruciating detail.

Bethany straightened and reminded herself to breathe.

Right. This was it—the moment of truth.

"Let's do this!"

CHAPTER 2

WELL BEGUN IS HALF DONE

Rose

The foursome slipped into the house one at a time. Bethany went in first. Bethany always went in first. She had her tactical flashlight set at a low level... just enough to see, but not bright enough to attract any unnecessary attention.

The black tactical flashlight was one of Bethany's most treasured possessions. Rose knew it had been one of the last gifts her dad ever gave her. She loved everything about it. She'd practically waxed rhapsodic about how the precision roughened grip of the military-grade titanium felt solid in her hand. Rose suspected the flashlight somehow boosted her confidence whenever she held it. Maybe it did. It was small enough to be concealed and carried easily, but very powerful in more ways than one. A good flashlight that left her slightly envious. Her own flashlight wasn't exactly special or even interesting, just an ordinary one she'd picked up at Lowe's.

Rose liked interesting devices. While mechanical things were more Jamie's world than hers, she still admired an object well-crafted and put to good use. Rose just liked her objects to do a little...more than most. If you could computerize a flashlight somehow, she'd be there.

On the other hand, would it be half as useful?

In addition to being a light source, a flashlight could double as a martial arts weapon. It was helpful in blocking an attack, and if you landed a solid punch with Bethany's prized little toy in your clenched fist, the other guy was going down hard! Besides, the light had several settings, including the ability to flash out "S.O.S." in Morse Code bright enough for a passing airplane to see.

As usual, Bethany had preset the light so that its current setting, "Low Glow," would be immediately followed by "Strobe Mode." One click of the button and the chip-activated LED would transform the light from a sleepy little moonbeam to a blinding disco blaze that could disable an opponent just long enough for Bethany to escape…or attack.

Okay, Bethany's flashlight was cool. No question. Forget the circuits.

Not that they'd be using any of those settings tonight or fighting off any attacks.

Hopefully.

Rose shuddered. Subterfuge really wasn't her thing.

Bethany gave the signal. Just like that, they were in motion, sneakers whispering across the gravel.

Rose would have preferred bringing up the rear. She didn't like this, not any part of it. It was the challenge she liked, not the mission itself. Of course, when it came down to it, breaking and entering was just another puzzle, which made it intriguing.

They made it to the house and stopped. Jamie signaled that the way was still clear, Bethany giving a short nod as she studied the rocks lining the walk. In the end, it took but a moment to spot the fake, finding the extra house key hidden underneath.

Rose snorted. Pathetic. Hardly a challenge at all.

Amy gave her a look. Right. Noise.

Rose rolled her eyes and hoped the expression wasn't too noisy for her.

Not that they noticed. The door was open, the way clear. Rose swallowed hard. The room beyond was black, darker than it was outside, without the benefit of the moon or the streetlights to give them light to see.

The others didn't hesitate. Amy entered right behind Bethany. The two of them had practiced entering and clearing rooms for several years, and the procedure had become second nature for both of them. Bethany would go in, scan high and to the right, sweeping the room quickly with her light for potential problems. Amy followed a split-second later, sweeping in the opposite direction and just a little more thoroughly. Lots of teen girls watch videos from apps on their cell phones and practice hip hop moves.

This was Bethany and Amy's dance, and they rocked it.

Rose blinked back the hot feeling at the back of her eyes she'd been feeling more and more lately. Amy and Bethany had always been close. It was only lately Rose had been feeling left out. What did it matter, their dance, their perfect synchronicity? It had never caused jealousy before.

Bethany wasn't dating my brother before.

There. That was it. The thought she'd been trying to ignore for far too long.

God, what am I supposed to do with these feelings?

The prayer formed itself naturally, surprising her. Rose hadn't been strong on talking to God, but lately, He'd seemed like the only thing she had to cling to, especially as she faced her own future with college just around the corner.

Which is why I shouldn't be wasting my time playing these silly games.

All the same, Rose followed the others, entering next, knowing Jamie was waiting for her to move and she was holding things up. Besides, she had a job to do. As she came in, it was up to her to check the room thoroughly for unforeseen alarms or for clues and information that would aid in their mission. She paused to inspect a fascinating collection of antique armaments mounted on the wall just to the left as they entered. She recognized a "Pennsylvania Rifle", used by snipers and light infantry in the Revolutionary War. German gunsmiths in Pennsylvania had developed the technique of creating twisting grooves or "rifling" on the inside of the barrel, which increased the range and accuracy by spinning the snugly fitted projectile. She'd wanted to examine one up close for a long time, and this was a recent addition to this particular collection. Rose also eyed a display of two crossed cavalry sabers from the Civil War, one Union, and one Confederate. It looked to Rose like they were authentic, not replicas. Probably very valuable. *Nice.*

She would have liked to pause and look further, but Jamie was already pressing in behind her. At six foot two and a hundred and ninety pounds, he was the least stealthy of the group, but that didn't matter so much. Having him in the rear ensured that the female group members would never have to worry about anybody sneaking up on them from behind while they were on a mission. He was constantly scanning their six and would always be ready with an escape route if necessary.

The problem was, Jamie knew her too well. He could see Rose was spending a little too long admiring the weapons on the wall. His nudge was almost a shove, steering her back toward the center of the room and back into the mission. Rose shot him a perturbed glare and moved along.

The house they had entered was over two hundred years old. It had originally been an inn during the Revolutionary War but had long since been converted to a private residence. The blue-gray limestone structure had been renovated dozens of times over the years, but the dynasty of owners had always been careful to keep its original style intact. Honestly, she would have liked to look around more. While computers were her thing, history fascinated her. Rose liked knowing where things came from. There were stories that it was used as a hospital during the Civil War and that the ghosts of both Union and Confederate soldiers still roamed the halls.

They moved through a colonial-style formal dining room with an antique hickory dining table and chairs. As her eyes adjusted to the semi-darkness, Rose could just make out the floral print curtains on the windows, which gathered with ornate cast iron holders in the shape of a fleur-de-lis. It was her turn to nudge Bethany. With the drapes still drawn back, the dancing beams from the flashlights would be clearly visible from outside. Bethany nodded and directed her light away, the beam dancing momentarily across the wall as she clicked the setting to dim it further.

In that flash, Rose had caught sight of the paintings on the walls, which were from local Virginia artists. In her mind's eye, she recreated them, having seen them recently in an article in the local paper. The collection was quite famous. Rose mentally cataloged each in her mind.

The first had depicted a boy at a grand piano. For some reason, the gangly child had made her think of Jamie, earnestly trying, always striving to be the best. Best at sports. Best son. Best of them all. His wild ambition was what brought them here tonight. If Jamie weren't challenging himself, he wasn't happy.

The next painting. She saw it now dimly between the other two—a pair of children sitting at a snowy window, playing a simple counting game. Had Jamie and she ever shared such a moment of quiet comradery? She couldn't remember quiet playtimes where they hadn't been competing with one another. The picture left her feeling unsettled, unhappy. Clearly not the intent of the artist.

She drew toward the final painting. Moonlight played against the canvas where children ice skated in what looked like a game of crack the whip on a frozen cow pond with a yellow stone farmhouse in the background. Rose stepped closer to this particular painting, wondering how it felt to be the anchor, the child in the pink coat in the middle. Too often of late, she'd felt like the one careening across the ice, loose and unrestrained, out of control and whirling away in what was someone else's mad adventure.

She shot a glance back toward the others.

Had they even noticed she'd fallen back, away from the others?

I don't belong here.

Bethany approached the door at the other end of the room. A giant grandfather clock stood just to the right of the door, like some kind of palace guard. Its steady tick was like a blacksmith's hammer on an anvil, echoing throughout the otherwise silent room. How bad was it that Rose felt like the old grandfather was impatiently urging her to keep the mission moving, as though even this towering antique had only censure for her?

She shook off the feeling, hurrying to catch up with the rest. The room was clear. She was dawdling now, dragging her feet. She'd committed to seeing this through. It was time she remembered that.

There were three steps leading up to the door, probably the result of this section of the house being from a different renovation than the next. Bethany bent over to examine the door, which had an antique cast-iron lock plate. She silently rocked the glossy knob back and forth using the glove, which should have been on her hand to keep the knob clean.

"It's locked," she whispered.

Well, duh. It wouldn't exactly have been left unlocked. Not with what was on the other side.

"I've got my pick set!" Amy replied, eager as ever as she pulled an oiled leather pouch out of her kit. The picks were fairly new, but the pouch looked as old as this lock. Amy loved the smell of the old leather pouch and couldn't help but bring it to her nose as though to reassure herself with its scent. To Rose, she looked like Bilbo Baggins, the heroic Hobbit thief, while she went to work. Amy would probably agree if she knew. She often saw herself as a character from literature when she was in situations like this. She said the images boosted her courage and gave her inspiration.

Rose peered over Amy's shoulder curiously. The strategy for these antique locks was different than the modern locks she worked on most of the time. A tension wrench would be useless since there was no rotating cylinder of pins like in most modern residential locks. Defeating this puzzle would just be a matter of pushing tumblers around until it was released.

The tumblers inside the old lock were stiff, and Amy had to use an unusually large, L-shaped tool to get enough leverage to move them. She couldn't get a firm enough grip on the tool with her leather gloves, so she stuck the pick between her teeth, slipped her right glove off, and put it into its designated pocket in her kit.

"Hurry up!" Bethany urged. She knew she didn't need to rush Amy, but maybe she felt what Rose did, that the clock seemed to be getting impatient with all of them.

"I got it!" Amy whispered as she felt the last tumbler give way. She turned the doorknob quietly and pulled the door open just a crack. Then she stepped back, deferring to Bethany, who would, of course, resume her position at point.

She could offer to give me a turn once in a while…

Bethany stepped forward, then turned around to address the team. "Okay, Amy and I go in quiet. Rose and Jamie, stay here and watch our backs until we're sure the next room is clear."

Watch their backs. "I still think Jamie and I should check outside again," Rose cut in, thinking that once she was safely outside, she could just as easily slip home without anyone noticing.

"No. We stick together. That way, there's less chance of getting caught."

Rose rolled her eyes. *Whatever.*

Bethany inched the door open slowly to keep it from creaking. She hated doing anything slowly. She mouthed words, speaking them half under her breath, which Rose wasn't sure she was supposed to hear. "Slow is smooth. Smooth is fast." No doubt one of her father's many mottos and sayings from his Special Forces experience.

Rose looked away, feeling more and more like a heel.

I wish I knew what was the matter with me. God, you have to help me with this. I don't want to be the person I'm becoming.

Finally! The door opened.

Bethany and Amy couldn't use their clearing procedure as effectively in the next room, as they were confronted with a short, narrow hallway. Bethany's expression said she didn't like being boxed in, but they didn't have a choice, so she moved ahead.

The hallway quickly opened up into a large library. Two of the walls showcased the vast collection with floor to ceiling walnut bookshelves. In the darkness, loomed ladders on wheels to help the reader reach the higher books. From her studies of the place, Rose knew the shelves had a number of arched alcoves with statuettes on pedestals. Each was a bust of a famous Virginia author... Willa Cather... Thomas Jefferson... Edgar Allan Poe...

The paintings in the library also connected to the history of the area, but these images seemed darker, not so much in their color palette as in their subject matter. There were depictions of battles from the Revolutionary and Civil wars, and one of Lee surrendering to Grant at Appomattox. There was also a large portrait of George Washington, whose original surveyor's office was in nearby Winchester and who may actually have stayed at this very home back in the 1700s when it was an inn.

Here the heavy drapes were pulled. Bethany snapped her light on a higher setting, casting a beam directly across from the entrance, illuminating their target. It was almost too easy. The pewter chalice sat right in the middle of a bookshelf. It was highlighted by a small spotlight in the ceiling that made it almost look like it was glowing. The shine of the chalice was almost hypnotic, and Rose found herself drawn immediately to it, trailing far behind the other girls who seemed likewise entranced.

It was Amy who remembered their mission and plans first. She turned and waved for Rose and Jamie to join them. Rose hastened her steps, almost running to join them, leaving Jamie alone to take one last look in the room behind them before he joined the others.

Heart beating wildly in her chest, Rose pushed past the others, seeing only the chalice, the end goal. Her doubts and desire to leave had fled at the sight of it. She stretched out her hand, needing to hold it. Wanting it more than she could remember wanting anything.

Bethany smacked her hand down.

"No, Rose! There could be an alarm!"

Rose jerked back, hand stinging, cheeks flushed. She shot a look at her brother, who only frowned at his sister's impatience. Rose could feel the frustration coming off in waves.

Amy's eyes lowered. Rose didn't need to see them to know her friend was disappointed in them. Amy's gentle soul rebelled against conflict, and she hated to see the others fighting.

Bethany seemed not to notice, her attention wholly on the chalice. She leaned in, letting the light play over the object's surface. "Jamie, check it out."

Rose backed away, and Jamie stepped up to the bookshelf. He turned his flashlight up one click brighter and spun the focus ring so that the beam of light narrowed from a broad flood to a tight spotlight. He carefully shone the light around the prize without touching anything. Nothing above but below…yep, there it was. Just like Bethany thought. A simple pressure switch that undoubtedly connected to an alarm.

Jamie pulled a multi-tool out of his kit and unfolded the scissors. He snipped the wire to deactivate the sensor, then he stepped back and bowed in a knightly fashion to Bethany. For just a second, her intensity softened, and there was a flash of a girlish giggle in her bright green eyes.

Rose sniffed. *Whatever.*

Bethany must have heard, for she stiffened slightly and turned hurriedly away. "See?" Her tone was a little bit smug as she reached forward to gently lifted the chalice from the shelf. Rose bit back a soft sigh as the chalice came into sharper focus. The pewter was a little tarnished, but there was an elegance about it that gave a hint to the fine workmanship which had created it. Rose drew in with the others to admire the prize in the light of their flashlights.

They were congratulating each other and just starting to move to their exit strategy when they heard the sound.

Three loud bangs behind them, so sharp they split the silence of the room. To Rose, each sounded like a shotgun blast.

CHAPTER 3

IF AT FIRST YOU DON'T SUCCEED

Amy

At the sound of the first bang, the room was flooded with light that was so bright all of the teens had to cover their eyes. Amy realized how vulnerable her team was, and her mind raced through any number of defensive options she and Bethany had planned for situations like this. She relived the room entry in her mind, wondering what had gone wrong. She quickly realized her mistake, and her heart sunk as she prepared for what was coming next.

Having immediately seen the chalice as they entered the room from the narrow hallway, the team had neglected their usual room-clearing procedure and rushed straight toward their goal. If they had only done what they had been supposed to, they would have noticed the lone figure who had been sitting silently in a darkened corner the whole time, almost as if he had anticipated their every move.

The three pops were actually three slow handclaps—sort of like the "slow golf clap" but with a much more sinister tone. The figure, seated in a brown leather chair, now rose and slowly buttoned the gray corduroy sport jacket with arm patches that covered his burgundy turtleneck. He was wearing World War I style aviator goggles, which made him look both menacing and, well, a little silly at the same time.

"Vell done, my leetle criminals!" His accent was an odd mashup of Boris and Natasha from the Bullwinkle cartoons and Gru from the Minions movies. He twiddled his fingers like a silent movie villain as he spoke. "You deed very vell, but chou forgot von thing." He said, waving his index finger at the frozen teenagers.

Amy's big green eyes, which were magnified even more by her thick glasses, HAD been wide open with terror and surprise. But now they abruptly narrowed as her expression melted into one of disappointment... and mild annoyance.

She groaned, knowing he wanted her to ask the question though she really didn't need to. Right now, she could make a list. "What did we do this time, dad?"

Dr. Martin Bradford pulled off his goggles. His attempt at a sinister grin turned into a warm smile as his demeanor transformed from that of an over-the-top Bond villain to a loving and compassionate father, who took tremendous joy in creating these educational experiences for his daughter and her friends.

"Well, honey," Dr. Bradford smiled almost apologetically as he dropped the villainous accent, "When you picked the lock, you took your glove off..." He waited a second for the hint to sink in. Once he saw the realization in his daughter's eyes, he continued gently. "Yeah, you left a fingerprint on the doorknob."

Beside her, Bethany sighed. Not so much for the mistake, but because Bethany knew Amy's dad was actually pretty awesome to go through this much trouble with all of them like this. That he kept calm, compassionate, and even loving when they messed up was not something every kid got to experience in their life. She knew Bethany envied her this and wished, not for the first time, that her best friend's father hadn't died the way he had.

In the meantime, Amy had other troubles. As easygoing as Amy was, she could be very hard on herself. She felt her shoulders slumping, deflating in a way that she knew made her appear smaller than ever. She closed her eyes a moment and prayed for calm, relying on the one Friend she knew she could count on to keep her from saying or doing something she might regret later. Not everyone in the group understood this, she knew. Lately, she'd been worrying about Rose, seeing the struggle in the other girl's eyes.

When Amy's eyes snapped open only a moment later, she was herself again, her expression smooth, though her tone had taken on an apologetic note. "I'm sorry, guys."

Bethany touched her shoulder sympathetically. She knew just how much Amy hated letting her friends down.

"Well, don't be too hard on yourself." Dr. Bradford addressed the rest of the group. "I deliberately put the chalice right across from the entrance to see if you'd let it distract you from doing a proper clearing of the room. I was sitting in that chair the whole time, and all four of you walked right past me."

"That one's totally on me, Doctor Bradford," said Bethany, her tone thoughtful. Amy could almost hear the wheels turning in her best friend's head. She was probably wondering the same thing she was. If he'd been sitting there the whole time, how did he know about the fingerprint?

"I commend you for taking responsibility Bethany, that's a mark of a good leader." He smiled warmly.

She accepted the encouragement with a nod, still working on the problem. Amy spotted a laptop on the floor next to the chair where Dr. Bradford had been sitting and hid a smile. Right. Webcam somewhere then...they'd all missed something tonight. She'd mention it to the others later. It was nice of him not to rub that particular failure in their faces. Too much negative feedback would only discourage. Maybe he, too, knew how hard Rose had been struggling lately.

Amy bit her lip. Maybe she'd try to talk to her later.

In the meantime, her father was still talking, and here she was, lost in thought.

"But other than that, you 'meddling kids' did a really great job. Like I keep saying in our forensic science class..." He put the goggles back on and resumed his accent, even more hokey than before. "Eev chou vant to catch a criminal, theen chou must THINK like a criminal! Muahahaha!"

The maniacal laugh was a little too much for Amy. It had been a long day, and like the rest of them, it was clear she was getting tired. "Okay, dad, we get it, and the goggles... seriously?" She adored her dad, but sometimes he could be SO EMBARASSING, especially in front of her friends. She shook her head, letting go of the worries and ever-circling thoughts that had been distracting her.

"Oh, Okay." Her father sheepishly removed the goggles and took the chalice from Bethany's hands. "Tell ya what, let's call it a night, and tomorrow afternoon in class, I'll show you how to lift the fingerprints off the doorknob using household glue."

The kids all nodded in agreement, and the promise of a new adventure lifted their spirits. They filed out the door with Amy following. She walked her friends out to the driveway, saying goodnight and urging them to drive safely. Rose lingered, her expression…wistful? Jamie was impatient, though, and in the end, Rose said nothing and got into her car, starting the engine with perhaps more force than necessary. The engine roared to life. If she took the turn out of the driveway a little faster than normal, then maybe that was par for the course.

Rose definitely had things on her mind.

Amy stayed where she was, long after the others had left, letting the quiet of the night in the Shenandoah Valley wrap around her. She tilted her head back to study the stars, thanking the Maker of them for the friends she had and the father who cared enough to give them such experiences. Peace washed over her, erasing the embarrassment of letting her friends down. Mostly. Well, as much as it was going to.

God might be perfect, but she certainly wasn't.

Laughing at herself, Amy returned to the library and threw herself down into the chair opposite where her father was deconstructing the 'crime scene,' pulling the fake pressure switch and wire from the bookshelves. "I can't believe I missed the glove thing! Ugh!"

He smiled as he coiled up the wire and tucked it with the switch into a drawer on his desk. "Don't beat yourself up, sweetheart. The whole point of these exercises, and of education in general, is to give you a safe environment to learn and explore so you'll be prepared for the world that awaits you. That's exactly what you're doing, and I treasure the chance to share these adventures with you and your friends."

"I know, dad." She considered this a moment and frowned. She wanted to say not everyone was enjoying the exercises as much as they used to, but she didn't know how to put her feelings about Rose into words. She wasn't sure she was reading things right and didn't want to speak out of turn. On the other hand, Rose was clearly chafing. She should have gone away to college this year, at the same time as Amy, but both had held back for different reasons. She wondered if Rose was regretting that now.

Well, whatever the case, Amy certainly wasn't. She treasured this extra year to study with Bethany, grateful that homeschooling allowed for this kind of freedom to pursue the things which would leave her better prepared for college when she did go.

"Where was the webcam?" she asked, knowing full well her father wouldn't tell her.

He only smiled as he bent to retrieve the laptop and return it to his desk. "Ve cannot have zou telling vall vour secruts," he replied with a merry glint in his eye.

Amy giggled and got up from the chair and stretched. "Whatever, Dad. I'm spent. I'm calling it a night."

Her father frowned at this pronouncement. "I can't tempt you to join me for some popcorn and reruns of the original Twilight Zone? I've got the one cued up with William Shatner and the airplane. It's our favorite." His tone was wheedling, the offer tempting.

If he hadn't been so wheedling, Amy might have agreed. "Not tonight, Dad."

He replied with a fake pout of disappointment. She both loved and hated when he did that. She smiled, wrapped her arms around him, and squeezed tight as he kissed the top of her head. "But thanks for the offer," she said softly.

They released each other, and Amy headed for the stairs. She paused with her hand on the newel post, looking back at him over her shoulder. "Love you, Daddy."

Maybe he was still "Dad" around her friends, but Amy knew it made her father happy that even though she had just turned nineteen and would soon be going off to college, at moments like this, he was still "Daddy." Deep down, she knew he always would be.

Amy's mom had died from a heart valve defect when Amy was twelve. Her father had built up enough tenure at his job to arrange for a flexible schedule so he could continue her homeschooling on his own, with the help of other local homeschool parents. The two of them had become pretty much inseparable, and while he'd been working with all his heart to prepare her to become a strong, independent adult, the thought of her moving off to college and possibly living somewhere else away from him was sometimes hard to even imagine.

And that's the truth of why I'm still here. It's not Bethany or even being ready to go. I'm just that much of a Daddy's girl, I guess.

Maybe that wasn't a bad thing to be after all.

"Love you too, baby," he called after her.

Baby. She might have been embarrassed by the pet name. Tonight, Amy only smiled and continued up the stairs to bed.

CHAPTER 4

THE BEST PART OF WAKING UP?

Bethany

Bethany Shanholtz woke up the next morning with a headache. She lay a long time staring at the ceiling, thinking she should have hydrated properly before bed. She should have done a lot of things before bed. Prayed, for example. Lately, her faith had been floundering a little when it came to conversation with the Lord. Like she wasn't altogether sure what He would think of her.

Rose last night. She'd seen it in her eyes, just how much it bugged her that Bethany was all gung-ho and take-charge. As though that had been her fault! Amy's dad had assigned her to lead the team. Being able to give orders was part of that. She couldn't become a federal agent someday if she faded into the background, especially when it came to taking an opportunity where it was given.

Or taken, a tiny voice reminded her.

Bethany cringed. She might have manipulated the conversation around a little bit to get what she wanted. She didn't like thinking back to the class the day the assignment was created and how she'd wheedled Dr. Bradford into giving her the lead.

Like you can make someone like Dr. Bradford do anything you want. He's an adult. He could have said no.

Somewhat mollified by this line of thinking, Bethany sat up and stretched, ignoring the niggling feeling she had that Dr. Bradford had known precisely what she was doing and was going to allow it for the sake of some lesson or another.

No. She was shrugging it off. Not going to go there. Rose could just get over her snit, and whatever Dr. Bradford thought she was going to learn...well, it was already learned, right? Things hadn't gone all that great in some regards, but they'd gotten through it.

Bethany wandered down the stairs of their farmhouse in her gym shorts and extra-long desert camouflage t-shirt. Not exactly dressed, given that this outfit was her current version of pajamas. The hall mirror gave her a glimpse of herself as she passed. Her long auburn hair was in serious bed-head mode, half-covering her face as she shuffled past like a creature in some old zombie horror movie.

"How did the crime club go last night?" her mom asked as she came into the kitchen.

Tina Shanholtz was frying bacon and sausage in the cast iron skillet. She knew Bethany had gotten in late last night and the smell of bacon was always the kindest way to get her oldest daughter out of bed in the morning. So far, it was working. Bethany's mouth had been watering since her eyes had opened.

In her mid-forties, Tina was a true Southern beauty. As it was late August, her deep tan from working in the orchard and farm was in full glow, making her blue eyes even brighter than usual. The few smile lines from working in the sun only accentuated her air of warmth and wisdom.

Bethany pulled her sports water bottle off the counter and trudged past her mom on the way to the sink, pausing for a moment to inhale the magnificent smell of the sizzling meat. She half-filled the bottle, drained it in one continuous guzzle, then refilled it completely, and plopped it on the kitchen table.

She then opened the refrigerator and pulled out a blue Gatorade. She spun the lid and drained half of it before setting it on the table beside her water. There. Hydrated. Her mom scowled at her choice of breakfast beverage.

"Gatorade? At this hour?"

Bethany groaned. "What? It's got electrolytes and carbohydrates and... things." She gave her mother what she hoped was a blue-tinted smile.

Tina raised an eyebrow. "For breakfast?"

"Would you like it better if I got an orange one instead?" Bethany snapped, not ready for one more confrontation so early in the day. After Rose's constant sniping last night, the last thing she needed was criticism first thing in the morning.

"Attitude, young lady," Tina cautioned.

Bethany stiffened, needing to count to ten before she trusted herself enough to speak.

"I'm sorry, mom. I apologize. But seriously, I'm doing both the Gatorade and the water to get rehydrated. I've got a splitting headache from dehydration, and I'm just trying to solve the problem so I can think again. I didn't mean to snap."

Her mother relaxed visibly, turning to flip the bacon over so it wouldn't burn. "So, what's up? Did the evil Doctor Bradford outwit you again? Muahahaha!" she teased.

Her impersonation of Martin Bradford was spot on. Not that Bethany would ever tell her that.

"No…" Bethany must not have been very convincing. Her mom's eyebrow went a little higher this time.

"Well… okay yeah… He totally beat us!" Once started, the frustrations just seemed to spill out before Bethany could stop them. "Rose slowed us down AGAIN, and Amy left a fingerprint. And to top it off, I rushed right past the bad guy without clearing the room."

"And Jamie?" There was a lilt in Tina's voice, a hint of a purr angling for the latest in what was not exactly America's Greatest Love Story.

"Jamie was fine," Bethany replied, striving to keep her tone nonchalant, as though his being there or not hadn't mattered in the least.

Tina grinned broadly. "'Fine,' was he?"

Bethany's lips twitched. Not that she was going to smile if it killed her. "I have utterly no idea what you're getting at," she responded primly, taking another gulp of her Gatorade and choking on it in her haste. She coughed wildly, glaring at her mom, letting her know that this too was all Tina Shanholtz's fault and that she wouldn't be hacking up a lung now if her mother hadn't been questioning her in that ridiculous, romantic tone. "Where's Joy?" she asked when she could breathe again.

"Your sister went down to the chicken coop to get some fresh eggs to make the pancakes. She should be back any minute now."

The back door opened, and Joy Shanholtz entered, carrying a wire basket with a large pile of brown and white eggs. Joy was a petite eight-year-old with light brown hair, big blue eyes, and the same high cheekbones and freckles as her older sister, though Bethany absolutely knew that after the summer they'd had being outside, her own freckles outnumbered those scattered across Joy's cheekbones.

The sisters shared the same skin as well, neither of them ever growing tan like their mom, taking after their fairer father. Joy had a fresh sunburn across her nose, showing a forgetfulness to using sunscreen, which Bethany had to learn through a painful lesson. Meaning Bethany no longer burned; she just freckled. Her mom said she looked "delightful," whatever that meant, as though almond-shaped green eyes and a bumper crop of freckles somehow made her more winsome.

What Bethany wanted was to be beautiful, not interesting. How was a girl supposed to compete with a classic dark-haired beauty like Elena with looks classified with words like 'endearing' or 'charming'?

Like her bed head was helping. Bethany sank into a chair at the table and buried her face in her hands, trying to smother a yawn. Oh yes, she was in top form today.

Joy, on the other hand, was proving herself to be accurately named as she carefully placed the basket on the counter, washed her hands in the sink, and started cracking the eggs into a bowl, all the while humming some tune she'd learned from Vacation Bible School over the summer.

"So, what's everybody's schedule today?" Tina asked as she brought the bacon and sausage to the table.

"It's Tuesday, so we've got co-op at the church in the afternoon," Joy replied as she mixed the batter with a wire whisk. She sounded eager and with good reason. With so many families taking vacations over the summer, this was their first true week where everyone would be back for classes. Their homeschool cooperative, or co-op, met twice a week in one of the Sunday School rooms at their church. Different parents took turns teaching classes and leading activities, especially subjects in which they had special knowledge and expertise. While Bethany knew deep down it was a great supplement to each child's home-based education—she loved the socialization of it as much as her sister did. The kids of her co-op were her best friends.

And Jamie? What was he?

Bethany frowned.

Both of the Shanholtz girls had been homeschooled their whole lives. Of course, Bethany and Joy loved having their mom as their primary teacher. Both were avid readers and used a combination of computer-assisted curricula, as well as the more traditional "books and workbooks" formats. Living on a farm and orchard gave them lots of opportunities to practice math, science, and other subjects in practical ways, and Tina was always finding opportunities to weave "life-lessons" into their chores.

Speaking of which…

"I'm staying after for Wushu class with Pastor Nehemiah, so Joy's gonna need a ride home. I want to get in some extra practice before the competition next month. Maybe she could take my chores?"

She held her breath on this. The girls weren't supposed to ditch jobs like this, their chores being as much a part of their curriculum as the books they read or problems they solved. But Bethany really needed the practice. Elena had come near to beating her last time out. Too near.

"No problem, I don't mind. I can even get a ride with Hannah," Joy said as she brought the first stack of pancakes over.

Their mom seemed to take a long time thinking this over. "It's all right, I suppose. For *today*," she said, emphasizing the last word. "And you need to take on some of your sister's duties tomorrow to make up for it. Deal?"

"Deal!" Bethany said quickly, with a thankful smile to her sister. Joy was a good kid. For that matter, her mom was pretty decent about it as well, even if she'd teased her about Jamie.

Joy sat down, and they all held hands. Today was Joy's turn to say grace.

"Heavenly Father, thank you for this day, for this food, and for each other. Help us to bring you honor and to be a blessing to those around us. In Jesus' Name, Amen."

Bethany bit back a smile. Joy had kept it short because she was hungry. Bethany envied her little sister. Life was so much easier at eight. So was faith, apparently. So, while the prayer might have been brief, it had been sincere.

Bethany, on the other hand, was a mess, inside and out. How many emotions had she wallowed through so far today? And it wasn't even eight o'clock in the morning.

She shoved her tangled hair back out of her face and settled in to eat despite the fact that she'd lost her appetite.

— CHAPTER 5 —

COUNTRY SONGS AND PICKUP TRUCKS

Jamie

Harlan Wood gave his wife Dana a goodbye hug. She handed him his lunch and he headed out the door. Jamie lingered long enough to finish his juice, still debating what to do.

Rose had been prickly ever since last night. The idea of driving into work with her wasn't really appealing right now. On the other hand, if he hurried, he could ride with his dad and talk to him about something which had been pressing on his mind for a while now.

Or he could just drive his own truck.

The problem was, they'd gotten in the habit of going their separate ways for a while now.

Harlan Wood had been highly successful as the owner-manager of Steven's Mill Shipping, so each of the kids had gotten a car as soon as they were old enough to pass the license exam. This was also practical since both of his teens were involved in a wide variety of sports and church activities along with their home-school studies and part-time jobs. Jamie imagined his mom and dad both had breathed a sigh of relief when Jamie and Rose had gotten their driver's licenses. His folks had had to have driven them around for thousands of miles over the years.

Jamie set his glass down and flew out the door calling a hasty goodbye to his mom, who had her arms full of laundry as she walked past on her way to the laundry room. He managed to give her a quick peck on the cheek, almost upsetting the precariously balanced load in her arms.

The door slammed shut behind him with a bang. Jamie winced. He hadn't meant to let it go like that. Still, if he didn't hurry, he'd be driving whether he wanted to or not.

It wasn't that he disliked his truck. On the contrary, he loved the beast. Sure, it wasn't as classy as Rose's vintage red Impala, nor did it have all the most recent bells and whistles like what some people drove, though it had a few. He supposed he might have done more, the way his sister had. The Impala had been priced above the amount their parents had set for her birthday car, but Rose, being Rose, had simply supplemented the cost with the money from her part-time job, which was where she was heading now.

And was where he was heading too if he didn't miss his ride.

"Dad! Wait up!"

Decision made, Jamie trotted across the yard, waving one hand that he hoped his father would see.

Harlan already had his own truck, a silver Ford F-350, started. Music blared through the open window playing that Country-Gospel station his father loved so much. It was playing some old song from the eighties that probably dated back to when his parents were dating or something.

His dad had seen him and was waiting, a smile on his face. Apparently, he didn't mind the company today. Not that he ever did, though lately, he'd seemed more worried about something. Distracted. Jamie didn't think Harlan had heard a word he'd said about last night's breaking and entering when he and Rose had talked about it at breakfast.

He climbed into the truck, amused when he heard his father singing along to the lyrics of whatever song was playing. Jamie had heard this one before, had even teased his father that this particular song might as well have been written about Harlan himself. In true country music fashion, the lyrics told a tale. In the first verse, a young farmhand meets a beautiful country girl and asks her father for her hand. The second verse describes them raising their family, with kids growing up strong and learning about Jesus. The last verse described the bittersweet goodbye of their children going off to college and then the joy of seeing them coming home to take over the family business. Between the verses, the chorus described how each season was a gift of God's grace. The song got to Harlan, as it often did. Jamie could see his father had taken advantage of the delay in picking up Jamie to close his eyes and bow his head the way he often did when this particular song came up. Praying.

Thankful for his life, Jamie supposed. Thankful for Rose and for *him*.

It was kind of humbling put that way, knowing your parent saw something good in you like that. It made a guy feel like he had something to live up to. Jamie was glad he'd left his own truck behind, feeling more than ever that this ride together into work had been the right move after all.

"Hey, Dad." Jamie tossed his backpack on the floor and buckled in. "Thought I'd ride with you today."

"You're always welcome, son."

Was that a hint of moisture in his Dad's eyes? Jamie pretended not to see, turning his attention out the window, seeing Rose leaving the house in a more orderly manner. She walked, head high, with an easy stride around to where her own car was parked. She waved as she crossed in front of them. "I'll be right behind you." She was dressed for working in the office of their Dad's transport company, her blouse crisp and professional. Jamie had been noticing more and more how girls seemed to put a lot of stock in looking nice.

He glanced down at his well-worn jeans and the work shirt he wore. Sure, it was clean now, but it wouldn't be by the time he finished his shift in the warehouse. Today was Tuesday, a homeschool co-op day. This meant they'd go straight over to the church from work.

Jamie swallowed hard. Lately, he'd had kind of a weird knot in his throat when he thought about classes over at the church.

The song ended as his father put the truck into gear. "It's nice to have you with. I was starting to think you didn't like riding with your old man anymore. Too grown-up for it."

Jamie chuckled. "Just seemed kind of silly for three people who live in the same house to be driving three cars to the same place for the day. Figured I could grab a ride with Rose for co-op and save the gas."

Harlan chuckled. "Thrifty. I like it."

An ad came on the radio. Harlan was still humming the refrain from the song he'd just been listening to as he backed the truck out onto the street.

Now that he was here, Jamie couldn't think how to start the conversation and talk about what had been preying on his mind. It used to be easier to talk about stuff. Now that he was seventeen, he found himself getting tongue-tied. Words tangled in his mind, half-formed into thoughts and wound around with emotion. They seemed impossible to express, especially when they had to do with... well...certain topics.

Bethany, for example.

"So how are things going in the shipping department, son? Anything I should know about?"

His father's voice broke so abruptly into Jamie's thoughts that it took him a moment to think about how to answer. He stared at his phone in his hands, as though he'd been flipping through texts while he struggled to mentally switch gears.

"Just that the traffic is getting heavier all the time," Jamie replied without looking up. "I think online orders have really boosted volume. We could really use some more help and at least two more forklifts. Mr. Darvishi says we just need to work harder. Sometimes I think he's picking on me."

He hadn't meant to say the last bit. It sounded childish. Whining. Jamie cringed, especially at the gentle, chiding tone from his father.

"Well, I told him not to give you any special treatment. You need to work your way up just like I did," Harlan said.

"Yes, sir." Jamie nodded, his fingers holding his phone so hard, it was a wonder the screen didn't shatter.

"Good observation about the capacity, though. If the deal goes through with the overseas investors, it'll give us a desperately needed shot in the arm. Then we can get caught up and take the old girl to a whole new level."

Jamie's head shot up. He hadn't expected the compliment. "Have you decided which group of investors you want to work with?" he asked, not because he was particularly interested, but because he was starting to see the way into what he actually wanted to talk about.

"I've narrowed it down to two companies. Omni Millennium and Omni Millennium."

Jamie chuckled. "So, what are they like, these investors?"

"Well, so far, we've only talked through lawyers by email. They're coming for the first plant visit next week." Harlan signaled for a turn, silent a moment as he navigated onto the busier state highway.

"They've got offices and locations all over the world. They seem to be solid people, and they've got a lot of resources that they could bring to the business and to the town. In addition to helping us expand our shipping company, I hear they're planning on making other investments all over the county. It could provide a lot of jobs and help us take the business into the next century."

"I like the town the way it is," Jamie replied. They were passing down the main street. He saw the ice cream shop, the clothing store his mother liked. Small businesses, not big chains. How would the model train shop survive if big-box competition came in and drove up things like rent? What about the bookstore? Or the place he used to buy candy as a kid? For a moment, he forgot his own troubles.

"I know, son, but change is inevitable. Hopefully, we can still keep all the things we love about the Valley and maybe make life even better."

Jamie nodded and went back to his phone. Without meaning to, he hit the icon, which took him to his photo album. Bethany's face filled the screen.

"Besides, who knows where you'll end up once you go away to business school. Have you made up your mind yet?"

College. Yes. That. Something else he needed to be worrying about.

"I'm still not sure, but I'm leaning toward Tech. They're strong in Business, Agriculture, and Engineering. I'm going to need a little of all of those for when I come back and take over your job." He shot his dad a grin.

Harlan chuckled. "Well, don't start painting your name on my door just yet. Last I heard you've got some work to do to get science back on track. I was kind of surprised when I heard I heard you didn't do so well on your last test."

No, he hadn't done well. Dr. Bradford had warned the kids that he'd test them on what they'd been going over. Jamie hadn't been listening or something because he'd read the wrong chapter completely. Jamie spent an hour making wild guesses, interspersed with prayer to the Almighty that He would see fit to work a miracle (He hadn't), and as a result, his grade had been less than stellar.

"I'm sorry, sir. I'll do better," Jamie mumbled, pushing the button to send his screen to black.

Harlan cleared his throat. "I suspect the problem had something to do with the ability to…concentrate?"

Jamie's eyes widened. "Sir?"

At this, his father burst out laughing. "Son, you're not the first boy to let a pretty face get in the way of what they were doing. I suspect Bethany Stanholtz might have something to do with the C- you brought home?"

Jamie felt the blood rush to his face. "Tell me it's not that obvious."

"Jamie, I hate to say this, but you've been mooning around since the semester began."

"I want to ask her out."

The word tumbled out of Jamie's mouth before he could stop them. He clamped his lips shut, horrified.

If he thought his face was burning before, it was an inferno now.

His father brought the truck to a halt. They'd pulled into the parking lot of the shipping company, but he made no move to turn off the engine or get out. Instead, he turned to face his son, his expression sympathetic. "I was right where you are now, not all that many years ago. Well, scratch that. It doesn't *seem* like all that long ago. I can promise you it gets easier, but at some point, you're going to have to take the first step. Have you given any thought where you'd like to go?"

It was all he'd been able to think about. "I haven't quite narrowed it down. I mean, a movie would be more like a…a date. But what if that seems too…"

Harlan nodded. "I can see where you're going with that—something more casual then. To test the waters might be better. When I asked your mother out on our first date, we went for ice cream."

"Ice cream." The weather had been chilly lately. Not exactly ice cream weather. At the same time, ice cream was a "friend" thing to do. Kind of. But doing it alone together would be sort of testing the waters. Seeing if there was mutual interest without committing to a full-on date.

"I can tell by that frown you're overthinking this. Worrying too much about it before you've even sat down to talk and see if this is a direction you want to go." Harlan glanced at the warehouse in front of them and frowned. "Kind of like I'm doing worrying about this big meeting with Omni."

"You're saying dating is like a business merger?"

"Well, there are elements in common. You know, your mother and I never exactly encouraged you or your sister to date when you were younger, the way some kids do. We'd hoped you'd instead focus on your studies until you were ready for college. But there's nothing wrong with enjoying the company of another person, especially one you like and respect. Bethany is a fine girl. Smart as a whip. Ambitious but tempered with compassion. But more important than any of those things is knowing she has a strong relationship with the Lord. Never contemplate a relationship with someone who doesn't know your God, son. It'll save you much heartache down the road."

Jamie thought about this a moment. "Does the same hold true for companies, Dad? What do these Omni folks believe?"

Harlan glanced at him, clearly startled. "Excellent question, Jamie. It'd be interesting to find out, wouldn't it?"

CHAPTER 6

THE MORE THINGS CHANGE, THE MORE THEY STAY THE SAME

Amy

One final twist of the screwdriver and the doorknob disconnected from the lock assembly. Amy scowled at it as it came off into her fully gloved hand. Her fault. The whole reason she was doing this was her fault.

Still mentally beating herself up for her slip last night, Amy tucked the doorknob into a bag with the word "EVIDENCE" written with a wide Sharpie in the biggest letters the bag would hold. She groaned and rolled her eyes as she looked at her dad's handwriting. Freckles, her beagle, looked up at her, head cocked to one side the way she did when she was trying to figure things out.

"Dad's trying to be cute again." She answered his unspoken question without thinking. To her, animals were perfectly capable of keeping up a conversation. Maybe not the same way humans did, but with a certain clarity all the same that made her wonder why other people didn't understand them the way she did.

She suspected she got this attitude from her father. From the time she was small, he'd encouraged her to be observant. Wasn't that the very cornerstone of communication with anyone, human or animal? To her, this was common sense.

Of course, her father lived and breathed the scientific method.

Martin Bradford's doctorate was in Forensic Science, but he also had advanced degrees in Chemistry and Microbiology. So, in some sense, he couldn't help but be logical, something which he tried hard to impart to his students. Amy had enjoyed the benefit of this logical mind since he'd started her first lessons barely out of babyhood.

The other kids? Well, they maybe weren't quite so quick to appreciate Dr. Bradford's unique approach to education. Rose seemed to chafe at his careful and meticulous experiments. Lately, Jamie had been distracted, his mind running more toward math and…other interests.

Bethany though. Bethany understood how Amy felt when a hypothesis fell into place. She seemed to delight in following the clues when it came to figuring things out. And though sometimes Bethany let her emotions run away with her, she had a keen sense of the logical. Making her the perfect best friend for Amy, and one of Dr. Bradford's most prized pupils.

Dr. Bradford loved teaching the kids at the co-op and was thankful that his supervisors allowed him to adjust his schedule to have Tuesday and Thursday afternoons free so he could work at the co-op.

At least for now.

In Steven's Mill, most of the adults were farmers, factory workers, or owners of the mom and pop businesses that filled the town. The few exceptions were folks, like her father, who worked at the Mount Hideaway facility, a secure government compound on a secluded mountain a few miles outside the town.

The official story was that Mount Hideaway was a satellite listening station, but none of the townsfolk believed that. They had developed a wide variety of rumors and conspiracy theories as alternate explanations. The more plausible ideas involved an underground bunker where the President and other top government leaders would shelter during an attack on Washington. This made some sense, as the town was just over an hour outside the DC Beltway. More imaginative theories involved secret spy training camps, scientific experiments, and of course—aliens.

Mount Hideaway employees never said exactly what they did, and a number of them, like her father, had skills and backgrounds that didn't seem to have anything to do with satellites. A number of employees were current or former military, especially from the Army and Air Force. Tina Shanholtz, who had degrees in Linguistics and Political Science, was known to have also worked there years ago but resigned a few months after her husband was killed in action to take over the orchard that her grandfather had started back in the 1800s.

The residents of Steven's Mill had long since learned not to ask about what really went on at the Mount Hideaway facility. If you asked a child, "What does your mom/dad do?" they would simply reply, "They work up on the mountain." and the subject would be dropped.

Mostly. Amy wondered. She knew Bethany did too. They hoped someday to do well enough in their chosen career paths that they could someday find out for themselves. Amy wanted to work there just to see how the puzzle unraveled and to find out the secrets they weren't being told. Bethany, though, had deeper ambitions. She wanted to succeed, to be someone who could change the world. Her pet theory was that whatever happened at Mount Hideaway, it had to be something pretty amazing if her mother had worked there. Knowing Dr. Bradford still was employed on the mountain had made him something of an awe-inspiring figure at times to Bethany.

To Amy, he was just her dad. And right now, he seemed pretty worried about something. Dr. Bradford wasn't the type to frown about things, but before last night, she hadn't seen him smile in ages. Even this morning, as they packed up for the co-op, he seemed distracted and out of sorts. The evidence bag was evidence in its own right, of her father trying too hard to let his daughter know everything was just fine.

And because his worry stemmed from Mount Hideaway, Amy knew she wasn't even allowed to ask if there was something she could do to help.

In silence, Amy and her father loaded the supplies for today's co-op class into the back of their big black Suburban. Martin's work for the government was important, and he took it very seriously. But, clearly having a flair for the dramatic, he enjoyed the idea that some folks thought of him as a mad scientist, working on freakish experiments in his secret mountain-top laboratory. He had deliberately chosen the Suburban because it looked like those cars that "scary government people" in the movies drive around in, and he had specifically requested the tinted windows option to enhance that image.

"Want me to drive, Dad?"

She asked the question hopefully, thinking maybe she could do this much to erase the worried lines on his forehead. She found herself actually wanting him to play the power-crazed mad scientist bent on world domination, if only to restore the balance to something resembling normalcy.

His answer was no more than a single word, clipped short. "Sure."

No. Not himself at all.

God, you're going to have to help him through this one. I can't when I don't even know what's going on.

Feeling better once she'd prayed and put the matter into the hands of Someone who could actually do something about whatever was going on, Amy shrugged and climbed up into the driver's seat.

Fortunately, the huge vehicle had one of those power-adjustable driver seats with memory. Amy was just five foot two, and her dad was over six feet tall. When she pressed the "Driver #2" button, she got a substantial ride forward and upward, so she could see over the dashboard, and her feet could reach the pedals.

Even if she was a tiny girl (and sitting up here, she certainly felt like one), she operated the big truck with confidence. She had grown up helping the Shanholtz girls and other friends with chores like bailing hay and driving tractors that towed the apple wagons. She and her friends had all been driving stick-shift vehicles through fields and dirt roads long before they were old enough to get a driver's license. Handling this SUV with power brakes and steering was not a challenge for her.

Traffic, as it turned out, was.

Halfway to the church, the car in front of her stopped suddenly. From her vantage point, she could see ahead to the intersection where the light was green, but nothing was moving.

"Dad?"

Her eyes were on the reason for their sudden stop. A group of protesters, waving signs, had stepped off the curb, blocking traffic. Police stood by, arms crossed. Stepping back to allow the demonstration.

Her father roused out of his stupor enough to sit up and look. "Now that's interesting."

"What do I do?"

The protesters seemed to be increasing in numbers. Surrounding the car. Chanting something. Signs reading "Say No to Change" bobbed over the sea of heads.

The More Things Change, the More They Stay the Same

"Take a deep breath, Amy. Tell me what you see."

That's right. Logic. Scientific method.

Amy kept her hands on the wheel, grip tight enough to turn her knuckles white. She wasn't supposed to be looking at that, though. She took in her surroundings. The stoplight, which had changed to red, uselessly as no one was moving in the intersection at all. The elderly woman driving the blue car in the lane next to them looked like she was about to cry. The car in front had a child's face pressed up against the glass, a frantic mother trying to get her offspring back where he belonged, likely to buckle him in again.

No. Not the other drivers. She needed to look outward. The crowd. What were they protesting?

"They're upset about a fast-food restaurant?" she asked, spotting the construction site to their left. Workers had left off in their work, the framework of the building behind them seeming frail and precarious. The men stood in a line. Some of them had their arms crossed. Others held tools loosely in their hands. A crowbar. A large mallet.

Amy swallowed hard.

"Look for the leaders."

At the construction site, it was easy to pick out the foreman. He stood to the side, snapping orders, pointing, and gesturing, trying to marshal his forces into what was fast looking like a defensive line. The police had their own leader, talking into his radio, face lined and tense. He was talking to someone else. One of the protesters. A woman with black hair. Glasses. She was shouting back. The cop, unperturbed by whatever noise she made, appeared to be holding his ground.

Amy read the signs. Looked between the protesters and the cops and the construction workers.

"They have to let us through, honey."

Her father's calm reassurance helped Amy to relax only marginally. Her hands tightened on the wheel despite her resolve. She felt sweat trickle down the back of her neck.

The light changed. Sure enough, the crowd parted. Not very far, though. Close enough to touch the vehicles as they drove through the intersection. Amy set her jaw and drove. Ignored both sides. No, all three sides now.

Behind them, the line closed up again. Taking over the street.

"Why don't they want things to change, Dad?" she asked softly as they drove away, the protest fading in the rearview. "It's just a fast-food restaurant."

"It's what it represents. Look...don't say anything about this to the others. If you can just take things in, I'd appreciate it. I'll be in as soon as I make a call."

The worried lines were back on Dr. Bradford's forehead, worse than ever.

—— CHAPTER 7 ——

WHO HAS CONTROL?

Amy

Steven's Mill Community Fellowship was a non-denominational church that had begun as a small home Bible Study back in the late sixties and had grown into a church of several hundred members. When they moved into their current building a few years back, they designated a suite of Sunday School classrooms as the "Homeschool Resource Center." It provided a central location for the dozen or so homeschooling families to share resources during the week and was one of Amy's favorite places to be.

Reverend Nehemiah McDaniel, or "Pastor Hemi," as most folks called him, was shooting basketball with some of the middle schoolers at the hoop in the corner of the church parking lot. When he saw Amy and Martin unloading the SUV, he bowed out of the game and went over to help them.

Amy watched him out of the corner of her eye, glad for the help. He was a tall, athletic African American man with graying hair and the physique of a body-builder. Pastor Hemi was another one of those people who had formerly worked "up on the Mountain." But several years back, he had taken his retirement package from the government, gotten his Divinity degree, and become the Senior Pastor of the congregation.

She, for one, was glad he had.

Secretly, she'd been hoping she could talk to Pastor Hemi about what they'd experienced on the drive-in. Pastor Hemi had helped her sort out other problems in her life, and she greatly respected his opinion. Besides, maybe he could do something to restore her father's peace of mind as well.

Pastor Hemi seemed to know something was wrong, for he exchanged quick hugs with the Bradford's and grabbed the large aquarium, leaving Dr. Bradford and Amy each with a cardboard box.

"What do y'all have in store for the kids today? Nothing explosive, I hope." He laughed.

"Oh, that only happened once, and we cleaned up the mess." Dr. Bradford chuckled, some of the worry leaving his eyes. "No, today we're going to lift a fingerprint using steam from household glue."

"Ah, the old cyanoacrylate fuming technique." The Reverend smiled and nodded.

For a fraction of a second, the scientist and the clergyman exchanged direct eye contact with a shared expression that jumped from recognition to caution, to a warm smile. The progression flashed so quickly that you'd need to have been looking right at their eyes to notice it.

Of course, Amy happened to be watching, just as she'd been trained to do, and she saw the exchange clearly. But she had lived in Steven's Mill her whole life, and it didn't surprise her a bit that the local minister, who taught Kung Fu classes and had biceps like an NFL quarterback, also knew advanced criminal investigation techniques. It was just another day in her little town, just outside the mysterious government facility where her dad worked.

"If you two don't mind going on ahead, I'll be inside in just a minute. I need to make a quick call."

Amy nodded and picked up her box from the tailgate, leaving her father leaning against the SUV; his phone already pressed against his ear. She walked silently next to Pastor Hemi, still trying to sort out what she'd driven through and honestly still feeling a little shaken from the experience.

"How about a detour by the kitchen for a cup of tea. You look like you could use a cup," Pastor Hemi said softly, and Amy nodded in relief. That he knew what she needed without her having to say a word just underscored what a great Pastor he was.

They dropped their burdens off in the classroom. Even with the traffic complication, they were still early enough that no one else from her group was there.

For once, Amy was glad Bethany wasn't there yet. She would have noticed immediately that something was off and would have demanded to know every last detail.

In the kitchen, Pastor Hemi grabbed a mug for each of them and motioned Amy over to the counter, where a pot of coffee percolated next to another pot of hot water for tea and hot chocolate. "I was thinking you wouldn't want the caffeine," Pastor Hemi said as he passed a basket full of assorted teas over to her.

Amy sighed. "Do I look that rattled?"

"Your father did."

This startled her. Amy hadn't thought of her father as being bothered by anything. Sure, he was off making some mysterious phone call, but she'd figured he was more reporting on the situation than anything. Though why he would need to call anyone about something so simple as a protest over a burger place, she had no idea.

She found herself spilling all this out to the Pastor, knowing full well he very likely didn't have the answers. Of if he did, the Mount Hideaway "code of silence" would keep him from saying anything. To her surprise, he did neither.

"Do you feel like God is in control?" he asked her when she'd finished.

For the second time in as many minutes, he'd given her something new to think about. "Mostly? I mean, yeah. Sure, God is in control; otherwise, a lot of what's in the Bible wouldn't be much use, would it? The things Jesus said would be so many words." She cupped her hands around her mug, taking the warmth from it while her tea steeped. The basement was chilly from the air conditioning, or maybe she still was from her encounter. "I think I see what you're getting at, though. You're saying God is still in control even when things look bad. Like the protest. For a minute there, I wasn't sure if there was going to be a fight or something, with us sitting right there in the middle of it."

"But you said the police were there. So, think about it. Are protests allowed by the law?"

"I guess so?" She answered doubtfully, trying to remember the class she'd had on government a couple of years ago. "With certain guidelines, though, right? They're supposed to be peaceful. Without violence. Otherwise, they become a riot."

"What do you think would have happened if someone had become violent. If say, the people assembled had somehow gotten into a fight with the construction workers."

This she felt a little surer about. "The police would have stopped it somehow."

"How?"

"I guess the one talking on the radio was working out plans with his superiors about what to do." She considered the possibilities. "Maybe they had backup coming or something else in mind."

"So, with the police there to uphold the law, you might say things were still under control even if you didn't see yourself what was going on behind the scenes to make sure of it."

"It didn't feel like it, though." Amy shuddered, tasting her tea cautiously to see if it was ready yet.

Pastor Hemi smiled. "Yet you were still allowed to drive through and arrive here no worse for wear. Maybe a little rattled but for the most part, ok."

Amy put this together in her mind with his first question. "So, what you're saying is God works that way too. That even when things don't feel under control around us, He's still working on things we might not see or even know about to make things work out."

"Bravo! Well done, Amy."

Amy stirred some sugar into her tea to sweeten it. "But what if the protesters had refused to move, or if someone had decided to get violent? I mean, someone could have chosen to break the law."

"Choice is the important word there. Here's where my analogy breaks down a little. We call that free will. Sometimes people choose to act in ways that are hurtful or even illegal. In a protest, this might create a loss of control, turning things into a riot. You'll notice, though, when you study in history times of upheaval, even the worst of these incidents is brought back under control again at some point by the authorities. With God, He's never out of control, even when things seem at their worst."

"Why let the bad things happen at all then?"

Pastor Hemi sipped his own tea, thinking before answering. Amy liked this about him—that he didn't just give the pat answers. "Scholars have asked that question for centuries, even millennia, Amy. Some say it's in trials and tribulations that we see God the clearest. Others will point out that sometimes what we think is a bad thing, is actually quite good. Many a great and honorable thing has sprung out of an injustice."

Amy stared into her cup. For a long time, she hadn't felt as though God could possibly be in control of anything. Not since her mom had died. To her way of thinking, God could have kept that from happening, but He hadn't. It had taken time to come to a place of peace within herself, and now here she was wrangling with her faith all over again, all because of what exactly? Because she'd felt surrounded by angry shouting people while driving to church?

No. It wasn't about being surrounded. It was about seeing people from her own town, people she very likely knew, acting in an angry and unpredictable way. It made her feel as though she couldn't trust anything quite the way she used to. Not when she was positive she'd seen Mr. Russell, the mailman shouting with those in the crowds, or Elena's mom standing front and center. In that instant, familiar faces had become strangers.

Was God in control even then?

Yes. He had to be. Otherwise, He wouldn't be God.

"I'm overreacting to everything, aren't I?" Amy laughed a little at herself and lifted her chin that she might look Pastor Hemi in the eye.

"I think you had something of a shock."

Amy noticed the clock over the door and winced. "I'm about to get another one if I don't get to class. I expect they're all waiting on me by now. Thanks for talking."

"Anytime, Amy." Pastor Hemi gave her a quick hug, and Amy hurried on her way.

CHAPTER 8

THE FINGERPRINT EXPERIMENT

Bethany

The "science and computer lab" was a large classroom with a table and chalkboard in front, a dozen or so lab tables, and a number of computer carrels lining the outside of the room. About half of the computer carrels were occupied by children ranging from preschool through high school ages, each working on various subjects using online curricula.

The Bradfords generally would have gotten to the classroom early so they could set up their project before the rest of the Criminal Science Study Group got there. Today things felt off-kilter. For once, Bethany had been the first one there. Then Dr. Bradford had shown up, seeming somewhat flustered and in a hurry. Even more intriguing was the fact Amy wasn't even there at all.

So intent was she on figuring out this new mystery that she barely noticed when Jamie slid into the seat next to her. He seemed out of breath but rather pleased with himself. Rose slammed into the chair on the other side of him, her mouth pursed in an unhappy expression, clearly put out.

"I can't believe you made me drive all the way home just so you could change," she muttered half under her breath.

Jamie scowled. "Well, in case you didn't know, I'd been working all day—"

"Like I wasn't?" Rose shot back as she opened her notebook.

"Not in a warehouse, you weren't."

"Hey guys, everything OK?" Bethany asked quietly, darting a quick look at Dr. Bradford, who was fussing with the old aquarium and what looked like the doorknob from his house.

"Fine. Great. Really great." Jamie shot her a smile, leaning in to whisper to her better. "I was thinking—"

Whatever he was thinking, Bethany wasn't going to find out. Amy shot into the room, one hand holding a ceramic mug with the string from a tea bag dangling from the side. She dropped into the seat next to Bethany.

"Bethany, you'll never guess what happened on the way here—"

"Bethany, about what I was saying. Maybe we could—"

"Bethany, could you kindly tell my brother—"

"ENOUGH!" Bethany slammed her palms down on the table in front of her. Every person in the room stopped what they were doing to look at her, including the preschoolers playing in the corner. Flushing, Bethany slid down in her seat. "I'm sorry, Dr. Bradford. Is there anything I can do to help set up what we're doing today?"

Dr. Bradford had put on his gloves and safety goggles while setting up the experiment. He looked at her now, his expression strangely like that of a startled bug. "Oh, um. No. Thank you, Bethany, that was nice of you to offer. Amy will help me today, won't you, sweetheart?"

He clearly wasn't himself. From the look of things, neither was anyone else.

At Bethany's outburst, Rose had huffed and turned away completely. Amy's lower lip was quivering like she might cry of all things as she stood and went to stand by her father, and Jamie? Jamie's face had gone beet red.

Great job, Bethany. Next time you might want to think first before reacting.

In the meantime, Dr. Bradford was talking, and shouldn't she be taking notes? Bethany scrambled to find a pen in her bag, only to have Jamie hand her one. Mouthing a silent thank you as she took it, she tried to ignore the spark of warmth as her fingertips brushed his.

Whatever she was going to write was instantly forgotten.

Martin took some aluminum foil and shaped it into a little round cup. At the bottom of the cup, he placed a round cotton makeup pad. He handed the contraption to Amy, who'd hastily donned her own goggles and leaned in to see what he is doing?

"Dad, did you raid my bathroom again?" Amy asked, eyeing the makeup pad critically.

Martin grinned and shrugged his shoulders innocently.

Amy snorted and placed the foil on top of an electric coffee cup warmer inside the aquarium, following her father's instructions exactly. She also placed a small tray of water beside the foil cup. Then she withdrew the dreaded doorknob from its bag, handling it only by the shaft so she wouldn't smudge the fingerprints. Her cheeks were flushed as she handled it. Bethany winced in sympathy, feeling her own stomach twinge about this particular mistake.

I should have thought of that myself. What kind of leader will I be if I make mistakes when handling my team?

Amy covered the top of the aquarium with aluminum foil, while Dr. Bradford informed the others it would be best if the group donned their protective masks and eyewear.

"Safety first!" he said cheerfully as he settled into lecture mode, explaining each step in detail as they went along.

Doctor Bradford lifted the aluminum foil lid from the aquarium and placed a few drops of glue from the tiny tube onto the cotton pad. He replaced the lid and plugged in the coffee warmer's power cord. Soon a fine mist was rising from the foil cup. The teens gathered around the table to get a better look as fine white lines began to appear on the doorknob.

Leaned in close like this, Bethany could feel Jamie's warm breath on her cheek. "Hey, want to go out for ice cream later?"

He whispered the words against her ear. It felt...ticklish. Bethany swatted at him to make him move, trying to figure out what in the world he was talking about. Ice cream? She might have nodded. She wasn't sure. Why in the world would Jamie be talking about ice cream at a time like this?

In the meantime, wasn't Dr. Bradford explaining something? He'd heard, hadn't he? From the way Dr. Bradford cleared his throat, it was highly likely.

"The cyanoacrylate from the glue polymerizes the moisture and oils from the skin. Remember, this only works on a non-porous surface. The dish of water adds moisture to the steam, which helps to rehydrate the print. You want to be sure to do this in a well-ventilated space and be sure that the bottom of your chamber is secure because the fumes are heavier than air."

The kids all nodded. Bethany was less interested in the terminology than in the way the steam spiraled around the knob. Magic. The prints appeared as though magic.

So cool. She forgot ice cream. She even forgot Jamie.

"And then when the glue is finished steaming, you can just dust for fingerprints as usual and lift it off with packing tape."

Amy chimed in, "And then you could even scan it and blow up the image in Photoshop to enhance the image even more!"

"That's right, Amy!"

Her father seemed surprised. Bethany hid a smile. Amy had read up on the procedure last night and called to tell her all about it. The process had sounded kind of dull then. It definitely was much more interesting in person.

Amy ducked her head modestly. "Thanks, dad."

"Don't you do this kind of stuff up at the Mount Hideaway facility?" Rose asked. Bethany blinked. Seriously? Asking about what went on behind those particular closed doors felt tantamount to treason or something.

She needn't have worried. Dr. Bradford shot that question down quickly. "Nice try, Rose. You know the work we do up there is classified."

Rose rolled her eyes.

Jamie shot his sister a look and shook his head. "Thanks again, Dr. Bradford, for leading this class. Forensic science really makes physics, chemistry, and even government a lot more interesting."

Ha. Like that didn't sound rehearsed. Bethany and Amy exchanged glances. Leave it to Jamie to try to gain a few extra points with Dr. Bradford. Still trying to make up for his last science grade, probably.

Dr. Bradford seemed pleased at the compliment all the same. "You're really welcome, Jamie. You know, with your dad helping to teach business and Bethany's mom helping out with social studies, you kids are getting some really great field trips and projects along with your home school curriculum."

"Raising fingerprints is awesome!" said Bethany, hardly able to take her eyes off the doorknob and the ghost prints now clearly visible. "I can't wait to go home and try it myself!"

Dr. Bradford chuckled. "That's great, Bethany, but be careful, and always remember to wear your protective equipment."

"I will," Bethany said with a hint of impatience in her voice. Not so much as to be disrespectful, but enough to let it be known that she had heard these instructions before. She was too busy dreaming about the future—one where she performed daring deeds. Solved crimes. Investigated crime scenes.

Beside her, Jamie tapped her elbow with his pencil.

"Hey..."

Oh yeah. Ice cream.

Her logical, analytical mind clicked on. His red face. The way he'd whispered the invitation in a way no one else could hear. Kind of. The urgent look on his face as he waited for her answer.

Wait a second, had he been asking her on a date? To go out for ice cream?

Bethany stifled a scream. She might have startled Dr. Bradford.

Amy and Rose stared. Jamie, if anything, went redder.

This time Bethany was sure of it. She definitely nodded, *yes.*

CHAPTER 9

TWO WEEKS LATER

Rose

Harlan Wood was sitting at the conference room table with his laptop computer in front of him and stacks of files around him. Rose entered, pushing a cart with two pitchers of ice water and several glasses. Harlan was dressed in his best black suit, the one that was usually reserved for funerals, weddings, and Easter Sunday. Rose hid a smile. Her father was going all out for this.

Rose herself wore a sharp blue dress and her one pair of dress heels. She was five-foot-eleven with long legs and big brown eyes and had a keen awareness of how she must look. The way Jamie had stared at her when she'd left the house told her that her appearance must have been some transformation. The funny thing was, once she'd gotten started, she couldn't seem to figure out where to stop. She had even curled some waves into her long dark hair, and today she looked just like a runway model.

Many girls her age would have enjoyed dressing up like this and knowing that they were turning heads, but normally Rose hated being stared at. She was much more comfortable in her sweatsuit with her hair pulled back in its usual tight ponytail. Yet the ponytail hadn't looked right with the dress. Then she'd added lip gloss because she was afraid of being too pale. The next thing she'd known, she was…this…and didn't know how to deal with it.

It's for Dad, she reminded herself firmly. This meeting was important to him. Because it was important, she would do this for him. Family was everything to her. A dress, curled hair, and a little makeup wasn't a hard price to pay when it came down to things that mattered.

Reassured, she tapped the door open a little further with her shoe that she might enter the room with her hands full. Rose's phone buzzed just as she placed the second water pitcher on the conference room table. She glanced at the message, her eyes widening.

"This is it, Dad. Uncle Donnie just texted and said they're leaving the airport, so they should be here in a few minutes."

"Okay, I guess we're as ready as we'll ever be." Harlan got up and buttoned his jacket. He headed out the door, probably to go to the men's room to give himself one more look. He wasn't any more comfortable than she was in all this finery. At the same time, the meeting was just this important. Both father and daughter wanted everything to go smoothly.

You have this, Dad.

Rose bit her lip as she watched him go. At a time like this, she should probably be praying. The problem was she didn't know what to ask. Was God interested in mergers, business acquisitions, and other stuff like this? It seemed kind of trivial when compared to other things, like world hunger or poverty.

Amy would pray.

Rose bit her lip. Maybe one small prayer wouldn't hurt.

"God, um. Just...whatever is your will. I guess."

It wasn't the most satisfying prayer, but it was the best she had. A few minutes later, a black luxury van from the airport limousine service pulled up to the office entrance of Steven's Mill Shipping. Rose followed her father out to meet them.

It was a few minutes after shift change, so there were more people in the parking lot than usual. Rose sucked in a breath when she saw the warehouse workers lingering at their cars, like so many gapers at the site of an accident. What would these Omni people think? It hardly looked professional, especially when all heads turned as the impeccably dressed entourage emerged from the van.

We look like a bunch of hicks or something.

More uneasy than ever, Rose trailed behind the rest, passing close to a knot of men near the door who were discussing the group which had just entered.

"That boy's suit probably cost more than my truck," one of the older freight loaders remarked. Donald Wood, Harlan's brother and the assistant manager, gave the crowd a frown through the glass door and came out to shoo them away. He waved his hands at them the way one might try to shoo birds off freshly planted seeds. "What did I tell you, boys? Get out of here! Your shift's over. Go home."

Great. They'd been told not to gawk when the city people arrived, and they had still shown up. Rose groaned and hurried past Uncle Donnie, trying to catch up with the rest before she too was scolded.

She found them in the lobby.

"Welcome to Steven's Mill Shipping!" Harlan beamed as he extended his hand to the woman he likely guessed in charge. "I'm Harlan Wood."

Apparently, he'd gotten it right, for the woman offered a tight-lipped smile along with her hand. "So wonderful to finally meet you, Mister Wood. Charity Clifton, vice president of business development for Omni Millennium."

Charity Clifton was a slender woman in her late fifties. Her straight blonde hair curled around her face like a pair of parentheses and was sprayed stiff so that not a single hair had the option to be out of place. She wore a blue-gray pantsuit with a crisp cream-colored blouse.

Sharp. Rose eyed her outfit, wondering how she would look in such a getup. Maybe a pants suit, finely tailored, would do better for business occasions. Right now, the dress felt like overkill, like Rose had dressed for a party.

Not that anyone noticed her. Thank goodness.

In the meantime, Ms. Clifton was busy introducing the rest of her staff. Dax, her personal assistant, was a slender twenty-something with dark wavy hair and a French-cut suit. Ms. Clifton's legal counsel, Ted, was a handsome African American man in his early fifties. Then there was Gustav, their Logistics Manager. He was about six foot four with a thick neck and broad shoulders and looked as though he would be more comfortable bench pressing trucks than sitting at a desk.

Uncle Donnie chose that moment to arrive, out of breath, and clearly agitated. Harlan gave his brother a look and smoothly incorporated him into his own introductions. "You've met Donald, my assistant manager."

Donnie nodded, smiling perhaps a little too eagerly. Rose bit her lip, wishing she could somehow tell him to calm down. He was clearly getting too worked up over these people. In fact, everyone was getting too worked up over these people. Hadn't Pastor Hemi reminded them just last week that in the eyes of God, everyone was equal? Didn't that kind of put everyone on equal footing?

She glanced again at the richly tailored suits, the expensive haircuts on the Omni crew. Equal. Yeah. Right. Some people were maybe a little more equal than others.

"And this is my daughter and office manager, Rose. If you all don't mind, she'll be joining us to take notes and as part of her management training."

Rose started. She hadn't expected to be included in the introductions.

"Well, hello, young lady." Ms. Clifton said, looking Rose up and down. "I'm impressed to see that your father includes you in the business at a leadership level. That's just the kind of forward-thinking we're looking for in our partnerships. Please call me Charity."

Charity reached out her hand to Rose enthusiastically.

Rose was ready to throttle her father for not keeping her in the background like she'd supposed. That Ms. Clifton…no…*Charity* was offering her hand was entirely unexpected. Rose somehow managed a smile and shook Charity's hand, making direct eye contact as her dad had taught her.

"Thank you, Ms. Clifton. Just let me know if you need anything during the meeting, and I'll be happy to go get it," Rose replied smoothly, as if she'd been interacting with corporate leaders her whole life.

Ha. Nailed it.

You'll at least know that I'm no hick, and neither is my father. We know what we're doing, or you wouldn't even be here.

The thought puffed her up a smidge, enough to help restore Rose's confidence. She shouldn't have needed it, but for whatever reason, this woman had left her rattled in those first moments. It took her back to when she was younger; a feeling Rose didn't like much.

When she was a small child, Rose's parents had noticed that she had strong leadership skills but tended to be a little withdrawn. So the couple had spent years helping her to develop self-confidence with a special emphasis on her social skills. They had adapted her curriculum and nudged her into activities like public speaking and debate. At first, she'd hated it, but she soon started winning contests and awards and embraced the talents that her parents had seen in her. Still, it shook her to see how easily she could revert to the old her. Maybe it was because deep down, Rose still preferred to be at home with her family.

But when I need to, I can still network with the best of them.

She wondered if Charity could see all that in her face, for the older woman smiled suddenly.

"Oh, nonsense. You're going to sit here at the table with us. I'm interested in your insights as well. If we need anything, I'll send Dax."

Dax nodded obediently.

Just like that, it was settled.

Rose was a little taken aback. She wasn't sure what "insights" she would have to share, but she wasn't about to let it show for so much as a second. Instead, she smiled warmly and took her seat at the table with the grownups as though she'd sat there every day of her life.

Her father's chest expanded as he waited for everyone to be seated that he might start the meeting.

Rose felt the warmth of his gaze upon her and knew she was making him proud. It felt...good.

For the next two hours, the group went over details. Lots and lots of details. Rose knew some of what they were talking about from conversations she'd overheard in the office and discussions around the dinner table at home. Some of it left her completely lost. Phrases were bandied about, things about ROI and fund managers. Occasionally Charity would pause the meeting and ask Rose a question or two, testing her, Rose realized.

To her surprise, to her *delight*, Rose found she could answer more often than not. At the very least, she discovered she had an opinion to offer, something she'd never even considered before.

In the end, it was decided they would meet again in a few days. The group would be in town for the next three weeks, talking to other local government and business leaders. There were matters which needed to be cleared up about zoning and permissions, whatever those were. Rose resolved to find out. She was tired of being a bystander, pouring coffee, and bringing in the day's mail.

Even college didn't seem quite so daunting. Who knew business could be so interesting?

As the meeting concluded, Harlan punched a button on the conference phone in the middle of the table, to let Uncle Donnie know it was time to take the visitors back to their hotel. In the past, it would have been Rose's job to see to such a minor detail.

Not anymore.

CHAPTER 10

"THE ONE THAT GOT AWAY"

Jamie

Jamie pulled his white F-150 pickup into the gravel turn-off at the side of the road near the low-water bridge. He shifted the truck into park and stomped the parking brake since the hill was steep. He walked around the truck and opened the door for Bethany, still marveling that after their first date, there had been another, and another after that. Maybe it was in part because Jamie insisted on opening doors for her. At first, she had found the whole idea annoying, but Jamie had assured her that it was a sign of respect and not by ANY means an indication that she wasn't perfectly capable of getting out of a truck on her own.

Besides, even if it was a little old-fashioned, what was wrong with showing manners?

At least she'd stopped fighting him on it. She stepped down from the truck, long legs unfolding elegantly. Jamie marveled at this too—that a girl so strong, so beautiful would even want to spend the afternoon fishing with a guy like him.

It sort of made a guy feel good inside, knowing a thing like that.

Head high and laughing at something Bethany said, Jamie felt a hundred feet tall as they grabbed their rods and tackle boxes out of the truck bed. They waved gnats away from their faces as they hiked down the dirt trail to the creek, talking as though they hadn't spent hours of the week together already, either on the phone or in class at the co-op.

The sun had just cleared the Blue Ridge Mountains, and it was already around eighty degrees. It was shaping up to be a typical August day in the Shenandoah Valley... hazy, hot, and humid. It was a nice change from the unseasonably chilly weather a couple of weeks ago when they'd done their breaking and entering at Amy's house.

How much had changed for all of them in that time?

Jamie wore an orange baseball cap with the logo of his dad's company. He drew it off now to swipe at the sweat under the brim gathering on his forehead. "Looks like summer is here to stay a while longer," he said cheerfully.

Bethany wore an olive drab Boonie Hat with three fly fishing lures attached. The military hat had also been her dad's. He tied those flies himself. He'd promised that one day he'd teach her how to tie flies, just like he had taught her other hunting, fishing, and camping skills, but that day would never come. Jamie studied the fly nearest and wondered how hard it would be to learn. Maybe he could teach her in her father's stead. Would that be creepy and weird, or something seen as romantic? He couldn't decide.

They sat down at their usual spot and set up shop. Jamie tossed out a soft plastic crawfish, Carolina rigged, with a red and white bobbing float. He found a "Y" shaped stick to use as a rod holder, placed his rod on it, and got comfortable.

He liked to just toss the lure out into the water and stare at the float until it jumped... or didn't. He didn't care that much. For him, fishing was mostly just about being outside. Watching the plastic ball dancing on the rippling water was absolutely hypnotic and gave him time to think.

Bethany did not have the patience to just sit and stare at a float all day. She was working a bright orange Hula Popper, an artificial top-water lure with a cupped mouth at the front and plastic tassels in the rear that resembled a hula skirt. It floated on the surface, and every once in awhile, she'd give the line a slight tug, causing the cup to make a little splash and a popping sound in the water. The lure imitated an injured bug that had fallen into the water, and it was a champ at attracting top feeders. She had bagged a number of smallmouth bass with this technique in the past and was going for another today.

"So, how are things going with the foreign investors?" Bethany asked quietly so as not to spook the fish.

Jamie tilted his head back, letting the light breeze off the water caress his face. "Dad and Rose say the talks are going really well."

"Rose?" Bethany seemed surprised to hear that Rose would know much about the meetings.

"I would have thought she'd have told you by now. Yeah, she was there to take notes, but apparently, the boss lady from Omni... Charity... something, kept including Rose in the discussion, asking her opinion and stuff. I'm not sure if it was her way of being polite or what. It all sounded a little weird to me."

Bethany tugged at her line, making the hula popper dance. "So you're saying it sounded weird to you that a powerful woman respected the opinion of another woman in a room full of men?" Bethany was smirking and sounded like she was mostly teasing, but there was a little bit of bite to her comment as well.

Jamie sat up. "No, I don't mean it that way... I just..." Jamie fumbled for a response, came up short, and finally just shrugged.

Bethany's eyebrow lifted. "Yes?"

Bethany stared at him; her hazel eyes narrowed as she held back a smile. She'd always enjoyed waiting for him to dig himself even deeper into the hole he'd gotten himself into. Now she was treating him like he was adorable when he was trying to get out of trouble, and he wasn't sure he liked it. It made him feel less like a man out on a date with the woman he...well...respected, and more like a stupid kid.

This dating thing was quickly growing more complicated than he expected.

"Look." He spoke slowly, wanting to get this right. "I'm not saying anything that has to do with one woman respecting the opinion of another. The point is, she's asking a kid. Someone our age." He caught Bethany's look. "Ok, maybe a little older than us. But still, Rose is only eighteen. Why should her opinion matter at all? It's not like she's trained in business or engineering or any of the things they were discussing. I mean, sure, she knows probably more than most people her age; she's homeschooled after all." Jamie paused here to grin cautiously at Bethany, who almost smiled in return. "But why would they want her opinion at all when there were people in the room, people with fancy degrees and years of experience who you think would have better answers?"

Bethany was quiet for a long time. Long enough that he really started to worry, thinking he'd messed things up for good with Bethany. She was frowning, biting her thumbnail the way she did when she was thinking things through. He waited her out, willing her to see it.

A powerful executive wouldn't have any reason to include a teen girl in a high-level business negotiation."

"I don't know," Bethany said finally. "Maybe they wanted a...I think my mom would call it a layman's opinion. You know, wanting to see things the way an outsider would."

She was still annoyed. Frustrated even. He could see it in the rigid way she held herself. He opened his mouth, wanting to ask her to explain further because he was intrigued by this, but was interrupted by a loud thrashing in the water. Bethany jolted upright, grabbing at the pole which had grown lax in her hands, fighting a strong tug on her line, hard enough to nearly send the pole into the water. Bethany yelped and yanked her pole to set the hook and started to reel in the flopping bass.

The battle was on. Jamie knew It would take a few minutes to tire the small-mouth out, pull him in, then let him go.

Jamie himself was off the hook.

For now.

—— CHAPTER 11 ——

THE INVITATION

Rose

Rose yawned. Work was slow. Files. Piles of files that somehow needed a pair of hands to find the appropriate place for them in the various cabinets which lined the wall. You'd think you could automate the process somehow. Create a device that would pick up each folder, scan the label, and drop it in the appropriate drawer. Instead, it fell upon her to bring order to chaos, while Rose's mind wandered, reliving the exercise in breaking and entering and her own role. Even after two weeks, she couldn't get it out of her mind.

Cringeworthy. She'd been cringeworthy the way she'd rushed in.

She paused, her hand on a folder marked, *Abbot, James* as though it weren't patently obvious it was meant for the drawer closest to the door to her father's office.

When will I ever learn to think?

It was a question she asked herself often, especially now as she had reached the cusp of going out into the world. College loomed, offering the enticement of a different sort of education. She felt far too advanced for the basic courses she would be forced to take in the waiting semester. Homeschooling had overprepared her in some ways. Would her obvious intellect be appreciated?

Would it be appreciated the way Ms. Clifton seemed to appreciate her?

Rose paused. It had been strange to be included in the meeting. Stranger still to be allowed to offer her opinion. On the other hand, she'd liked how she felt when everyone in the room had looked at her, waiting for her to speak. It was a new feeling. One she kind of wanted to explore again.

Behind her, the office phone rang. Her duty to answer it, but she was across the room. Her father called to her through the open door. "I've got it, honey," followed by a click, the sound of a phone being set on the desk. "Ms. Clifton! What a surprise!" Harlan Wood tended to like working hands-free so he could make notes. Rose had gotten used to tuning him out.

"Mr. Wood, I hate to impose on you, but I was wondering if I could ask a favor of you. If it's not too much of an inconvenience." Charity Clifton's voice filled the room, strident, even demanding in tone. Unaware she was on the speaker, she spoke with confidence though Rose guessed she'd sound the same in front of an audience. She'd seemed that type.

"Of course. How can I help you?"

Rose slipped the folder in the appropriate drawer and turned, curious now.

Her father shuffled papers on his desk. Beside him, the monitor showed financial spreadsheets. He leaned forward now in his chair, obviously hunting something to write with. Rose bit back a smile and went forward to pluck a pen from where it protruded from underneath several printouts and handed it to him. He mouthed his thanks.

She shook her head, drifting from the room to pick up the next file from the desk by the door. *Watkins, Felicity.* Last drawer. Or second last, maybe. There were a lot of W's.

Rose knelt, glad they had no appointments today, thankful to be able to wear jeans and a loose shirt. Who knew filing could be a workout? She paused, considering the idea, wondering if there was a way to incorporate that somehow. Phys-ed through clerical work? She should have thought of it years ago.

Behind her, she heard the rumble of her father's voice—a reply. Ms. Clifton spoke too loudly, impossible to ignore. "Well, while we've researched your town quite thoroughly, this is our first in-person visit, and we'd really like to have someone local who could show us around."

Her father cleared his throat. Rose could almost hear him thinking how this would be a waste of his time when he had better things to do than play host. This entire visit had seemed to put him on edge. "Oh certainly, I'm sure I could spare Donnie, I mean, Donald for a few days."

Rose snickered and grabbed the next file. *Moskewitz, Franklin.* Poor Donnie. She could only imagine how that would go.

"Actually...again, if it's not an imposition, I was hoping that Rose could be our... liaison. If that's okay, Dax will pick her up in our rental car tomorrow at noon. She will have lunch with the team, and then we'll have her help us with some of our... social calendars and things. "

Rose froze, twisted to stare at her dad, who was already nodding though there was no way Ms. Clifton could see him. She gestured wildly, nearly losing the folder as she tried to convey that no, this was not a good idea. While she had been flattered by the attention the other day, being one on one with the woman scared her half to death.

Not that he noticed. His tone was surprised, his attention on the caller, not her. "Uh, sure. Certainly, that would be just fine."

Rose stared. He wouldn't. He hadn't even asked her. Like she was some kid and not an adult ready to leave for college in a few months. She sagged, the folder drooping in her hand. Numb with shock, she slid open a drawer and dropped the folder in without looking, snapping it back with more force than was necessary. Her father hung up as she came into the room.

"So...what's going on? Was that the Omni people?" she asked as she came into the room, struggling to keep a tone of studied casualness as if she hadn't been listening to the whole conversation for the last five minutes.

Harlan looked up and smiled, though she could see he was clearly distracted. "Why yes. It was Ms. Clifton, though I suppose you heard. Be hard not to, being right there and all." He chuckled as she winced, heat coming into her face though she told herself it was hardly her fault when he'd been the one to put it on speaker.

Rose drew herself up stiffly and crossed her arms across her chest, not liking the prickling feeling of guilt which crept over her. *Not that I had to listen. I could have closed his door. Given him some privacy.*

"You seem to have impressed them, Rose. They want a local person to kinda be their tour guide, and they specifically asked for you." He scribbled something on a paper and handed it to her. Details, she saw. Date and time.

"Why me? I don't know the first thing about being a tour guide."

The words burst out without her intending her to say him. Her father only laughed. "Only one way to find out. I expect you'll discover more when they pick you up. You might want to dress a little more…professionally," he added, with a wink.

At this, she had to laugh. With no meetings, her father had somehow escaped the house wearing what looked like his oldest jeans and a football jersey with his favorite team on the back.

"Yeah, nice one, Dad. I'll try to remember that." She shook her arm at him so that her many bracelets jangled, reminding them that even dressed casually, there was never a moment where she wasn't put together. Her loose shirt might have been grabbed because it was comfortable and easy to move in, but she knew she looked fabulous from the trim boots which graced her feet to the top of her head where her silky brown hair was pulled up in a casually chic topknot. If she'd learned anything this past week, it was maybe to wear something a little classier than sweats paired with a ponytail.

Rose shook her hand and turned away to go back to her filing. "Just remember, this Dad, when it all blows up in your face," she called over her shoulder as she picked up the next folder.

She wondered idly which drawer *Moskewitz, Franklin* had wound up in.

CHAPTER 12

DAX AND DISCOVERY

Rose

A stretch limousine pulled up in front of the office of Steven's Mill Shipping. You'd think everyone would have something better to do than to stand around making comments. Rose would have scowled if she weren't working so hard to give the right impression. After all, she was in a sense representing her father and company both in this ridiculous errand.

Somewhat impatiently, she waited as the driver got out and opened the door for her. It felt weird to be called "Miss" by the driver and to be ushered into the car as though she were royalty.

She missed the old her. She wanted her sweats and to pull her hair out of the careful French braid she wore and to put it back into a ponytail. She took a deep breath and stepped into the vehicle, surprised to find Dax alone in the car, working on his laptop. "Um. Hello."

Dax didn't answer immediately. Rose frowned a little and looked around for a seatbelt, wondering at the same time if people wore seatbelts in limousines. Dax wasn't wearing one, so maybe one didn't?

When in Rome…

Rose settled in the seat next to him in the back, waiting Dax out. So far as she was concerned, she'd done her part in saying hello. It was obvious he was busy. So be it. She glanced around, taking in the strangeness of being inside a vehicle that was so long with such plush seating. The controls nearest her were intriguing, offering different options for lighting, sound, and climate controls.

I bet you there's some amazing speakers in here if you were playing music.

"Sorry, I'll be right with you. Would you like a bottled water or anything?" Dax offered, barely looking up from his screen.

"Uh, no. Thanks, I'm good." Rose replied, with an uneasy glance at the bar along the length of the limo.

It looked quite impressive and was in all likelihood well-stocked with far more than just water.

While Dax's head was down, Rose counted seats. It would comfortably seat the whole Omni entourage. She amused herself by placing each person around the vehicle in her mind. She supposed Ms. Clifton…Charity…would likely sit in the back where Rose was now. Kind of like being the head at a conference table. Likely the ranking would place less important people along the side with the least important riding backward up near the driver.

She wondered if Dax had very deliberately chosen his seat because he'd never be allowed to sit there when the rest of the group was along. It amused her, thinking this way, as Dax seemed like such a puffed-up wannabe last time she met him. Had he even looked at her directly once in the course of that entire meeting?

He was good-looking, though. She studied him surreptitiously, noting the professional styling to his hair, the cut of his suit. Dax stared intently at his screen and typed so quickly; she was amazed the computer could keep up with him. She found herself staring at his hands, admiring the agility of his fingers on the keys. It was almost like watching a musician playing a fine piece of music.

Finally, he looked up with a big sigh of relief. "O… kay! I am so sorry. I had to finish writing a speech for Charity to give to your Chamber of Commerce tomorrow."

Rose smiled a touch awkwardly, caught unprepared by his friendliness. "Oh, that's fine. I could see you were busy and didn't mind waiting you out." She glanced out the window, noting they were already coming into town. The car slowed as it turned onto what was considered the main drag. "So, can I ask… just what am I supposed to do?" She gestured with one hand at the passing scenery out the window. "I'm supposed to be some kind of tour guide?"

Dax laughed at that, not in any way which was critical, but as though they were friends, which she found she kind of liked. "We just need someone with local knowledge to point us to the good restaurants and talk to us about some of the 'behind the scenes' things that go on in the town. You know, the stuff they don't talk about in the business meetings."

Rose frowned. What she wanted was to point out was that they could get just as much information from Yelp. There was something else going on here. Instead, she chose the safer route. "But why me? My dad was surprised that you asked for me over Uncle Donnie. I mean, he knows so much more than I would. I hardly visit fancy restaurants. I mean, I'll be honest. I can point you at the best place for a hamburger or milkshake, but fine dining?"

"No, it's okay, I understand." Dax might have been laughing a moment before, but he wasn't now. His smile seemed a touch forced. "There were basically two reasons to get in touch with you. First, if you haven't already noticed, my boss is a real visionary. She has become incredibly successful because she's always planning ten steps ahead of everybody else. When she looks at a project like this, she's looking at the future, and she likes you."

Okay, that was...unexpected. Rose wasn't entirely sure how to react to this piece of news, especially when coupled with the fact that Dax didn't seem entirely comfortable with Rose being recruited in this way. Jealousy? She wasn't sure. "Wow. Okay, you said there were two reasons?"

Dax hesitated. His eyes sheepishly wandered around the car for a second. It was the first time she'd seen this young man, or anybody from Omni, appear to be anything other than smooth and confident. It made him human and real. "Well, she believes in including opinions from her trusted staff, so she asked me who I'd prefer to work with." Dax looked up into her eyes. This time when he looked at her, his smile was genuine, and even a little bit shy.

"Oh... I'm..." Now Rose was the one to hesitate. A number of local boys had expressed interest in her over the years, but she hadn't really liked any of them. Honestly, they'd seemed childish in their attention, juvenile in the way they preened and smirked at her as though they were doing her a favor if she would just go out with them.

Dax though. Well, she hadn't considered him in quite this way before. She did now, seeing the maturity and confidence he wore easily, as though accustomed to both. Maybe he wasn't entirely happy about something his boss wanted from her, but right now, Dax was looking at *her*, Rose Beatrice Wood, as though she were someone worth getting to know.

Rose was suddenly glad she'd taken the time to braid her hair, to dress up a little, as now these things helped her find the confidence to reply without stammering. "Thank you. I'm honored."

"Well, it was between you and your Uncle Donnie."

His words were perfectly timed. For the first time since she got in the car, Rose found herself unbending enough to laugh with him.

"But seriously, you and I will be working pretty closely together to just keep things running smoothly while we're in town. We're having a lunch meeting now where Charity will fill you in on some of the details, and then you and I will get to work."

The car pulled into the covered entrance of the hotel. It was strange, though. While Rose had been understandably nervous when she'd set out on this expedition, she wasn't now. Something about having Dax at her side seemed to help. They went in together; Rose relaxed enough to tell him about a time she'd been in this very hotel for her father's birthday dinner. She'd been five and had thought the desserts displayed were meant for anyone to eat. As a result, both started laughing when they entered the restaurant and spotted the dessert cart right near the podium where the maitre d was waiting.

The greeter ushered them to the private dining room, Rose still fighting a bad case of the giggles right up until she spotted Charity Clifton, her lawyer, and Gustav the Logistics guy, all seated at a large table with a white tablecloth where a feast had been laid out for them. Shrimp cocktail, fruit and cheese plates, smoked salmon with onion and cream cheese, and an assortment of tiny decorative pastries.

Charity stood up, seeming delighted to see them. "Welcome, Miss Wood! We are so glad that you could join us. Do sit down."

Apparently, the charcuterie board was meant only as an appetizer, for a server appeared as if by magic to take their orders for lunch. Feeling somewhat out of her depth again as things started happening too rapidly around her, Rose seized upon the special of the day as though it were a lifeline, agreeing to it without even hearing what it was she was ordering.

Rose reached for her water glass as Dax ordered his meal, admiring his calm assurance. Watching him now, she found herself praying for his kind of calm. *Lord, if you can hear this, help me to be more like him.*

It seemed a reasonable prayer, especially given the company she was in. Whatever the case, it definitely helped, meaning maybe Amy had something after all with all this constant praying thing she seemed so good at. Calmer now and more reassured, Rose sipped her water, answering greetings from around the table as the waiter disappeared and left her alone with the Omni representatives.

Charity was kindness itself, waiting until Rose had set her glass down before asking. "So please... tell me about yourself."

Well, that seemed easy enough. Rose straightened and smiled, calling upon her speech training from countless forensics meets to be able to answer clearly and in as professional a tone as possible. "There's really not that much to tell. I've lived in Steven's Mill my whole life. My brother and I are homeschooled, and I work at our family business."

There. That wasn't so hard.

"Hmmm." Charity took a sip from her own water glass. "That tells me more than you may realize."

Rose frowned, not sure where this was going. "It does?"

"Why, yes, it does. It tells me that you're a leader from a family of leaders."

Nope, definitely not following.

Charity seemed to know exactly what Rose was thinking, for she smiled knowingly and continued. "Your father is a successful, self-made businessman, and your parents have taken it upon themselves to oversee your education personally. They've given you and your brother both academic training AND practical, vocational education. Furthermore, when we first met, you looked me in the eye and shook my hand with confidence, while many girls your age would have been intimidated."

Well, at least she hadn't *looked* intimidated. Though looking back, had she really been? Rose had never thought about herself quite this way before, and she rather liked this version of herself, seen through a professional and powerful woman's eyes. Rose found herself sitting a little straighter, maybe with a touch of pride now.

Yes. Of course. She really hadn't been intimidated at all. Only a touch nervous, if that. "It was kind of you to notice," she murmured, ducking her head demurely. "Though I still fail to understand entirely why I'm here."

Charity seemed pleased at her response, for she leaned toward Rose, as though genuinely interested in what the girl had to say. "I'm hoping to bring this area into a whole new era and to connect it with the rest of the world. Have you traveled much?"

Rose blinked. "Not really. We've been to the Bahamas on a few vacations, and I've gone on church mission trips to Haiti and Guatemala."

"I see. That's a good start."

A good start? Rose smiled and nodded politely. She had no idea what Charity meant by that, but she was certainly intrigued. What had Dax said in the car? Something about Charity seeing ten steps ahead and liking Rose. Which meant...what exactly? Coupled with questions about travel, there seemed to be a hint of a plan here. Something involving...her? An internship, perhaps?

Charity seemed not to notice Rose's preoccupation. She sat back now, addressing the table with enthusiasm, gesturing at something only she could see. "I have a vision to bring the world together...taking the best of different regions and cultures and lifting the quality of life for all. I see so much potential in this town and its people." She turned and fastened her gaze firmly on Rose. "And you in particular."

"Me?"

The door at the end of the dining room opened. Several uniformed waiters stepped in, each bearing a tray heavy-laden with delicious smelling food.

Charity reached over and patted Rose's hand. "As you spend time with us over the next few days, we'll discuss this more."

"Um...sure."

Charity turned her attention on the plate set before her. "Enough business, don't you think? I'm famished. Eat up, my dear; we have a long day ahead of us." Charity picked up her fork, dismissing their conversation entirely, and not seeming to notice the way Rose bowed her head quickly to at least *think* a blessing over the food, since it seemed no one else was inclined to pray.

When she looked up, only Dax was looking at her. His forehead was creased in worry, his eyes dark and with no trace of the humor or even the friendship they'd shared only half an hour before.

CHAPTER 13

TABLE TALK

Jamie

"Hey, isn't it Rose's turn to set the table?" Jamie asked as he set out silverware in each spot. "I could have sworn I did this just last night."

Harlan Wood was already seated, scrolling through messages on his phone and frowning. "I don't know. Does it matter?"

It did matter, but it seemed childish to bring it up. Jamie shrugged and finished the job, sitting down just as his mom came through the kitchen door with the mashed potatoes. She set the steaming bowl on the table next to the chicken and sat down. In truth, tonight's dinner was everyone's favorite, not just his. Fried chicken done to perfection mounded the serving plate next to green beans from the garden, which had been stewing with a big chunk of fatty pork for most of the day.

"Heaven has to be something like this," Jamie said without thinking, making his mother laugh.

"I highly doubt my cooking is on quite that level, but thanks all the same." Dana Wood was blonde like her son, with fair skin which showed every blush just as easily as Jamie did, much to his consternation. His mother was blushing now, though, on her, it looked nice.

"You're cooking is always tops," Harlan said as he turned his phone off and slipped it into his pocket.

"Rose texted a few minutes ago. She said she'd be here anytime, but to go on without her."

"Works for me," said Jamie, reaching for a drumstick.

His mother smacked his hand. "Grace first."

"Sorry, mom." He knew better. He knew he knew better, but he'd worked hard all day and was hungry. Drat it all, there was that blush. He moved quickly, covering his embarrassment by reaching for his parent's hands. The family bowed their heads together as Jamie offered thanks, maybe a little more hastily than was warranted.

While their heads were still down, the screen door slammed loudly, startling everybody.

"Sorry," Rose murmured as she slipped into her seat while around her, the family straightened and got down to the business of serving up the food.

Dana handed the mashed potatoes to her daughter, eyes bright with curiosity. "So, tell us all about your day with the people from Omni Millennium."

Jamie snorted. Yeah. Good old Omni Millennium. That's all they'd talked about all day at work. Like he wanted to sit in on more. He bit into the drumstick and resolved to refrain from the conversation. Eat, then get out of here. Maybe see if Bethany wanted to take in a movie.

Rose was excited. Talking with her hands excited, which was something Rose didn't do. The words seemed to spill out of her in a torrent. "I had lunch with the whole team, and Charity told me more about her vision for the company and all the good it will do for the town. She's amazing. Did you know that she's originally from Georgia, the country, not the state? And she's lived in over twenty countries."

Jamie stared at his sister. He'd never heard her talk so much at one time in his life.

"So what? Georgia, the country, not the state, is a million miles from here. Who cares? Oh, don't tell me. She's adopting you and is going to take you there on the next flight out."

"Jamie!" Dana didn't like bickering, especially at the table. After forgetting to pray, this felt like strike two. From the look in her eyes, the bases were loaded, and he was just about to lose the game. Big time. Jamie clamped his lips shut, realized he needed to be able to eat, and shoveled in green beans before he did anything stupid.

Besides, Rose was totally ignoring him. Where was the fun in teasing her if she didn't even notice?

"So, as I was saying before I was so rudely interrupted..."

Oh, she had noticed. Jamie stifled a grin. One point for him.

"...after lunch, Dax and I spent the afternoon going over the team's schedule for the next two weeks and planning..." Rose faltered her, glancing around the table somewhat uneasily. "Well, *things*."

"Things?" Harlan looked up sharply.

"Dax?" asked Dana, clearly more interested in the human side of the equation.

Rose brightened. "Yes. He's originally from Belgium, but he went to a business school in New York City. He just started working for Omni Millennium a few months ago."

Rose giggled. She actually giggled, something Jamie hadn't seen her do since she was twelve and had decided she was too old for such things. Or too cool. Something.

In fact, Rose seemed positively loony as she leaned forward in her chair, elbows on the table as her hands danced over her food while she gestured. "We actually spent most of the afternoon planning out the meals and the social events the team will be attending when they're not in business meetings. Dax seemed really interested in my ideas. And you have to admit, it's pretty amazing that Charity...I mean the team from Omni Millennium, is so interested in learning everything about our community. They really seem to care about the impact they have on the community."

That did it. It was bad enough that Rose wasn't being Rose anymore, but this stream of enthusiasm for Omni, Dax, and whoever this Charity person was just too much. "Well, while you were wining and dining with *Dax*. I was signing in all the incoming and outgoing shipments for Mr. Darvishi. That logistics guy, Gus or whatever..."

"Gustav." Rose interrupted, her tone a little too smug and superior.

"Whatever." Jamie snapped. "*Gustav* was getting Mr. Darvishi to show him all around the shipping and loading area. Dad, did you know they're talking about installing a whole automated system for the packages, like robots and stuff?" Jaime threw his napkin on the table and crossed his arms across his chest. "Robots!" He repeated the word just to make sure they understood.

"Well, it's not the kind of robots like you see in the movies, but yeah, that's part of what they're talking about. Like I've been saying, we've got to modernize to keep up." Harlan said, though there was a hesitation in his voice, like maybe he wasn't quite so on board with the idea either.

"But won't that put all the guys in the loading dock out of work? A few of the boys are starting to get antsy about losing their jobs." Jamie stared at his father, not liking the way Dad seemed to draw inward the more Jamie talked.

"Part of our agreement with having Omni as investors is that all the current employees would keep their jobs. I'm insisting on that," Harlan replied, but the forcefulness of his words was at odds with the doubt in his voice.

"Good grief, Jamie, what's gotten into you?" Rose seemed to notice her food for the first time and grabbed a forkful of beans. She kept talking, this time gesturing with the fork, threatening their mother's tablecloth as the buttery beans rose and dipped over Grandma Esther's embroidered roses. "If Charity said they'd keep their jobs, they'll keep their jobs."

Both parents were staring at him now, his father with a worried frown, his mother with that long-suffering, 'why can't everyone get along' expression she got when her children were fighting. Rose sat in the middle of it all, calmly eating her beans as though she hadn't been the one to stir up the hornet's nest.

"Mom, thank you for dinner. It was delicious. Dad, if I might be excused?" Jamie rose stiffly, collecting his plate and silverware, to take to the kitchen. He didn't bother waiting for an answer. Honestly, he'd had enough.

The problem was, he expected his sister to be naïve. She was young and didn't pay attention to how the world worked the way he did. Money and economies meant little to her.

Unlike him. He found the whole idea fascinating. He loved rags to riches stories, things about self-starters. People who went out and tried, putting together hard work and a solid dream together with savvy business skills.

What he didn't like was big companies diving in on little companies and remaking them into their own image with no care or concern for how things had been done in the past. How many corporate takeovers had promised no firings only to go back on it later?

Rose didn't get it. He expected more from his dad, though, and was suddenly uneasy that his father might be a human being, and worse, be capable of mistakes after all.

It was a new thought, and one he was not comfortable with.

But most of all, he didn't like this chatty, hyped-up version of his sister. Rose wasn't being Rose, and he suspected this Dax person had a lot to do with it. Except she'd been acting kind of weird for a while now—since the lesson in Breaking and Entering.

Jamie shut himself in his room and sank down into the chair at his desk. To his left was his Bible, a little dusty admittedly but a good source of wisdom, especially when he was troubled like he was now.

To his right was his phone. Bethany would be done with dinner by now. Also, since she was a girl, he could count on her to give some unique insight into what was going on with Rose lately and whether he should be worried or not about this Dax character.

He glanced at his Bible again, considering the problem, layering in the way his father had been so strangely defensive—like his own company didn't even matter anymore.

In the end, Jamie reached for his phone first.

---- CHAPTER 14 ----

THE DAY THE WORLD CHANGED

Amy

"While we mostly hear the phrase 'blood spatter,' there are actually three distinct types of patterns: blood spatter, blood drip stains, and blood transfer patterns. The term 'spatter' indicates that the blood is acted upon by forces other than gravity. The term 'drip' means a pattern caused by gravity alone. And transfer patterns happen when the blood comes into contact with another object, such as a hand, a shoe, or a weapon."

It was co-op day again, and Dr. Bradford had the full attention of the class.

"An amazing amount of information can be gathered from these patterns, including the distance from the blood source to the target, the direction of travel, the speed or force of travel, and even the sequence of events that caused the blood to be shed. Be taking notes because this will all be on the quiz next week."

Amy glanced up, startled. Of course, she'd been taking notes. This stuff was fascinating.

Ah. Not for everyone. Jamie's paper in front of him was just about blank. Amy's gaze slid over Bethany's notebook, surprised to see her usually meticulous friend had likewise been…distracted? Amy's eyes narrowed as she looked from one to the other.

Dr. Bradford launched into the history of blood spatter analysis. He was just talking about some of the ways people had done experiments in blood splatter by shooting bullets through sponges soaked with blood, for example, when he was interrupted by a loud rumbling noise in the distance. For a second time, Amy looked up from her notes. It sounded like thunder, but that was unlikely since the sun was shining and a quick glance out the window showed there were no clouds in the sky.

In that instant, the entire building shook in what felt like an earthquake. People cried out, grabbing at the table and each other.

It was over in a second.

"Dad?" Amy half rose from her seat, finding she wasn't the only one on her feet. Rose stood on the other side of the table from her, her face pale and eyes wide behind her glasses.

"Everybody just stay still!" Dr. Bradford cautioned, going to the window. He was quickly joined by a couple of the other adults. Not about to be left behind, despite orders to the contrary, Amy hurried after him, arriving in time to see a string of police cars, fire trucks, and ambulances rush by the church. Their lights flashed, and sirens blared. They sped past the church building except for one police car, which peeled off from the rest and pulled into the church parking lot.

"You kids stay here. I'll go see what's going on."

Never had Amy's father spoken quite so sharply. He meant business. There wasn't a one among them who would have dared follow outside. Amy retreated to the window to watch through the glass the drama playing out in the parking lot. The others followed.

Dr. Bradford and Pastor Hemi wasted no time in rushing out to speak to the officer. That both men seemed upset left knots in Amy's stomach, she felt Bethany's hand in hers and took strength from the fact her best friend was right there with her.

You too, Lord. You're here too.

Somewhat reassured, she squeezed Bethany's hand, hoping to convey a little of the calm over to her friend.

"What do you think they're saying?" Rose asked, her voice small.

Jamie shook his head. Being taller than the rest, the others turned to him now, as though his better vantage point would somehow lend some understanding to the conversation happening outside.

"I have no idea, guys. I've never seen Pastor Hemi so rattled."

The same could be said for her dad. As the men turned away, it was clear both men were shaken. Dr. Bradford seemed to have aged in those few moments, his steps heavy as they returned to the building.

Martin was met with a barrage of "What happened?" and "What's going on?" from the kids as he returned to the room.

"Guys. There's been an explosion at the Shipping company." His eyes sought out Rose and Jamie.

Jamie staggered, the blood draining from his face. "Dad?"

Dr. Bradford could only shake his head. "We don't know anything else yet."

Rose grabbed his arm. "Jamie, let's go!" Her voice caught on a sob. "We need to go see if dad's okay."

Bethany grabbed her purse from "I'm coming too!"

Dr. Bradford raised a hand to stop them. "Rose, the police are saying that everybody needs to stay as far away as possible in case there's another explosion or the fire spreads."

"Are you kidding? That's my *Dad*!"

Amy stared. Rose had her hands on her hips, squaring off in front of Dr. Bradford in a defiant attitude, which, well, wasn't like Rose at all. At the same time, Amy couldn't deny the sick feeling of what she'd feel like if it were her father, who was in danger.

Rose didn't so much as say another word. She spun on one heel and simply walked out. Jamie bolted after her. Bethany seemed torn. In the end, she swung her bag over her shoulder. "I'm sorry," she said to Dr. Bradford and took off after them.

The sick feeling in the pit of Amy's stomach intensified. "What are we gonna do, dad?" Amy asked.

"There's only one thing we can do right now. Let's go downstairs." Martin replied, reaching out to draw his daughter to him. He hugged her hard and led the way to the prayer chapel.

Built in the 1920s, the prayer chapel had been the original sanctuary of the church, complete with stained glass windows, wooden pews, and an organ with gold pipes that reached to the vaulted ceiling. Most services were now held in the modern auditorium with the stage, sound system, and lighting, but the atmosphere of this room lent itself to times of quiet, fervent prayer.

Pastor Nehemiah was already there kneeling at the steps in front of the altar. Martin and Amy knelt beside him. Amy closed her eyes and let the peace of God wash over her.

What was it Pastor Hemi had said the day she'd had to drive through the protest? Know that God was in control? That meant even now that she could trust that whatever was happening as the shipping company that God was there. He was there as her friends sped into danger.

Trust. It was about trust, wasn't it?

Amy brushed at the tears on her cheeks, thankful that whatever happened next, that none of them had to face it alone. *Be with them, Lord. Just...be with them.*

She repeated the prayer silently as the three knelt in silence for several minutes. The darkness hanging over them seemed to fade. The knots in Amy's stomach loosened. When she looked up, she saw them doing the same. She hadn't been the only one crying.

Of one accord, they each quietly turned around and sat on the steps.

"How can we help?" Amy asked the pastor.

"Martha is calling all of the parents to come and get the younger kids, but a few of them might need a hand to hold and possibly a ride home."

"I'm on it," Amy said, thankful for the chance to be useful.

***

The Reverend watched to make sure Amy had completely left the chapel. Only when he was sure she was out of earshot, did he speak quietly to Martin. "It looks like you might have been right."

Martin took a shaky breath. "It's starting sooner than I expected, though. I usually like being right, but not this time. This is going to get really ugly, really fast."

The pastor only shook his head, his eyes solemn and sad. "It already *is* ugly. God in heaven, protect us all."

"Amen."

CHAPTER 15

INFERNOS AND INTERFERENCE

Bethany

Rose, Jamie, and Bethany sped toward the chaos in Rose's red Impala. Rose always drove a little too fast, and both Bethany and Jamie had ridden with her many times. Today she was so frantic that Bethany and Jamie exchanged concerned glances. But neither of them dared to tell her to slow down. That didn't mean Bethany's heart wasn't in her throat as the car careened around corners, tires squealing. She put out a hand to brace herself against the door, praying they'd make it in one piece.

That they were allowed to make the turn on the road up to the shipping company was proof God had to be looking out for them. A siren behind them caused her to look back. The police had arrived and were setting up a roadblock behind them, limiting traffic.

Except for emergency vehicles, she guessed. There was no way they'd get anywhere close to the place. She started running through possible ways for them to get to where they wanted to be if they were stopped.

We can do this. It would have to be like the breaking and entering exercise all over again, working together as a team. If they were pulled over, they could go through the woods.

As it turned out, they didn't need Bethany's unspoken plans. They were stopped at the service road, outside the parking lot's security fence. Smoke billowed up through the trees beyond them. From this vantage point, it was impossible to see anything at all; there were so many fire trucks in place.

"Dead end," Bethany murmured under her breath, the reality of the situation crushing her to where her skin felt too tight. She was crushing Jamie's hand before she realized she'd taken it in her own. They looked at each other, faces pale. Rose's eyes glittered dangerously, her jaw set. It was she who reached first for the door, scrambling from the car and ignoring the officer who'd been trying to explain through her open window just why they couldn't go on.

Bethany and Jamie were right behind her. Bethany was the one who thought to apologize. It wasn't the young officer's fault they were disobeying. He just didn't understand their connection to the situation.

"Sorry. We're just…"

What they were 'just' she never said. Bethany could only shrug, helpless, trailing Rose and blinking back tears. The entire situation seemed so unreal. So terrifying.

Focus. You have to focus. An agent wouldn't lose their cool.

But even an agent would be rattled if it were their own family inside that burning building. And to Bethany at least, she'd spent enough dinners over at Jamie and Rose's house that their father was kind of like a father to her too.

Behind them, the young officer shouted. Thinking quickly, Bethany spun, thinking to at least delay him long enough to allow Jamie and Rose to get closer, to find out what was going on. They were intercepted by Brian Foreman, the son of the Sheriff and a second cousin of Donnie's wife, Clara.

Only he wasn't any happier to see them than the other officer had been.

He stepped out in front of the trio, putting up his hands to stop them. "I'm sorry, Rose, you have to turn back."

Rose wasn't listening. The closer they got to the building, the wilder her eyes became. She tried to sidestep him, dodging first one way then another. When Brian moved with her, she gave a small scream of frustration, whirling on him angrily, stepping up until her nose was an inch from his. "We've got to get in there!"

Brian drew himself up, his voice loud, but not angry. "I can't let you in, Rose, you know that. Let the responders do their work."

This was a plea for her to understand, for Rose to allow him to do his job. Bethany's heart went out to the man. This was his family in there too, and he was only trying to do his job. Bethany reached for Rose, thinking to draw her back, but Rose was having none of that. Rose shook her off roughly, drawing herself up in a way that didn't seem Rose-like at all.

"You can't stop me! This is, this is my property! My dad owns this place. Dad and Uncle Donnie are IN THERE!" The last two words became a wild shriek.

With that, she shoved him. Brian had his hands full, grabbing at the girl and pushing her back forcibly. She struggled against him—in a second, things were going to get serious. "Rose, I need you to calm down!" Brian turned toward Jamie, who in all of this had stood, pale and undecided, his lips working like he wanted to say something but couldn't get the words out. "Jamie, can ya help me out here?"

Bethany was already in motion. Jamie got there first. "It's okay, Brian. I've got this. Come on, Rose." He put his arms around Rose as around them the roar of the fire increased. Something crashed down inside the building. Firefighters shouted and ran, changing the direction of their hoses, making whatever just flared up a priority.

Rose struggled against Jamie initially, finally sagging against him with a sob as the heat forced them all to take several steps back. Brian's face was as pale as their own as they came to a stop at the car.

"Get out of here, kids. You don't need to see this," he said hoarsely. Whatever else he might have said was lost as his radio crackled to life. He bent his head, pressing a button, responding to whatever message had just been sent.

They should probably go, but Bethany knew there was no way any of them were leaving until this was over. Jamie's voice was hoarse when he spoke. "I'll move the car."

They watched as they pulled the car into a grassy spot just outside the commotion, coming back to where they stood on the other side of the fence where they'd be out of the way. There were more vehicles arriving every second. Even Rose seemed to understand they were only in the way now. This had become an inferno in minutes, the smoke so thick they periodically lost sight of the firefighters as they worked to put out the blaze.

They had to walk down a ways to get a clear view of what was going on. They followed the fence along the perimeter of the property until they reached a spot where they could see the building through the trees. The three teens pressed their faces into the crisscrossed aluminum fence and watched the scene in horror. Bethany noticed Rose's knuckles growing white. She was clutching the fence so hard, and she wondered if the metal was slicing into her friend's hands. She didn't have the heart to try and move Rose's fists.

Jamie looked as if his heart had been torn from him. It wasn't just the smoke that caused the wetness in his eyes.

Emergency vehicles surrounded the loading dock area of Steven's Mill Shipping. Black smoke poured out of a huge hole in the roof. That must have been what they'd heard cave in. The loading bays stood open, letting out smoke, allowing entry for the teams of firefighters working the blaze. Not that anyone was going in right now. Orange flames danced around the openings. Firefighters in heavy gear held hoses, aiming streams of water on the flames. Even from here, the noise and the smell were both overwhelming.

Rose growled deep in her throat, hitting the fence hard with the palms of her hands. "We've got to get in there!"

Bethany shook her head. "We can't. The police will just stop us again. We're lucky we weren't arrested already."

"You don't understand. It's not like it's your dad in there!"

"I understand enough to know I'd get in the way of the people trained to deal with this!" Bethany shouted back, stung, and trying hard to remind herself that Rose was terrified and hurting right now.

Rose ignored her, grabbing Jamie and tugging at his arm, trying to draw him away from the fence.

"Jamie, come on, we've got to do something."

"Jamie, don't." Bethany stepped closer to him, prepared to grab him if he did something stupid, and tried to go with Rose.

She needn't have worried. He might as well have been carved of stone. When he spoke, his voice seemed to come from someplace far away. "Two hours later, and Rose and I would have been in that building. The center of the flames is right where I drove the forklift yesterday. What if...what if I did something wrong when I left it there?"

Bethany swallowed hard. "You can't think like that. Accidents happen. None of this had anything to do with you."

He shook his head. "There's something…off…about this." He frowned, curling his fingers around the fence, leaning forward as though he could see through the smoke, through the building itself into the heart of the fire if he only stared hard enough.

Rose was having none of that. She grabbed Jamie's arm again, shaking him hard. "JAMIE!"

Jamie blinked and stared at her as though seeing her for the first time. "No, Rose. Bethany is right. We need to let the responders do their jobs."

"Are you kidding?" Rose pushed him away from her and ran back down the fenceline toward the gate. There she was stopped by a burly police officer, someone they didn't know. Even from where they stood, Bethany and Jamie could clearly see the conversation wasn't going well. Rose had started out talking. In moments things had escalated. She'd faced off with the cop and was shouting loud enough for them to hear her from where they stood, even if they couldn't quite make out the words.

Bethany and Jamie looked at each other and raced down to join her.

Jamie got there first, but just barely. Rose stood, livid and fuming, glaring at the cop who looked about an inch away from calling for back-up.

"Rose…"

Bethany didn't have the words to say. She didn't know how to defuse the situation. The officer was clearly not about to let any of them pass.

The radio on the cop's shoulder chose that moment to spit out words and phrases, things hard to hear against all that noise. The phrase "fully involved" came through loud and clear, though, as did "Hazmat situation."

That did it. Bethany straightened. It was time to take care of her team. Besides, if it was turning that bad, there was no way they would be allowed to stay even this close. Hazmat meant evacuations, removing people in the vicinity from what was fast becoming a dangerous situation.

"Rose, we need to go."

The radio gave one last squawk as they turned away.

"Multiple fatalities."

Rose screamed and sank to the ground, collapsing so quickly there was no way to catch her. She buried her face in her hands and did the most un-Rose-like thing Bethany had ever seen her do.

She wept. Bethany knew then that the sound of Rose's grief would never leave her; she would hear that for the rest of her life. It was the first time she'd heard true suffering and pain.

Bethany fell to her knees to help, to comfort, to do something, *anything* for her friend. Rose wasn't even aware of her. It was as if the part of her that mattered had gotten into that burning skeleton of a building and would never come out again.

If Rose's father died that day, a part of Rose would die too. All Bethany could do was lay down beside her and hold her as she wept, praying she could somehow keep her friend from slipping away from her entirely.

CHAPTER 16

PRAYERS AND PROTESTS

Bethany

The small prayer chapel was nearly full. From what Bethany heard as she entered, Pastor Hemi considered moving the group to the main auditorium, but this room just felt like the right place for this meeting. Silently she agreed. The intimacy of the room encouraged warm compassion. The parishioners filed in quietly, exchanging whispers and hugs as the organ played softly. It felt like coming home. Some of the knots in Bethany's stomach eased.

Tina, Bethany, and Joy Shanholtz had entered together. Bethany paused just inside the doorway, hunting for her friends. She saw Amy and Martin Bradford seated in the third pew from the back. Amy motioned for them to sit beside her. There was just enough room.

Seated next to her best friend, Bethany looked around the room, scanning for people she recognized and noticing who was absent. The church had several hundred members, but it felt like the folks in this room, just over a hundred or so, were all family—some she knew really well, and others were just faces that she would nod or wave to when she saw them in the grocery store. But they all gave her a sense of stability, of belonging. Her mom had grown up in this town, and even when they had moved around to military bases all over the world, this place and these faces had been an anchor for her.

Jamie, Rose, and Dana Wood were all seated in the front row. There was a twelve-year-old girl sitting with them. Bethany wondered who she was. The pale, drawn face wasn't familiar to her.

Pastor Hemi rose and nodded to Martha, the organist. She brought the old hymn in for a landing as the pastor stood behind the carved wooden pulpit and cleared his throat.

"Friends and family." He paused and looked around the room, as though making sure to encompass each of them personally in this greeting. His eyes were somber but filled with such love and compassion that Bethany found herself feeling comforted, even now in the midst of tragedy. Never had she experienced a gaze that felt so much like a hug.

Pastor Hemi cleared his throat and continued speaking. "It's in times like this that it can be difficult to feel God's mercy and His presence. But it does my heart good to see His love reflected in all of you. There's no doubt, this is a time of pain and confusion, of mourning and questioning. But it's also a time for us to support each other and to be the kind of salt and light unto the world that I know we all want to be."

Around her, members of the congregation nodded. Bethany blinked back sudden tears.

"Our hearts and our prayers especially go out today to the families with loved ones whose lives were lost in the terrible accident."

Somewhere someone sobbed. *Lost.* There had been lives lost.

Bethany swallowed hard, willing herself not to cry. Amy's hand in hers helped her to hold steady. She had to remind herself that at least Jamie and Rose's dad was alive. Mr. Wood was at the hospital even now, with some doubt as to whether or not he would wake up. Jamie had told Bethany his family was coming to the service because prayer was all they had left, and if that was the case, they were going where the most people were praying.

Speaking of which, shouldn't she be doing just that?

Bethany bowed her head, shoving aside the chaos of her own thoughts, trying desperately to find God in all this turmoil. Around her, she sensed more than saw others doing the same. The Pastor was still talking, but the words washed over her, meaningless when so many things were going through her mind.

God, you know what we need. You know why we're here. Help. Help us all. Comfort those who are hurting. And for the rest, give them…give us your healing grace. Oh please, Lord, you're here aren't you? You're listening to what I'm saying?

She was crying, after all. Bethany felt Amy tighten her hold on her hand, silent companionship and commiseration. Bethany swiped at tears with her other hand, thankful for the friendship. She wondered how Jamie was doing in all this and turned her prayers to him and his family.

Let Mr. Wood be okay, Lord. I ask this in Jesus' name that you heal him, that you heal all who are injured…

Beside her, Amy gasped.

Bethany's head came up sharply. Two figures who must have arrived late were heading for the front of the chapel, where there were still a few remaining seats.

Elena?

The dark-haired girl trailed behind her mother, a silent shadow, clearly not happy about being there. The girl slouched her way up the aisle, dropping heavily into the empty seat her mother indicated, looking for all the world like she wanted to disappear. She had good reason to. Throughout the church, prayer was abandoned for the sake of a quiet buzz of conversation.

There was an almost imperceptible chill that followed the girl, as though she were made of ice that cooled the air in her wake. It moved with them, affecting each row as they strode head held defiantly high through the church.

Pastor Hemi cleared his throat, reminding those there of their task. The hum died out, though more than one head bowed somewhat reluctantly. Bethany frowned, bending her head closer to Amy's.

"What's going on?" she asked in a hoarse whisper.

"Later."

The service continued but had lost some of the intimacy. There was an undercurrent in the room which spoke of more than grief and loss. A hint of anger coursed through the room, so faint as to be almost unnoticeable unless you were looking for it.

And right now, Bethany was looking for it.

By the time the service ended, Bethany had recognized two very important facts. First, the anger in the congregation wasn't being directed at Elena so much as it was at Elena's mother. Second, that even good Christians like Amy had trouble concentrating sometimes.

It's not just me then, Lord? I'm kind of relieved...and at the same time, sorry. It should be easier to focus on you, especially when stuff goes wrong. Maybe we're all works in progress.

When the service eventually broke up, it was on a quiet note. Voices hushed, people filed out of the chapel. Bethany was torn between wanting to find Jamie and her desire to know just what had happened. Usually, the members of Steven's Mill Community Fellowship were more welcoming to guests. And with a town as small as Steven's Mill, it wasn't as though Catherine Krezinski was a stranger to any of them.

As they left the chapel, Bethany turned to Amy to ask, but Amy sometimes understood her better than she did herself, and she pushed her away. "Go find Jamie. I know you want to see him before he goes."

"But—"

"We can talk later." Amy's eyes were solemn behind her glasses. "In fact, I think I should say hello to Elena. She looks like she needs a friend."

Bethany flinched. For a moment, she experienced a flash of anger herself. Amy befriending Elena seemed wrong on the deepest level. Elena was...well, Elena was trouble. Now Amy was trying to be *nice* to her?

"You do what you need to," Bethany said, struggling to keep her tone even.

Amy heard what wasn't being said, all the same, her chin coming up in that way it did when she was being stubborn. "I do what my Lord needs me to," she replied and turned away.

Bethany flinched. *Fine.*

But as she pushed her way through the crowd, trying to find the Wood family before they left, she realized just how astute Amy had been. People were talking. Everyone here was talking and saying just how violently opposed to the expansion of the shipping company certain people in this town were. Certain people defied progress at every turn and would do anything to keep out new business.

Anything.

As what they were saying sank in, Bethany started seeing people she'd known her entire life in a new way. Not that everyone here was agreeing with what was said. On the contrary, the gossip breaking out in what was supposed to be a fellowship hall wasn't conspiratorial so much as divisive. Sides were being drawn, and Bethany was surrounded suddenly by people she didn't feel like she knew at all. They were blaming without cause, without any kind of proof. Hinting without ever coming out and saying what they meant to say.

They blamed Elena's mother for the explosion at the shipping company.

It was no wonder Elena had looked so tragic, and why her mother had been so… well, almost defiant in the way she stood off to the side of the room, talking to the pastor brightly, as though she were an actor in a play. Only she was floundering with her lines and seemed to have no idea of the emotion she was supposed to be conveying to the audience.

And because of the protest, the congregation had decided Catherine Krezinski was guilty without the benefit of a trial or even an investigation.

This was why Amy had gasped. She'd felt it too and hadn't been immune to thinking the same thing. Amy had told Bethany about driving through the protest a couple of weeks ago. Had even Amy thought Elena's mom was guilty somehow?

Bethany stopped walking. She couldn't find Jamie anyway. From the look of things, he'd already left. Besides, what could she even say that would help? She'd already told him she would be praying, that she was there for him. She could call later, or better yet, text, as it would be less intrusive while he waited at the hospital for a miracle.

In the meantime, Bethany turned in a slow circle, wondering at the difference an hour made in how she saw the world. Grief. Fear. Worry. Anger. This wasn't the congregation she knew, and it filled her with…what? Disappointment? Or something deeper? A sadness perhaps that people weren't as perfect as she'd always thought they were. Even Amy was acting in unexpected ways.

Speaking of which…

Across the room, Amy was talking to Elena. Bethany watched them a long time without moving. This was the love of Christ in action, wasn't it? To stand with someone when they were unfairly being persecuted.

Bethany bit her lip. Maybe she'd been wrong. In fact, the more she thought about it, the more certain she was. She couldn't control anyone else in the room. She couldn't stop a single person there from saying mean things about Elena's mom. It wasn't up to her to change their hearts. She could only control herself and trust God to take care of the rest.

So be it, Lord. Help me to follow Amy's example.

Bethany took a deep breath and started toward them, thinking that for today at least, she could try to lay aside the natural animosity she'd felt toward Elena ever since their last meet. Of course, some of this was Elena's fault. Elena had very ungraciously beaten Bethany at martial arts and had not let her forget it since.

It was a good plan, but not quite so easy to carry out as she had supposed it would be. Someone stepped in front of her, blocking her way. Another cut off the only avenue of escape. Bethany was surrounded in moments, swallowed up by the crowd.

Behind her, she heard a woman's voice, harsh and grating. "Did you hear? Wood did it himself. Trying to get out of the deal with Omni."

And just like that, the tide turned. New gossip formed, this time even uglier than the last.

Bethany froze.

Were they kidding?

She twisted, turning, fighting her way through the crowd, but whoever spoke she could not be sure. There were too many women and no way to know which one said it.

CHAPTER 17

DIGGING FOR ANSWERS

Dr. Martin Bradford

"This wasn't an accident."

Martin Bradford's steps seemed heavier even to him as he crossed the parking lot to where yellow tape fluttered in the wind. The fire was long since out. It had taken hours and a good deal of outside help to make that happen. All that remained of the main warehouse now were twisted girders stretching to the sky, ash, and broken dreams painfully coupled with the sacrifice of good men.

That the children had borne witness to this pained his soul—his only reassurance was that his precious Amy hadn't been there to see this. If the others had nightmares for years to come of those horrifying moments, he would not be surprised.

Major Lance Piper stepped past him, ignoring the police tape as though it weren't there. Martin's eyebrow rose. While the bodies had been removed, this was still a crime scene as far as he knew. "I thought the fire investigator wasn't done yet."

"We're not touching anything."

The reasoning was shaky at best. Martin understood suddenly why he was the one to be asked to come on this particular expedition. Being their crime scene specialist, it would be up to him to make sure they did no harm. Morally this was shaky ground. They ought to be out here with authorities, not standing where the ruins still smoked at dawn before anyone else was up. The whole thing stank of subterfuge.

"What are you looking for?"

"An idea as to how this started." Lance's tone was distracted. He stepped carefully along the edges of the ruins, bending to peer carefully at the charred remains of the building. "Tell me which side you think the scorch marks seem thicker."

"You already have a theory," Martin remarked, joining him with great care in where he placed his feet.

"You're looking to prove your hypothesis."

Lance bristled at this. "What of it?"

Martin stopped and stood where he was, arms crossed over his chest. "It's not good scientific method, Lance. Come on; you know that. Even my middle school kids that I teach science to know it. The point of testing a hypothesis is to try and prove it wrong, not right."

Lance straightened and stared at him. "You're refusing to assist?"

Martin fought to control his breathing, to hold on to his calm. "I want to know why we're here and what makes you think this isn't some terrible accident."

Lance kept walking, entering the building itself, kicking aside debris to see better what was underneath.

"Martin, you know better than that. There's been talk—"

"There's always talk, and twice as many conspiracies. Ever since they built Mount Hideaway, you've got people looking under bushes and behind trees for spies. Sometimes a fire is just a fire." He pointed at the scraps of wood and metal under Martin's feet. "You might want to quit messing around in that."

Lance drew back, one foot balanced on a twisted I-beam. "And sometimes it's not. Sometimes people try to start something."

"The protest group?" Martin laughed, drawing in too much smoke and ending on a cough. "Look," he said when he'd recovered, "Those folks are just trying to keep the town the way it is, the way it's always been. I hardly see them burning down a business just to stop expansion."

"It wouldn't be the first time a group like that got a little carried away with their own agenda."

Martin shook his head, raising his hands in a sign of protest. "I give up. The next thing I know, you'll be spouting some dark conspiracy saying Omni did it to drive down the price. Or Harlan Wood was trying to use the fire to back out of the deal for some reason."

"You know as well as I do that there's something fishy going on out here. You said so yourself to that pastor friend of yours."

Martin stopped breathing. "You're watching me."

"You think there's anyone at Mount Hideaway who isn't under surveillance?" Lance laughed. There was no mirth in the sound. "Since 9/11, there's been a policy in place making it crystal clear we exercise due caution when it comes to our people. We told you that when we hired you."

"Since when does 'due caution' mean you listen in on my every conversation?" Martin snapped, drawing back, away from the ruins. "Never mind. There's no point in your answering. I can tell right now you'd be lying to me." He started to walk away.

"I don't lie to you, Martin. You know that."

Martin stopped. The two men stared at each other for a long time. Lance's icy gaze never so much as wavered.

"No, you don't. That makes it worse somehow. Then you know the rest of the conversation. What's going on, Lance? We've all seen how security is ramping up. Something has been cooking for a long time. Yes, we wondered if this had something to do with that. Buildings don't just explode out of the blue." Martin's eyes narrowed. "Wait. Tell me we didn't have something to do with this."

"What?" Lance snapped the question, fumbling for a handkerchief which he used to blot sweat and soot from his rather bald head.

Martin stepped in close, drawing himself up in a way that even Amy would know meant trouble. Martin didn't lose his temper often, but he felt the traces of it now, in the way his hands shook, trembling from the effort to not form into fists. "Tell me we're here to look for evidence. Not to plant it."

"Do you think so little of me?"

"I think that much of you. Your patriotism knows no limits. And I can tell right now, if you thought you were doing the right thing, there's nothing you wouldn't do."

"Put like that; it sounds like a bad thing." Lance shrugged. "Maybe it is."

"So, what are we doing here, then?"

"Looking for this." Lance moved a few feet to the right of where he stood, bending to pick up and push over a file cabinet. "This is where it started."

"You know that for certain?" Martin asked, stepping carefully across the debris to join him. He ran a practiced eye over the charred remains of furniture and melted plastic. His training had given him the rudiments of fire investigation, enough to know that Lance was very likely right.

If so, they were certainly looking at arson.

"You destroyed a crime scene to get a look at this. I hope you have some reason for doing this outside of satisfying your curiosity. People died, Lance. What will their families do when they're told they'll get no answers, much less satisfaction when they can't even trust law enforcement to do their jobs."

"They are doing their jobs, Martin. Now take a look quick and tell me what we're staring at. In half an hour, the cops will be all over this site with their own arson investigator, not to mention a whole crime scene crew brought in from the next county." He pulled some papers from his pocket and handed them to Marten, who paged through them rapidly.

"How did you get this? It says here you have the authority to take charge of the investigation in whatever means you see fit."

"You've been at Mount Hideaway how long and still ask that? Martin, I need you to trust me." Lance's expression was serious, his eyes somber. "Tell me what you think you see. I trust you more than I trust anyone I know. You'll be fair and impartial, but we're running out of time."

Martin drew himself up stiffly. "I need to offer you an apology, then. But this isn't the way things are done. Can I ask if my findings will be made official?"

"That depends on what you find." Lance smiled mirthlessly. "You were right about one thing, Martin. I'll put my country first every time. Can you do the same?"

CHAPTER 18

BEIRUT AND THE MINDING OF BOYS

Charity Clifton

Charity Clifton drew herself up stiffly, not an easy task when seated around a conference table. "It seemed you are having a hard time hearing me, for I've asked my questions now three times without a satisfactory response."

Ted and Gustav glanced uneasily at each other. "We answered your questions; you just don't like the answers," Gustav muttered half under his breath. Ted elbowed the other man sharply in the side, hard enough for Gustav to expel his breath hard in a loud sigh. He was going to be a problem, but she decided to wait and see how Ted handled him. Maybe she wouldn't have to intervene herself.

Still, Gustav was becoming more and more of an annoyance. Sooner or later, he would have to be dealt with. Fine. Sooner rather than later.

Charity's lips pursed. "You have got to be kidding me. I could have sworn you just questioned my authority."

Gustav drew himself up, eyes flashing. "I was questioning your *sanity*," he said carefully, his accent making his words thick. "Ma'am." His eyes were hard, but she could feel the uncertainty in him.

Ted clapped a hand over the other man's mouth. "What my associate is trying so hard to say is that we don't know any more than you do. The whole place went up like it was Beirut all over again." He gave Gustav a hard look, drew his hand away, and wiped it fastidiously upon a napkin.

"Except to my knowledge, there was no ammonium nitrate being stored in the warehouse." Charity's eyes narrowed. "Or was there? Maybe I should be questioning your whereabouts last August? Are you perhaps taking side jobs? Things which do not fit within the vision for Omni Millennium?"

"I'm a lawyer, not a terrorist." Ted's words were clipped, his expression hard.

"From where I sit, there is not always much difference." She put up a hand to stop his obvious protest. "No matter. How you use your vacation time matters little so long as it doesn't impact the company. It might raise some rather interesting questions of loyalty, though." She raised a single eyebrow and allowed one corner of her mouth to curl into what could charitably be called a smile. Ted had been with her long enough to know better, of course, which was why she allowed him to see it.

"Speaking of loyalty, I might ask the same of you. Your little protégé is notably missing," Ted commented, carefully casual as he reached for the carafe of coffee at the center of the table to refill his cup. "Maybe you might ask him about where he was when the building blew. Unless you already know."

"Is that a statement or a question, Mr. Walters?" Charity's lip curled as she lifted her arm to examine the sleeve of her tailored suit to flick at a speck of imaginary lint.

"Given I am your legal counsel, it would help if I knew whether there was something which we needed to protect ourselves against."

"And you feel Dax is something we need to be protected against?"

Ted drew himself up to look her square in the eye. "I think Dax has his own agenda."

"As do you, Mr. Walters," Charity reminded him, her tone sharp. "But I take your meaning." She reached for her bottle of water, a very expensive variety they had had to bring with them. Stupid tiny town, filled with small, insignificant people and their funny little church-going ways. She was starting to hate this job. Though it had its perks, she'd rather enjoyed playing with that little girl who was easy to mold, like modeling clay.

Rose. What a ridiculous old-fashioned name. Still, she was coming along nicely. Maybe she'd consent to a name change. Something more in keeping with the persona she was trying to develop. Something like Rae. No. Rue. Like the plant. A solid, intimidating name.

Yes, she rather liked it—her little Rue.

Which, of course, reminded her that Dax had been the one to bring Rose to her. He had even gone so far as to suggest the girl might make a suitable… companion.

Charity considered this a long moment. "You are certain Dax was behaving in defiance to my orders?" she asked Gustav directly.

The man hesitated, eyeing Ted warily. "I don't trust him."

Charity ran several scenarios through her head. Much as she disliked Gustav on principle sometimes, he was no dummy. He knew logistics and risk management. Right now, he was saying Dax was a risk. She would be a fool to ignore that. The trick was to not allow him to know she was taking his advice. It wouldn't do to let him question her in this manner.

"Watch him," she said finally. "And see what you can find out about what happened yesterday at the shipping company. That little explosion is drawing too much attention."

"It was done badly," Ted murmured, half under his breath. "It could have been done with half the explosives."

"Mr. Walters, we really do need to talk about what you did on your summer vacation last year," Charity said with a dry chuckle. "I might have to redefine your duties somewhat. Starting with our little problem child." She gave the lid of the water bottle a savage twist. It made a satisfying sound.

Ted eyed her, cautious now, and more than a little wary. "How do you mean?"

"Only this. See to it that Dax does what he's told, Mr. Waters." Charity smiled. It was not a nice smile. "Or else."

There. The balance was restored; Ted was afraid of her again. Let that little upstart Gustav believe he could override *her* authority; Ted at least knew better. Ted would keep his partner in line as well as Dax. He was the key. Keep Ted under tight rein, and the rest would fall nicely into place.

CHAPTER 19

COMAS AND CONFRONTATIONS

Rose

"Why do we have to be here?"

They'd been at the hospital for ages. Rose stretched, trying to get comfortable on the hard plastic chair placed next to the bed. She hated being in the room with him, finding it easier to be supportive from the relative safety and comfort of the waiting room. But Mom had asked them to sit with him while she stepped out to get a refill on her coffee. Now here they sat, staring at their Dad, which would have been weird enough if he'd only been sleeping.

Except he wasn't, was he? The burns were extensive; the damage to his body when the ceiling had caved in was considerable.

Rose shivered. "Why do *we* have to be here?" She repeated the question, this time adding a nudge with her foot against Jamie's thigh. He sprawled, not so much sitting as draped across another such chair placed next to hers. He lay back, one arm draped over his eyes. "Jamie!"

"He's our Dad, Rose. I can't believe you want to go home and just…walk out on him."

"What's the point when he's not even awake? The doctors or someone will tell us if anything changes." She stared at the monitor next to the bed, endless green lines dancing up and down, showing respiration, heart rate, oxygen. Things whirred and clicked around him. Some kind of weird inflating thing on his legs expanded and contracted like something alive. She didn't understand what it was doing, what any of the machines were doing, and she didn't want to know, didn't want to think of him hooked into a bunch of lifeless machines, her father dependent on a few green lines on a screen.

What was worse was the fact her father was in there somewhere. Underneath tubes and sensors, wires and bandages lay the man who used to teasingly call her Daddy's Girl until she made him stop a year ago. A very quiet part of her mind longed to hear him call her that one more time, a whispered voice she ruthlessly squashed. He looked small when tucked into bed like that and was sleeping—only without the possibility of waking up.

Rose slouched deeper into her chair, arms crossed. "He's in a medically induced coma, Jamie. It's not like he's aware we're here or is even going to wake up. What's the point? I don't understand any of this."

"We're here for him, Rose, and for mom. She needs us right now too."

"She stepped out for *coffee*!" Rose snapped, sitting up abruptly. "Coffee I could have gotten!"

Coffee which would have enabled her to escape from this awful room, with its even more awful machines. There was a smell in a hospital room, a smell of forced cleanliness, chemical, and unnatural smell. Rose would have gone for coffee just to be able to hold that under her nose for a while to mask the smell of disinfectant and sterile instruments in sterile containers.

"She needed to get out of this room for a few minutes. You don't think this is hard for her to see Dad lying there like this?"

Rose hated that scolding tone Jamie used on her when he thought she was in the wrong. He'd been using it on her a lot lately. "It's hard on us too!" she reminded him harshly, getting up to move around the room. Standing at the window with her back to the bed and the machines made it easier somehow. As if Dad wasn't actually here. The reflection in the window was like finding her escape blocked, and it made her angrier.

"What if he dies?"

Jamie shot to his feet. "That's it; we're having this out in the hallway." He grabbed her arm and propelled her from the room.

"What?" Rose struggled, stumbling after him. He shoved open the door to the room and pushed her through it, into the hallway and the nurse's station. She rounded on him, realizing for the first time just how much taller he'd grown over this past year. He seemed to tower over her, more man than little brother, as he reached one hand back to slide the door shut behind him. The blood ran into his face, making his features almost frightening. He was angry at her, but she couldn't seem to stop.

"We are not talking about Dad like he's not even there," Jamie growled the words, bending close to speak without raising his voice.

"How do you know he is?" Rose drew herself up. "What if he already left, and that's only his body in there, being kept alive by machines? What if everything that made Dad...Dad is gone forever?"

"We don't know that. They said there was brain activity, things going on in his head."

"*Minimal* brain wave activity," Rose countered, lowering her voice to match Jamie's tone as a nurse hurried past on her way to another room.

Jamie drew back. His face was unnaturally pale, his eyes bright with unshed tears. "Even if Dad is gone, his soul isn't exactly lost. Pastor Hemi says—"

Rose blinked back angry tears. "Pastor Hemi says a lot of things. Where was God when everything blew up? Where was God when the fire started?"

"It wasn't God who started the fire." Jamie's words were clipped.

"Then who did?"

Rose and Jamie stared at each other. A trio of food service workers paused to join the staring match, a heavy metal cart carrying trays between them. The tallest worker cleared his throat awkwardly. Rose stepped back, allowing them room enough to pass between them. She and her brother were frozen in a tableau, neither of them willing to be the first to break eye contact.

They waited while the cart trundled past, Rose cheeks scarlet with anger and shame. Her fingers curled into fists at her side. "Whatever you think, that's not Dad lying in that bed. That's something else that isn't Dad. That's just his body, and his soul is...well...doing what souls do when they're between heaven and earth. I can't stand around hoping he'll open his eyes...or that he'll come back to us. It's not *fair*, Jamie. And it's cruel to just stand around watching like that."

"You're the one being cruel, Rose," Jamie said softly, his shoulders slumping. "We don't stay here for us. We do it for him." The anger and frustration had just leaked out of him. He seemed defeated, deflated. Rose decided she would rather see him angry; at least then, he had some life to him.

"Well, Dad wouldn't want us hovering over him when we could be out doing something," Rose countered.

Jamie's eyes narrowed. "Doing what, Rose?"

"Something. I don't know." Her phone bleeped at her from her pocket. Rose grabbed at it, grateful for the distraction, a feeling of relief washing over her as she read the message on the screen. "Dax is here. I just need to grab my bag, and I'm out of here."

"Wait, what?" Jamie sidestepped, getting between her and the doorway to her father's room.

"I'm leaving, Jamie. You can tell mom I'm out with a friend."

"What kind of 'friend' takes you away from your family at a time like this?" A vein throbbed in Jamie's forehead. "You're not seriously going to go with that jerk, are you?"

"A jerk?" Rose almost shrieked the word. "How dare you!"

Jamie glared. "Only a jerk would show up at a time like this and just...what... lure you away with him? What do you even know about that guy?"

"Enough to know that he at least cares about how I'm feeling right now." Rose crossed her arms, beyond furious now.

"We're all hurting, Rose. You don't see me running away."

"Jamie, you can't run away if you never go anywhere in the first place. You're so caught up being the perfect son...no...the perfect *Christian*, that you're terrified of actually doing anything at all to rock the boat. You won't even tell Dad you want to go into real estate, not shipping. You keep right on pretending you're going to take over the family business someday."

"I never said—"

"You think I don't know? The way I know you've got your life all mapped out, nice and careful and without making any waves or doing anything daring. You're so much like Dad; it hurts to look at you. Maybe if he hadn't been dragging his feet on this merger, none of this would even have happened." There was a catch in her voice, but she refused to allow it to come back again.

She might as well have struck him. Jamie staggered back a step until his back was right up against the door. "Wait a minute, what are you saying?"

Too much, apparently. The fact that he hadn't seen it when Charity and even Dax so clearly had was somewhat disconcerting. This here was the heart of why she was so angry and why she wasn't going to stand by and watch her father's husk wither away without him inside it. Harlan Wood had made a deadly mistake, and it had cost him dearly.

Now it was costing the rest of them something as well.

"Rose, explain yourself."

Jamie. Poor deluded Jamie standing there, drawing himself up like she'd been the one to attack him when he was the one to drag her out into the hall in the first place. He deserved it.

Rose compressed her lips into a tight line. It was definitely time to go.

"Move."

Jamie drew himself up. "No."

Their voices had risen to where the staff was paying attention. Nurses at the nearby station had stopped work and were staring. The one nearest slid off the high stool where she perched working at a computer and approached. Her expression spelled trouble.

Well, we are causing a disturbance.

Normally Rose would have backed down. She might have even been apologetic. That was the old Rose, though, the one she'd been raised to be, all quiet and obedient. She was a new creation, Rose reminded herself. Charity had taught her that you got nowhere in life by holding back. It was time to be assertive. Strong. Powerful.

"You know something? There isn't a thing in my purse I actually need. I've got my phone and twenty bucks in my pocket. I'm good. See you around, Jamie."

With that, Rose spun on her heel and left, the heels of her boots tapping on the floor in a comforting series of clicks, which carried her quickly to the doors out of the horrifying nightmare. Behind her, Jamie stood as still as death. She could almost picture him, immobilized with that dopey look on his face, all self-righteous outrage.

At least he wouldn't shout after her or do anything to cause a scene. Jamie was too well-bred for that. Or maybe he was just too frightened. It made her exit that much more satisfying, knowing he was helpless to do anything to stop her.

Her hand slapped the big silver button, which marked the exit. She waited impatiently for the heavy doors to open, slipping through before they were halfway there.

Dax was waiting just on the other side, his dark wavy hair mussed, a motorcycle helmet in one hand. He looked incredible in his fine suits, but Dax in a black leather jacket was another matter entirely. For a moment, he took her breath away, making her forget everything she was leaving behind.

Right now, she needed that. To forget. To be someone else for a while. To leave the old Rose behind completely.

She was almost running by the time she reached him. If she surprised him by the way she flung herself into his arms, he gave no sign of that.

"Get me out of here," she said, as he folded her into his arms in a long hug. "I just need to get out of here."

He was even kind enough to ignore the fact that she was crying.

CHAPTER 20

GOSSIP AND LASAGNA

Amy

"It's okay, Jamie. I understand."

Bethany hung up the phone and sat for a long moment, staring at it. She was sitting cross-legged on Amy's bed, shoulders slumped, looking more defeated than Amy could ever remember seeing her.

"No news?" Amy asked, sympathy causing her to reach out and tug at her friend's sleeve, reminding her that she was still here.

"Worse. He got into some sort of argument with Rose. Next thing you know, Rose took off with Dax. Just walked out."

"Dax?" Amy wrinkled her nose in distaste. "When her Dad is in the hospital and everything? Wow."

She didn't ask questions. While curious, Amy could see that talking about this was only upsetting Bethany further. Amy thought for a second and leaned back in the desk chair until she could reach the bureau drawer behind her. "I would suggest we need to pray about this, but right now, you look like you need something more than even God."

Bethany's head came up. "You're kidding. Tell me you didn't just say that."

Amy's eyes flashed with suppressed humor as she fished around in the drawer and came up quite triumphantly with an unopened bag of M&Ms. "Chocolate first."

Bethany burst out laughing. "Now that's why you're my best friend."

Amy opened the bag and handed it off to her after grabbing a quick handful of the candy for herself first. "We should probably pray," she spoke seriously again, frowning. "Though I'm not entirely sure what to pray for. Obviously, that Mr. Wood be okay, but Rose is another matter entirely."

"She's being awful to everyone!" Bethany burst out. "And she left!"

"She's also hurting a lot right now. She's always been really close to her dad. Don't you think that maybe seeing him like that is bothering her a great deal? It's no wonder she wants to run away."

"Is that what she's doing?" Bethany leaned back against the wall and popped several M&Ms in her mouth as she thought about this. "Running away?"

"Do you think we were the only ones to hear what was being said about the fire? And her dad? You can bet she's heard it herself. People can be really cruel without meaning to be." Amy bit her lip. "When my mom was sick, they used to talk about her too. Wondering if she'd done something to make herself sick. Someone even asked my dad once what my mom did that was so sinful that God would take away her health."

Bethany sat up with a jolt. "You never told me that!"

"I wasn't supposed to hear it. I was little, and it wasn't long after the funeral. Dad had put me to bed, but I couldn't sleep. I heard someone at the door and came downstairs, wondering what was going on. It was someone dropping off a casserole for us, and they were standing there going on and on. I never saw my dad look so angry in my entire life."

Bethany's eyes had gone round. "What did he do?"

"He simply handed them back their casserole dish and politely told them he would be appreciative if they didn't come around again."

"That's it?"

"That's it." Amy looked down at her hands, clasped in her lap. "I expected him to shout or want to hit them or something because that's the way I was feeling, standing there in the shadows. I'd never heard such evil, vile words in my life. But Dad only said, "God doesn't work that way, peanut. He never has. He never will." Then he came over and hugged me so tight I couldn't breathe. I never forgot because I could hear him praying when he did so, like he needed to remind himself that was true too."

"Oh, Amy." Bethany scooched over to the edge of the bed, tackling Amy in such a hug that they both wound up on the floor. M&Ms scattered everywhere, and they both lay there giggling like goons because it felt so silly and normal and right to do so.

Amy felt something relax in her that had been tense for days.

"So, what now?" Bethany sat up and starting picking candy off the rug. "I hate that Jamie is hurting so much, and yeah, that Rose is too. But there's also nothing we can do to make it better."

"There is prayer," Amy reminded her, rolling over on her stomach to grab the candy which had rolled under the desk. "It goes back to what Pastor Hemi said. God's got things under control, even if it doesn't look like it. If that's truly the case, shouldn't we just get out of God's way and let Him work?" Amy tried to back out from under the desk and clonked her head soundly on the edge.

"Maybe that's your answer," Bethany said, as Amy rubbed at the sore spot on her head. "If it's all just a matter of getting out of the way, then all anyone would ever need to do would be to do nothing at all."

Amy sat up, gingerly. "True…" Her tone was somewhat doubtful. "You know, every time I think I have this whole living the Christian life thing down, it turns out I haven't gotten it figured out at all." Her eyes went to her Bible sitting on the edge of her desk. The cover was bent and worn, the pages much thumbed. "There is definitely some argument that God also wants us to do the right thing…"

"Now, you're talking." Bethany scrambled to her feet and bent down to help Amy to hers. "Doing implies action. But this is going to take more than a handful of candy to figure out. We need real food."

"For what?"

"A planning session. You have to admit there's something strange about this whole explosion thing, or people wouldn't be talking about it like this. If it was just an accident, people would straight up say so. It would still be tragic, but there wouldn't be so many questions or investigations."

"I think even accidents are investigated pretty thoroughly," Amy said, tossing the candy from the floor into the wastebasket next to her desk. "But I catch your meaning. Even my dad was called out there today, I guess."

Bethany paused, her hand on the doorknob to the bedroom door. "What do you mean?"

"I went over to the church this morning to drop off some muffins I made to go into the baskets they're putting together for families of the victims. Someone there said they saw Dad wandering around ruins out at the shipping company this morning. 'Bright and early,' she said. With someone else."

"Who could possibly tell that from the road? There're too many trees down there. Besides, that's not exactly a residential area."

Amy shifted awkwardly. "I probably shouldn't say because it seems a little too much like gossip, but it was Mrs. Gunnerson."

"Ah." Bethany nodded, understanding in her eyes. Mrs. Gunnerson was something of a busybody, especially since her husband had died last year. That she would drive up to gawk at the sight of the tragedy was not exactly unexpected. It was quite likely she would have gotten as close as she could safely get away with just to 'take a peek.'

"Exactly." Amy shook her head. "If the local police hired her, they'd probably find the thief who's been breaking into area businesses and stealing computer equipment. C'mon, you mentioned food. Now I'm hungry. I think there's still lasagna in the fridge from last night."

"Yum. Wait. Computer equipment?" Bethany trotted to keep up with Amy, who was already halfway down the stairs.

"It's probably nothing. They were talking about that at church too."

Bethany stopped in her tracks, her head tilted to one side as she considered this. "Huh. Maybe someone broke into the shipping company to steal equipment? The explosion happened early in the day. The thief might have knocked over something or done something which might have left something smoldering."

Amy laughed, looking up at her from the landing. "Weren't you listening at all when Dad was teaching us all that breaking and entering stuff for class? He also reminded us somewhere in that lecture about Occam's Razor?"

Bethany frowned but followed Amy downstairs all the same. She was still frowning when they reached the kitchen. "Okay, I give up. Occam's Razor rings a bell, but for the life of me, I can't remember what it's about."

Amy withdrew a casserole dish from the refrigerator and set it on the counter while Bethany got out plates and silverware. As she dished up the first portion onto a plate and set it in the microwave, she drew herself up and took a lecturing tone. "Occam's razor is a scientific and philosophical rule that entities should not be multiplied unnecessarily."

Bethany stared at her. "Um. I know your brain retains terrifying amounts of information, but even that one lost me. I mean, I understand the words, but what in the world does that even mean?"

Amy laughed and grabbed two glasses from the cupboard, motioning for Bethany to grab the milk from the refrigerator. "It's really not that complex."

"So explain it to me."

"It's what I just said. 'It's really not that complex.'" Amy laughed at her expression. "Think of it this way: Most things generally aren't as complicated as we think. Occam's Razor tells us that if we have to do all kinds of mental gymnastics to make a theory work, it's likely not the right one. Most things are a whole lot simpler than we think they are."

"So, by extension, we look for the simple solutions." Bethany sat down on a stool at the counter and placed her chin in her hands as she thought. "So...a long drawn out story about some thief coming along to steal things as I said is likely not it, because there are just too many variables. There's a lot of things that would have to come together to make the theory work. I get it." She sat up as the microwave beeped, and Amy put the second plate in to heat up. "Then what's the simple solution?"

"I'm not sure." Amy slid the first plate across to Bethany, trying to keep from burning her fingers as she did so. She couldn't escape the feeling that she was missing something important. Like the answer had already been presented, or at the very least hinted at. She just couldn't put her finger on exactly what it would be.

At that moment the door opened, and her father came into the kitchen from the garage. He paused for a moment to close the door, then resumed walking as if they weren't there at all. He moved heavily, his head down, forehead furrowed in thought. Not like himself at all.

Amy and Bethany exchanged glances.

"Dad?"

Bethany even waved. "Hi, Dr. Bradford."

He didn't seem to notice they were even there. In fact, he walked right past without saying anything at all, heading toward his study in a single-minded, even grim determination.

"He looks as though he just lost his best friend," Bethany murmured behind her.

Amy started, a knot forming in her stomach. "You mean, Mr. Wood?"

As one, they looked at Bethany's phone, where it rested on the counter next to her plate of lasagna. The screen was blank.

"Okay, so it's not that," Bethany said, her hand pressed to her abdomen like she was going to be sick.

"Jamie would have called. For a minute there…"

"I know. I felt it too." The microwave beeped a second time. Amy stood, torn between rescuing her food or going after her father. The only reason this was a debate at all stemmed from the way her father had walked through the room, head down. As if he had not only been upset about something, but that he was also thinking just that hard about something incredibly important. The last thing she wanted to do was to interrupt his thought process, no matter how much she wanted to know what was going on.

"Something's up, though," she said finally as she grabbed her own plate from the microwave.

"Something suspicious, you mean," Bethany said. She stared at her plate. "Suddenly, I'm not hungry, after all."

Amy stared at her lasagna. As good as it smelled, neither was she.

CHAPTER 21

HALLELUJAH AND HANDCUFFS

Jamie

The room was silent except for the hum of machines and the pastor's quiet murmur as he brought Harlan Wood to the foot of the Father's almighty throne. Jamie sat hunched over, unable to focus on the pastor's prayers or his own. His mother wept softly beside him, her prayers taking the form of tears.

Wasn't there something in the Bible about that he'd just read? How sometimes the Holy Spirit interceded in groans too deep for words. These then were the prayers of his mother, of himself.

He took comfort in this, in knowing God was smart enough to figure out the intent without it having to be defined for him.

Jamie liked thinking about things this way. He enjoyed things that made logical sense, like math. Finding the beauty of numbers and logic in the Bible had been a surprise. Finding it here now, at his father's bedside, even more so. As though God wasn't as far out of reach as he'd seemed in the week since the shipping company had burned, and his father had entered the hospital.

"Today is the day for miracles!"

Jamie's head came up as the words rang out, filling the room. Pastor Hemi continued on, claiming these words as truth. Jamie sat turning these over in his mind, puzzling through what it would mean if this were true.

Miracles. Miracles didn't fit well with logic. They required too much faith, and lately, that had been in short supply.

His mother's head was still bent. Pastor Hemi stood, his hands upon his father's, which had been arranged neatly over his chest. Harlan Wood looked too much like the dead already, arranged like that.

"Today, he's going to wake." His mother touched Jamie's arm lightly. When he looked at her, the worried lines had eased around her eyes and mouth. "Today he's going to wake," she said again, her faith shining out through tear-washed eyes before turning away to gaze with love and tenderness upon her husband's slumbering form.

Jamie looked away, feeling like an intruder on something too private for him to bear witness to. The pastor was busy talking, holding his mother's hand, and saying something. Jamie didn't know what he was supposed to do now that the praying part was done. He stood up and went to the window but was too restless to stand around. Finally, thinking to give the pastor and his mom some privacy, he stepped into the hallway.

Maybe that was a God thing because he was the one who saw them coming before anyone else did.

He recognized the first cop from that day out at the fire. Not the young one who'd at least been passably nice, but the other. The one who'd been at the gate later, who'd made them leave. He strode out next to Brian, whom he honestly didn't know all that well.

He knew him well enough to recognize trouble when he saw it, though. The men were grim-faced. Each step spoke of purpose and a dark business, they had no wish to carry out.

Jamie's heart leapt into his throat.

Dad!

Jamie whirled and slipped back into the room. "They're coming for him," he said fast, to get their attention, still looking over his shoulder. "They can't do anything, though, can they?"

"Jamie, look, your father..."

It was the joy in his mother's voice that broke through the fog of fear and pain blanketing Jamie. He turned, dreading what he would see, feeling faint when he saw his father's face, his father's eyes open for the first time in a week.

His mother stood over her husband, radiant. She clasped his hand between her own, crying again, this time tears of joy. It was Pastor Hemi who recognized something was wrong. He started forward, smile fading. "What is it, son?" He didn't wait for an answer but reached past Jamie to look for himself.

It was too late. They were already there.

"Dad!" Jamie rushed forward, bending low over his father, crying now. He'd protect him if he could, but there was nothing he could do. No battle he could fight. Oh, why had he chosen this moment to open his eyes?

The door opened. Pastor Hemi was pushed out of the way even as he tried to block them. Jamie buried his face against his father's shoulder and wept. "Dad."

Behind him, someone cleared his throat.

"Harlan Augustus Wood? You're under arrest for criminal negligence leading to the deaths of Mario Rodriguez, Ernest Walsh, Thomas..."

The names droned on. Jamie felt his father's hand in his hair, impossibly weak. Trying to make him feel better. The words whispered were raspy, from a voice left too long unused. "It'll be okay, son."

CHAPTER 22

DETERMINATION AND DESOLATION

Bethany

Bethany couldn't decide if she'd picked the right shirt or the wrong shirt, given what they were doing. The red tee was her favorite, and proclaimed bravely across the front, "LIVE IN THE MOMENT." Right now, she was feeling decidedly impulsive in coming over to the Wood's house, especially without an invitation. She took a deep breath before knocking, trying to find calm and courage. A quick prayer helped too.

At least Jamie seemed glad to see her.

"It will be all right," she assured him with a hug. "We'll figure this out."

"Figure out what?" It was Rose, who'd come home to meet the disaster head-on. Given how much time she'd been spending with Dax lately, this was saying something. At least she looked more like the old Rose. Kind of. Her ponytail had been replaced by an updo which, while charming, was more care than Rose used to give to her appearance. She spoke with more intensity, as though she were waiting for something, but what, Bethany couldn't say.

"Everything. Your Dad. What really happened."

Rose stared at her, her lower lip quivering ever so slightly before she drew herself up, face hardening.

"There's nothing to figure out. He did it."

"He didn't!" Jamie exploded in the same instant Bethany answered as well.

"We can prove his innocence."

Rose glared and stomped across the room to sit on the couch, flipping channels on the TV. Jamie drew Bethany to the dining room table, inviting her to sit with him. "Tell me what you're thinking," he said, his eyes brightening for the first time in days he saw hope.

"I have a plan."

Bethany talked quickly. The entire building hadn't burned. There were offices, places where there might still be information. People they could talk to. Someone had to have seen something. There had to be something the investigators missed. She spoke with the conviction of one who had spent a great deal of thought and even prayer on her words before speaking them. And Jamie, *her* Jamie was listening.

So too, was Rose, who eventually abandoned the TV and came to sit down with them.

Bethany summed up her thoughts and leaned in as she finished, clasping her hands on the table, even smiling now because she was so sure of what she was saying. "Guys, I really think we can do this."

Rose immediately shook her head, no. "Everybody in the town says our dad was responsible for the explosion that killed those workers. How can we fight that?"

"By proving that he didn't do it!" Jamie jumped in quickly, his expression fierce. "We know somebody set him up to take the fall, and…" here he looked at Bethany, meeting her eyes. "…there must be evidence somewhere."

"We're just high school kids. We can't do anything." Rose's voice trembled as she drew back into herself. Gone was the confidence of the new Rose. Here was the hesitant girl Bethany had known for years.

"That's the point," Bethany hastened to reassure her, reaching for Rose's hand and stopping when Rose drew back so far she might as well have climbed over her chair to get away. Bethany paused, drawing back her hand as though she had only been making a gesture and that she hadn't been reaching for Rose at all.

Bethany took a breath, struggling to keep her voice calm, even reasonable. Hoping Rose would be the same. "Rose, listen. Nobody will be paying any attention to us. And Amy can help. Her dad is working with the police." She paused, unsure if she should have said that. Amy had only found that out recently, and it wasn't exactly public news. "She hears stuff."

Well, that part was true enough anyway.

Rose reacted as if struck. "Just leave our family alone, Bethany!"

"Rose!" Jamie stared at his sister as if he'd never seen her before.

"We've been through enough!" Rose snapped, throwing up her hands and shoving herself away from the table.

Bethany recoiled, blinking back tears. This was the Rose Jamie had been telling her about. She didn't know this Rose but was quickly finding she didn't like her very much. She struggled to speak, willing herself not to cry. "Rose, what's going on with you. We *are* family. You know that."

But Rose had turned away, arms crossed. Staring at something only she could see. She seemed almost above them at that moment, sitting there with so much silent dignity and even derision, and something else she couldn't quite identify. In that instant, Rose became a stranger.

And Bethany no longer knew how to reach her.

Bethany opened her mouth to try again, but Jamie waved her to silence. She smiled at him gratefully as he leaned forward to touch his sister's shoulder, speaking urgently, though she gave no sign she was even listening.

"Rose, I'm gonna see our dad's name cleared."

Nothing. No reaction at all.

Jamie's face hardened. "Fine. You know what? Bethany, at least, is going to help me. Even if you won't."

Well, that did it. Rose was pulled in so tight it was as if she were trying to keep herself from breaking. Her voice broke into a sob as she glared at him, at them both. "Fine! Just keep me out of it!" She snapped the words, throwing up her hands in disgust as she launched herself from her chair and ran from the room.

Bethany was right behind her. "Rose!"

Jamie reached out and caught her arm, holding her back. "Let her go, Beth."

"But…" Bethany bit her lip and sank back down into her chair. She wanted to say it felt wrong to let Rose go when she was obviously so angry at both of them.

On the other hand, Jamie was still holding her hand.

She looked down, then up at him. Something tight in her eased as he smiled and drew her closer.

Oh my.

"We've got this."

Bethany forgot Rose. She forgot everything as she lifted her head and gazed into Jamie's eyes. Their fingers intertwined, intimate, and perfect. When he looked at her like that, she even forgot to breathe.

He was absolutely right. Rose obviously needed her space to cool down and think things through. In the meantime, Bethany would stay right where she was, so Rose would know where to find her.

CHAPTER 23

WAGGING TAILS AND WILD GUESSES

Amy

"Dad! Look out!"

The eminent Dr. Martin Bradford was entirely in the way of too many dogs. Not his fault. He just happened to be bringing takeout into the house from the car when Amy showed up with the Patterson hounds who were quite impossibly taking her for a walk.

The dogs descended upon Martin in a flurry of yips, yelps, and excitement, tails wagging. Every last one of them had only one object in mind: the bag of kung pao chicken being waved high over his head out of reach of the wild pack of dogs who were convinced this was a new game.

"I'd go in and make this easier on everyone if I weren't tied up like an Egyptian mummy!" he shouted, as the leashes wound around his ankles with alarming precision.

"I'm sorry, Dad. My timing was horrible." Amy bent to untangle one leash from another.

"I didn't know you were dog-sitting today."

"The Pattersons had to go out of town for the day." Amy drew the yelping pack away from her father somewhat regretfully. "Let me put them in their run next door, and maybe I can join you for dinner? You got something for me, didn't you?" It smelled wonderful, and she couldn't blame the dogs for wanting their share.

"Szechwan Chili Broccoli with steamed dumplings."

"Dad, I love you!" Amy drew the pack of dogs down the street to their own home, where she returned them to their grateful owners who were just now getting back. On her way back to her house, Amy found her steps lighter than they had been lately. It wasn't just the prospect of hot food. Her dad had seemed normal again. Cheerful. Even somewhat dorky as he danced around trying to keep their dinner from the dogs. It was the Dad she knew, the one she'd been missing.

Maybe everything was finally going back to normal?

She arrived back out of breath and eager to sit down to dinner. As she washed up, she even rehearsed what she wanted to say. She'd been holding back her thoughts for days about the arrest of Mr. Wood and the fact that Bethany and Jamie were trying to conduct their own investigation. By the time she found her dad in the kitchen dishing up the food, she'd even convinced herself that he would be proud of them for using the skills he had been teaching them in his class on forensic science. Even if they hadn't really found anything yet, she even imagined him beaming at her as she reported to him.

"You seem chipper, Amy," her dad said he handed her a heavy-laden plate and motioned her over to the table.

The food smelled wonderful. Life was good. "Maybe I am, Dad." She sat down and bowed her head, waiting for her father to say grace.

"Lord Jesus, we thank you for this fine dinner and even finer company. Use both to strengthen us through these difficult times."

Amy's eyebrow lifted. She murmured, "Amen," and reached for the chopsticks. "Um...Dad. Are things still looking so...difficult?" The words tumbled over each other in her eagerness to speak. "You don't think Mr. Wood did it either, do you? That's what you mean? Neither do we. None of us, except maybe Rose. That's why we're..."

She faltered and stopped when she realized her father was staring at her, chopsticks heavy laden about an inch from his mouth. A piece of chicken fell off and hit the table with a wet splat. The silence was profound.

"Um...Amy?"

Amy tried to laugh. The sound came out wrong, though. From the way her father was frowning at her, he wasn't pleased in the least by his only child's babbling, and she was quite possibly in for a heavy storm unless she acted fast.

"Okay, Dad, before you start saying that none of this is any of our business, you have to understand that it is. I mean, this is Rose and Jamie's father we're talking about." Amy dropped her chopsticks, gesturing quickly because sometimes it took her hands a second to keep up with her thoughts. "And because none of us think he actually had anything to do with the explosion, doesn't that make it the responsibility of well, *every* good citizen to be diligent of their surroundings. I might even go so far as to say to keep their eyes open in case something would come up which might be *helpful*—"

"Amy." Her father was looking at her, not angry, but in that way he did when he was both amused and concerned. Like when he was cautioning Bethany not to blow up the house in trying his experiments at home.

Amy sighed. She kind of knew what was coming.

"Honey, you're going to need to let this go."

"But why, Dad?" Amy retrieved her chopsticks but made no move to poke at her food, however good it smelled. "You know the right thing hasn't been done, or Mr. Wood wouldn't have to go to jail as soon as he's well enough to leave the hospital. It's bad enough there has to be a guard outside his door like he's some kind of—"

She couldn't say the word 'criminal' as it was too terrible. Not for Mr. Wood.

"So, you don't think justice was done?" Her father sat back, watching her intently, his food all but forgotten.

"No, Dad, I don't. And neither do you. I've seen how upset you've been since the fire. And I know you went over the crime scene with a fine-toothed comb."

Martin sat up abruptly. "Wait, you know about that?"

By now, Amy was exasperated. "*Dad*, everyone knows about it. They were talking about it at church."

Her father was clearly not happy with this news. The corners of his mouth turned down, several heavy creases settled upon his brow. "So much for national security."

"You found something, didn't you? We've been looking all over for evidence, and we haven't found a thing because everyone had been walking all over the place by the time we got out there. But I think we found the point of origin, and the char patterns indicated—"

One eyebrow lifted. "Char patterns? Point of origin? I don't recall arson investigation being part of our studies."

"We might have engaged in something of an independent study."

"I'm impressed." Her father scooped up the stray piece of kung pao and returned it to the edge of his plate. "Still, I don't think this is a game you kids should be messing around in."

"Game?" Amy went hot and cold, all at once. "How can you say that? And we're not children, not really. We're all going to college soon. I'm actually an adult, Dad. Or have you forgotten?"

For a long moment, he stared at his bowl before carefully extracting a new piece of chicken and thoughtfully popping it into his mouth.

This was it. He wasn't going to answer. Because he never answered. Not when the topic of her growing up or going away came up. Instead, he got all funny looking around the eyes and went silent as he did now. Only now that she really needed him, he wasn't even listening. "Dad, this is important. A man's life is at stake."

"Hardly his life. Even if he's found guilty, he's being charged with criminal negligence. You're talking about years in prison, worst-case scenario. And with a good lawyer—"

"I can't believe you're saying this!" Amy was on her feet now, angrier than she'd ever been in her life. "What about justice? What about doing the right thing? Did you even try to clear him from guilt when you went out to the crime scene? Or did you just find what they told you to?"

"Maybe I'm talking the way I am because it isn't his life in danger, but yours? Have you considered that?" Her father no longer looked jolly or even comfortable the way she'd always thought of him. Gone was the dorky dad who embarrassed her with goofy goggles and stupid dad jokes. This was a man she didn't know. This was the agent who worked out at Mount Hideaway. This man was stiff and unyielding, with a gaze so hard, his eyes might have been carved out of granite.

And while she loved her dad and even respected *Dr. Martin Bradford*, she wasn't sure she particularly liked the government agent standing in front of her.

"Are you going to forbid me to investigate?" she asked when she found her voice.

"Would you listen if I tried to talk you out of it?"

Amy thought about this. "No. I don't think so. Not this time, Dad. I still love you, and I want to honor you the way the Bible says. But I also have to love my neighbor, and that means doing what I can to save an innocent man who's being punished for a crime he didn't commit." Amy looked regretfully at her dinner. She really was hungry, but she'd made her stand. To take her plate would only appear childish, and that wasn't the way to make a graceful exit.

Besides, she'd just realized something.

"Dad?" She hesitated in the doorway, wondering if she should say it or not. "You taught me to follow the clues. Well, the very fact you're still sitting there and not forbidding me to leave the house until I'm forty kind of tells me something very important that you might not have realized."

"What's that, honey?" Martin's voice was hoarse. He watched her carefully without moving.

She almost said it but couldn't force herself to say the words. They were there, though on the tip of her tongue. *You believe he's innocent too, don't you, Dad. But because of your job you're not allowed to do anything about it. I think deep down; you want us to find the truth after all, even if you're saying otherwise right now.*

But this wasn't the only thing she'd figured out in the last ten minutes.

"That you're starting to see me as an adult after all."

With that, she turned to go, feeling older and sadder than she'd expected to feel at the first fluttering of true adulthood. This didn't feel like a moment to celebrate at all. In fact, she'd have given anything to be able to return to the dining room and crawl into her daddy's lap the way she did when she was five and had fallen down and skinned her knee.

The silence from the dining room behind her told her that maybe he felt it too. In fact, given how echoing every room was, the entire house seemed to ache.

CHAPTER 24

RUNS AND REVELATIONS

Rose

Rose could feel her blood pounding in her ears. Her sneakers slapped the pavement; her breath came in short sobs. She could hear him behind her, and any minute now, he would catch up. He would—

Rose threw herself down on the grass at the side of the trail. "Darn it, Dax!" she said between pants as he came to a halt beside her. Though 'halt' wasn't exactly the right word. He kept his body moving, annoyingly jogging in place while still somehow managing to reach down and draw her to her feet.

"You almost had me that time Rose. Another hundred yards and you would have had me beat."

"Another hundred yards, and you'd be explaining to the authorities how I came to drop dead on a jogging trail. I told you before, Dax, I don't run. Nor do I see how this could possibly be anyone's idea of fun."

"I never said it was fun; I said it was a distraction." Dax blotted at the sweat beaded on his face with his towel. "Keep moving, Rose, or you're going to cramp up."

"Like I haven't already?" Rose imitated his actions, wiping at the sweat on her own face, thinking she needed a shower more than she needed some stupid little hand towel. And after that, a pint of rocky road to help her recover. But first, air. She needed air.

Dax caught her hand, pulling her closer, so they could walk together back to her car. At least it wasn't far. To be honest, she was kind of proud that she'd almost made it to the finish line. This near-victory was made even sweeter by the fact that Dax walked with her, holding her hand, and making a big deal about how far she'd run. She found herself preening under the attention.

For the first time ever, Rose thought of herself as capable. Strong and sure. Powerful.

Like Charity Clifton. Speaking of which…

"Dax, are you sure Ms. Clifton said it was all right for you to be spending the day with me? Don't you have work to do?"

The team from Omni had stayed in town throughout this whole mess. They said they were waiting to see what happened because, in their minds, the offer was still on the table. Even with the grave situation Steven's Mill Shipping was experiencing as a company, Omni still saw the property as valuable and even was willing to help rebuild, especially given the fire had only destroyed one of the buildings and done very minor damage to the rest, thanks to the efforts of the firefighters.

"You *are* my work for the day. Charity likes you. She knew you'd be at loose ends with your father's arraignment this afternoon. She thought a distraction might do you good while waiting to go to court."

Rose glanced at him sharply. "I'm not going to court."

Dax's eyebrow lifted ever so slightly. If she hadn't come to know him as well as she had over the past couple of weeks, she might have missed it entirely. Fine. So, she'd surprised him. But she wasn't about to be convinced no matter what he might say. To her way of thinking, she wanted nothing to do with the court or anything which came after. What her father did had nothing to do with her.

In the end, he actually surprised her by not talking further about it. They'd reached the car, and it was time to go. "Want to meet for lunch after you shower and change then? I mean, since you're free?" Dax asked, pausing with one hand on the door.

Rose smiled, relieved that this wouldn't have to be a fight. "Actually, yes. I'd like that. But after lunch, I pick the activity. Jogging was definitely a distraction, but I'm sure we can do better."

Dax grinned. "Better than jogging? Surely you're kidding!"

She flung her towel at him and got in the car.

***

An hour later, when Rose showed up at the hotel, she was told to come to the conference room, the Omni group had commandeered while they were there. She expected to find Dax up to his eyeballs in work, about to apologize for blowing her off. Instead, she found Charity sitting alone at the long table, her laptop open in front of her.

Charity gently closed the laptop and got up to meet her halfway. "Rose! Do come in. How are you holding up? Here, let me get you some water. You must be absolutely devastated!"

"I'm fine. Well. Not exactly fine, but mostly am. Oh, I don't even know anymore. Mom is always at the hospital, and Jamie is always around Bethany, and I just feel so *alone*!"

The next thing Rose knew, she was seated at the table, an overpriced bottle of water in her hand, and pouring out her troubles to a very sympathetic ear. She told Charity about the argument she'd had with her brother at the hospital. About the arrest and how it made her feel when she'd heard about it. Charity sat next to her, alternately patting her hand in commiseration and nodding her understanding.

"I wasn't even there. Maybe I should have been, but I was with you that day because you'd wanted that information about the company, and you'd said I was the one who could find the files you need. They were the right ones, weren't they?"

"They were perfect. That you could find anything at all with all that going on is a wonder. I don't know how you do it."

Rose shook her head, vehemently. "I'm not a wonder. In fact, sometimes I don't know what I am at all."

Rose had a lot of things pent up which she hadn't known what to do with. Here, in this quiet setting, with the attention of a refined and intelligent companion, it was easy to pour out her doubts and worries. To her horror, she began to cry. Once started, she couldn't seem to stop. It was the first time someone was willing to *listen*, and she had so much to say.

"Jamie doesn't believe Dad had anything to do with it. I don't know what to think. I mean, accidents happen all the time, but that doesn't make it criminal, does it? Or maybe someone else did something, something that didn't have to do with Dad at all. Jamie's nuts, thinking he and Bethany can sort that out and clear Dad somehow. I keep thinking they ought to leave well enough alone, but no one listens to me. But they never have listened to me, have they? Bethany always does whatever she wants, and now she's got Jamie following her around everywhere. Who do I have?"

"Oh, my dear..." Charity pushed a box of tissues toward her. "It seems I was wrong in forcing Dax's company on you this morning. Men can be so callous without meaning to be, do you not agree? I have no doubt his idea of activity didn't measure up to your needs at all."

Rose blew her nose hard, embarrassed now that she'd been crying. "Dax? No, Dax is fine. A little clueless, but jogging was kind of fun. He's good at distractions."

"Yes, well, Dax has rather a skill at making one see what he wants you to see."

There was something unsettling in this tone. Rose went back over what she'd said in her mind, wondering if she'd overstepped some line. From where she sat, she very likely did. She'd just been crying in front of a woman who was a very important executive in a company doing a business deal with her father.

Oh, she'd definitely gone overboard. And somehow had gotten Dax in trouble at the same time.

"Dax is extremely loyal to the company," Rose said, trying hard to do damage control before she made things worse.

Charity patted Rose's hand one last time and got up from the table. "I'm sure you're right, dear. I would caution you, though, that Dax is one who, first and foremost, always has his own best interests at heart. Still, he has his uses. Right now, that would be taking you to lunch somewhere nice—my treat. You need a little spoiling after what you've gone through. Make sure he gives you proper attention. No more of his favorite activities. Tell him you want to do what *you* want to do for the rest of the day."

Rose giggled. "I like that. But I must look an absolute wreck…"

Charity waved that off. "Nonsense. You're young enough to look pretty when you cry. Why not go tidy up, and I'll let Dax know you'll be out in a minute." She picked up her cell phone and made a shooing motion to Rose, pointing in the general direction of where Rose knew the restrooms to be.

Feeling lighter than she had in a long time, Rose left the room, swinging her purse from one hand. Maybe she'd needed a good cry to clear the air. She certainly felt better than she did when she was moping about the house or trying to endure one more long prayer session at church.

She also rather liked the idea of getting to do whatever she wanted. Only…what had Charity meant by Dax having his own agenda?

Did that mean she couldn't trust him after all?

CHAPTER 25

PROTÉGÉES AND BETRAYALS

Charity Clifton

"Where's Rose?"

Dax hurried in, out of breath, his hair still damp from his shower. Charity liked seeing him flustered, liked knowing he was off balance. After all, fair was fair. Wasn't she somewhat off-balance as well, put there by this young upstart who had only recently been her fondest creation?

"She will be out in a moment. She felt the need to freshen up after our little talk."

Why she gave him any explanation at all, she didn't precisely know. Of course, he would wonder now what they'd been talking about. If she were honest with herself, she wanted him to wonder. She wanted him to ask, the way anyone else would. The fact that he stood there now, shifting uneasily from one foot to the next and fussing at how his hair lay over his forehead, told her that he would ask Rose, rather than confront her. That meant he still feared her.

Well, good. He should. She didn't let that show, but she did allow herself a little smile at his fears. She hoped she showed amused tolerance, that he would understand that she knew more about him than she let on.

He glanced at her now. Uneasiness in that look. Yes. He was hiding something. People who were honest with each other had no fear in asking questions. It meant they were comfortable enough with whom they were talking to be willing to answer questions in return.

Dax was giving off a veritable cloud of non-verbal signals which screamed he didn't want to be asked anything at all. It was rather darling, the way he thought he was hiding from her. The very act of his silence was by itself as revealing as if he had written a confession. She might have taught him well, but it was she that had the experience, and he was no match for her.

She amused herself with analyzing each signal, starting from the top down.

Head turned slightly away, not quite meeting her eyes? Check. One arm crossed across his body, the other fiddling with his hair, then reverting to a stance with crossed arms, as though holding himself protectively away from her? Check. Only this particular gesture annoyed her, as it looked too much like he was shielding himself from a blow. As though she'd do something so crass as to physically strike him.

Let's see, where was she?

Body angled at 45 degrees, not turned fully toward her? Check. Of course, he could argue he was watching the door for Rose's return, but all the same, being presented with a shoulder did tend to warn off conversation.

Stance rigid? Check. Definitely steeling himself for something. What?

It was all so terribly subtle and delightfully droll. He thought he was keeping things from her so terribly well, when all he was truly doing was telegraphing his desperation. Something was decidedly off about him.

No. He was not one to be trusted at all.

To her delight, when Rose returned, she seemed to be thinking along those same lines. When Dax reached for her hand, she hesitated. Her eyes seemed uncertain when she glanced up, her gaze skittering away to Charity's. Checking with her, Charity realized, for some signal. Asking a silent question which delighted Charity to no end.

Oh, her precious Rose was looking to her for guidance. The girl was such an intriguing puzzle, so open, so utterly pure. It was such a joy to weed out the odd beliefs which were holding the child captive. Here then was an opportunity to teach her yet again.

She gave a hint of a nod, a tacit approval for Rose to go with Dax. Let the girl become embroiled in whatever the little betrayer was up to, and then she, Charity Clifton, would ride to the rescue. The grateful Rose would be hers to mold.

No. My Rue. She will change her name. Become my protégé to replace…him. She will be a force to be reckoned with by the time I'm done with her.

The key was timing. Things were certain to come to a head. She would see to it. But Rose needed to be there to witness the destruction.

"I hope you both have a lovely time," she said, her smile calculated to be gracious. Pleasant. "Dax, I have told Rose you will take her somewhere absolutely lovely for lunch. This is her day, after all. My treat."

Rose's smile blossomed, but she was looking at Charity, not at Dax. Oh, yes, perfect. Absolutely perfect.

"Thank you, Ms. Clifton. You are too kind." Rose smoothed her skirt with one hand, the action a little strained, the girl obviously a little nervous. But she had spunk, for she managed to smile even if a bit uncertainly, at Dax. "Shall we go?"

Dax's eyes had narrowed. He was trying to read the subtext of the situation, the way she'd taught him.

"By all means, let's. Charity. I will see you tonight." He gave a short bow and tucked Rose's hand through the crook in his arm, playing the gallant as he escorted Rose from the room.

Charity watched him go, amused by the display and thinking how best to destroy him.

She waited until she was alone to hit a button on the phone. Her little pet enforcer answered immediately.

"Gustav, tell me you're with Ted still. You are? Good. Put me on speaker. I want you both to be very clear about what I'm going to say. That situation we talked about earlier? I want you to deal with it."

CHAPTER 26

RAINSTORMS AND ROSE

Bethany

Thunder rumbled in the distance. A storm was coming, and Bethany was a long way from her car. She wasn't exactly dressed for mad sprints either.

It had been her own fault. She'd parked at the store to get her mom the items she needed for dinner but had run into a group of girls she knew from church. When they'd suggested walking down to Cones & Candy together for ice cream, it had seemed like a great idea. Only they'd been so busy talking, none of them had paid attention to the weather at all. It had been good to connect with them, though, and the visit was just what Bethany had needed, a break to put some distance between her and the craziness that had been going on the past week.

Feeling like any second the sky would open and attempt to drown her, Bethany considered her options. Getting back to her car was something she'd have to figure out entirely on her own. Her friends were going in the opposite direction.

"Thanks for coming out with us, Bethany!"

The girls waved goodbye and took off at a dead run, hoping to beat the storm.

Bethany watched them go, thinking if the group had been smaller, they would have all crammed into her car at the store, and she wouldn't be in this mess. Maybe if the car was bigger? Well, what was done was done. She licked her ice cream cone thoughtfully and drafted a hypothesis.

If she ran, she might just make it but would likely lose her ice cream cone in the process. On the other hand, walking might be possible if she stuck to the east side of the street and made use of the awnings most of the downtown business seemed to have. She turned a calculating eye to that side of the street.

Most. Not all. There would be some dashing involved if it actually started raining.

Which it did. The first drop plunked Bethany squarely on the forehead. She tilted her head back to glare at the sky. "Right. It's only a little water," she told herself firmly and decided to take the slower option and enjoy her treat.

Unless…

About a block up, she saw Rose's car out in front of the town's only theatre. The Downtown Theatre was a landmark in Steven's Mill and only had two screens. Bethany considered the facts. With only two shows, one starting at 7:00 and the other at 7:15, it was highly likely that the previous show would be letting out soon. Very soon. If she timed it right, she could be waiting under the awning when the picture let out, and she could snag a ride from her friend.

Not that this was a great solution. Things were still pretty stiff between her and Rose.

She glanced again at the sky. "I don't know, God. I'm starting to think you engineered this. The rain. Rose's car. Are you trying to tell me it's time to mend fences?"

There was no answer other than an increase in rain. This was no gentle sprinkle but an actual downpour. Bethany squealed and ducked under the awning of the ice cream shop.

She definitely wanted a ride to her car. If she were to be completely honest with herself, she wanted her friend back even more. It was the process of getting Rose back that made her hesitate; the gap between them was wide and growing larger.

She pitched the cone into a nearby trash can and ran for it, only getting somewhat drenched by the time she reached the theater. She leaned against the building, feeling somewhat like a drowned rat, and used her phone to check the time.

Good. Any minute now.

Sure enough, the door beside her opened. People exited in a rush, couples holding hands. A few parents with children. The occasional knot of teenagers. They exclaimed about the rain, with the look of those coming back to earth after having visited somewhere far away only find this world was getting drenched. Bethany was buffeted by them despite her proximity to the building. It was the awning, of course; everyone wanted to stay dry.

Bethany stood on tiptoe, trying to see over heads. When she saw Rose, she felt a profound relief, the kind of warmth that's supposed to happen when you see a friend. "Rose!"

Bethany jumped, waving her hand, trying to be noticed. When that didn't work, she ducked down and forced her way through the mass, arriving at Rose's car just as Rose did.

Along with someone else. Dax hovered a half step behind Rose, dark and brooding. He wasn't in a good mood, and it showed. For that matter, Rose didn't look much happier. Add to that the fact that neither of them was particularly delighted to see Bethany, and she knew immediately she had made a horrible mistake. The warm feeling began to turn chilly, and the relief became awkward as Bethany's mind tried to keep up with the change.

She almost gave up then and there. She might have—had thunder not crashed loud enough. It seemed to echo off the buildings around them. All three of them flinched.

"I was...um...hoping for a ride," Bethany stammered, looking from one to the other. "I didn't know you were on a...date? I'm sorry, Rose. I kind of wanted to talk, but I'll just be...um...leaving." She turned to go. They were all getting soaked right now because of her.

Lightning lit up the sky, the thunder coming on so fast in the wake of the flash that they seemed to come almost together. The storm had swept in insanely fast and wasn't playing around.

"Bethany, wait!"

Rose tossed her keys to an increasingly soaked Dax. It was the old Rose who caught at Bethany's hand and drew her back under the awning where others still huddled debating the storm. She kept going until they were back where the rain couldn't hit them. Not that it didn't try.

"What did you want to talk about?"

Bethany had hoped they could clear the air; now she wasn't so sure that was possible. She was fast coming to realize that maybe she should have tried sooner than this. Called Rose, *something*. Now, as her friend stood there, arms crossed, dark eyes fastened on her face with a sort of angry defiance, Bethany couldn't help but feel deeply just how much wider than she'd realized the chasm between them had become.

Lord, give me the words.

The prayer, brief as it was, gave her strength, and with that, certainty. "Please, Rose. I know you don't want things to end this way. I feel like we're at odds all the time lately, and I...I miss my friend."

For a moment, Rose seemed to soften. Not that she smiled or anything, she was still miles away from that, but she did relax her stance a little, to the point where she wasn't holding herself quite so rigidly.

"I'm listening."

Okay, maybe not the best beginning, but through God's grace, she had a chance. Bethany flung herself into that opening, talking quickly before Rose changed her mind. "Look, I maybe shouldn't have pushed so hard the other day. I know you said you wanted nothing to do with trying to clear your father, and I wasn't listening. That didn't make me a very good friend."

Rose took a breath. She almost spoke, but whatever she was going to say was lost in a violent crash of thunder. Both girls looked up at the awning above them and giggled when they realized simultaneously there was, of course, nothing to see.

Beyond the awning, the rain came down harder than ever.

"So we're good?" Bethany asked as they drew a little closer together as wind kicked rain under the awning.

"Yeah. I think so."

For the first time in what seemed weeks, Rose smiled at her. Bethany heaved a sigh of relief. "Thank you." She hugged her, thinking that if she had to walk all the way back to her car in the rain, it was worth it just for that smile. In fact, since things were going so well, she couldn't help but think maybe she could broach one more topic. "Um, Rose?"

Rose was craning her neck. Checking the car. Making sure her date hadn't left without her? Bethany hesitated. Maybe this wasn't the time or place?

Or maybe it was. They were here. Together. On good terms. Definitely the time and place. A God thing even. "Rose...Today, your father was let out on bail, but they're still charging him. There's going to be a *trial*, Rose. Now more than ever, he needs our help. I was wondering if maybe you wanted to help Jamie and me in our investigation."

Rose stared at her for a long moment. The smile faded. When she spoke, her voice was bitter. "Really? Here I'd made myself perfectly clear I wanted no part in this, and now, when I think you're going to apologize, you have the...the *audacity* to stand there and think you can tell me what to do. Again? A full 30 seconds after you *apologized*?"

Thunder boomed. Hail hit the pavement, tiny shards of ice which ricocheted off of concrete and bounced off their feet.

"What?" Bethany felt like she had to shout to be heard over the storm. Or maybe it was to be heard over whatever thoughts were running through Rose's head. "Are you kidding? This is your *dad* we're talking about!"

"*My* dad, Bethany. Not yours. You need to butt out where you're not welcome. Whatever my dad did is on him—"

"You think he did it?" Bethany stared at her incredulous. "Rose, you can't be serious! This is your father we're talking about. Harlan Wood would never do anything to hurt another living soul. People died, Rose, and he could go to jail the rest of his life for that!"

"Grow up, Bethany. That's what happens to people who break the law. They go to jail."

"Rose, you worked with him. You know how your father felt about the workers. He would never do anything that would put any of them in danger. You worked out there. Rose, think. Think about how your Dad treated everyone. In fact..."

Bethany paused. There was something there she wasn't quite seeing. Or hadn't seen but was starting to. She grabbed Rose's arm. "Rose, you knew everyone there. If someone wanted to do harm to your father or the company, maybe someone who worked there who had a grudge or was angry with your father, you'd know about it, right? Someone who would benefit from him being framed for the explosion?"

Rose shook her off. "I don't know what you're talking about. Honestly, Bethany, people are staring. What's wrong with you? You're talking crazy." Rose's words tumbled over themselves; her hands flew, emphasizing her words, nearly hitting the woman next to her.

People were starting to stare. The little drama under the awning was nearly as violent as the rain lashing the pavement. Bethany opened her mouth to speak when something very important clicked.

Rose always talked fast when she was nervous.

"You've thought of someone, haven't you? Rose, who is it?"

"I don't know what you're talking about. Look, you might have all day to stand here talking, but in case you haven't noticed, I'm on a date. I came over here to do you a favor. You said you wanted to talk. I even was fool enough to think your apology was sincere. Now you attack me out of nowhere and expect me to be happy about it?"

"Attack!" Bethany tried to wrap her mind around the word, but she couldn't make it fit. *Attack?*

But Rose was clearly done with the conversation. The rain was tapering off, and she was already pushing through the dispersing crowds, her shoes sending up a fine spray of water against her skirt as she ran for the car. She threw herself in the driver's seat as thunder rumbled, distant now though it still echoed against the buildings.

Rose's car disappeared down the street. Bethany watched until the taillights disappeared in the distance. Then, with no other option open to her, she ran all the way back to her car.

Whatever good intentions she'd had at the start of the conversation, they were gone now. In fact, Bethany didn't much care if she never saw Rose again.

CHAPTER 27

ARGUMENTS AND ASSASSINATIONS

Rose

Rose normally loved driving in the rain. The lights from the businesses along Main street reflected upon the wet pavement. She would send the small car careening through rainbows, enjoying the beat of wipers in time to the music blaring on the radio. It was playing in puddles, like when she was a kid.

Today though, the music only irritated her. She jabbed at the button three times to make it stop, and even then, Dax had to do it for her. It was as though her car was a stranger; nothing fit right. The car wasn't even obeying correctly and careened around the next corner, too fast, and sliding for a moment before she regained control. She held it firm against the fishtail.

"Think you might want to slow down?" Dax asked.

"Think you might want to keep your thoughts to yourself?" Rose shot back, taking the next turn, if anything, a bit faster than the last. It was childish and petty, but that's how she was feeling.

Dax shrugged, but a glance at his pale face showed he was rattled. Good. Maybe she liked him rattled. "You know," she said as she slowed to a stop for a red light. "If you'd proven yourself to be a creep by trying to do something in the movie theatre, I'd probably be less mad at you than I am right now."

"You mean I had a chance—"

It was a good thing the light was still red because Rose couldn't possibly slap him across the face while driving in this downpour. Her hand stung as she replaced it on the wheel, the sound of her palm striking his cheek still ringing through the car. The position of the front seats made for an awkward strike, but judging from the way her palm tingled, it was effective enough.

"I guess that's my answer." Dax experimentally stretched his jaw.

"You think this is funny?" The light changed, and Rose gunned the engine. "I trusted you!" She stifled a scream and sent the car sliding through an intersection, narrowly missing a bicyclist. "Are you kidding? Who's on a bicycle in this mess?"

"Look, Rose, I don't know what happened back there with your friend, but you need to slow down." Dax reached a hand across to touch hers, where it clutched the steering wheel so tight her knuckles seemed almost white in the semi-darkness. "Actually, things haven't been exactly right between us since we went to lunch. Maybe we can pull off somewhere? Talk?"

"Talk? Why is it all anyone ever wants to do is talk?"

"Because it sounds safer than you taking your frustrations out on a wet road in a car not exactly equipped for stunt driving. Rose, look out!"

They narrowly missed a truck which had loomed seemingly out of nowhere. Rose felt the blood drain from her face as she struggled to keep the car from running into someone's yard when she swerved to avoid them. Her heart was in her throat, and she fought an urge to shiver.

"Yeah, maybe you're right."

It cost her to admit it, but things hadn't been right all day. How much of it was the fault of her father and his arraignment, and how much was on the fact that she was liking Dax less and less as the day wore on, was hard to say. Bethany had only been the icing on a very miserable cake. In truth, it was this betrayal that had stung the most. After a horrible day, sometimes it was good to have a friend to count on, but when that's taken away too, it just makes the rest of the day that much worse.

Rose paused at the next stop sign and looked around her in surprise. Without a clear destination, she'd followed the road out to her dad's shipping company without thinking. They were only about a quarter-mile out. With nowhere better to go, and thinking they might talk better if they had privacy, she made the turn, arriving in the empty parking lot a few minutes later.

The rain had let up, giving a sodden and forlorn air to the place. Crime scene tape fluttered in the wind, caught on the fence that encircled the property. They'd been in the process of removing the ruins, but there was a lot of work to be done and the skeletal remains in the waning light of day created a scene straight out of a gothic novel.

Only this was no Heathcliff beside her, nor was an empty shipping company any semblance of Wuthering Heights. Though the theme of loss certainly permeated the air.

Rose shook off the gloomy thoughts and put the car in park. Headlights lit up what remained of the shipping office before she snapped them off. She really didn't want to sit and stare at the ruins in front of her.

"Well, this is certainly romantic," Dax said and raised a hand defensively to protect his face when she gave him a sharp glance.

Rose lifted a hand to rub at her face. Never had she felt so tired, so strung out. "Look, I'm sorry, Dax. None of this is your fault. I mean, you were pretty much ordered to distract me today and to cater to my every whim. I didn't even want to see that movie; I only wanted to know how far you'd go to try and please me."

"You mean you're not into animated aliens who sing and dance on rainbows?"

Rose fought a smile. "Absolutely not. It just…well I just kept thinking about something Charity had said."

"You'd be wise not to listen to everything Charity says," Dax said, frowning. "I won't even ask. I would expect her to have pointed out a laundry list of my flaws." He turned toward Rose, reaching for her hand. "Yes, I'm ambitious, Rose. Even self-interested to a certain extent. But I do like you, and even respect you." He touched his cheek with his other hand. In the lights from the dash, she could still see her fading handprint upon his skin. "More so now. Not a lot of girls have such high standards or even morals. And it's kind of nice. Like you know you're worth something. It makes me value you more, if that makes sense."

Rose flushed. "If I'd known that, I'd have hit you sooner," she said, trying to make light of the matter, but in truth, she was pleased. It was nice to know he thought highly of her. She found herself relaxing a little against the seat. "I'm sorry for giving you such a crummy day. Just…with all that, and my dad, and Bethany…I've been mad at you since lunch for no reason, and that's not fair."

"You want to talk about it?"

Rose snorted. "Hardly. Should I?"

"Sometimes, it helps to get things out rather than stew on them."

It had stopped raining. The lights in the parking lot should have come on by now, but they appeared to not be working. In the darkness of the car, it felt almost too close. Intimate. "Would you mind if we walked while we talked?"

"Not at all."

The fact that Dax understood made it easier to like him. She stepped out of the car into humidity. She could still hear rumbles of thunder in the distance, and there were flashes of light along the horizon. Another storm coming? Or just the traces of the one which had just left?

Dax took her hand as they walked toward the main building. While scorched, it was still fairly intact. She'd been through that door a thousand times and never thought that someday everything would change. Not like this. It felt almost as though the building itself had betrayed her. It was supposed to be eternal, unchanging. It was supposed to be always there for her, without thinking about it.

"I hate this place now," she said fiercely, kicking at a rock, sending it careening into the darkness.

"If it was your call, what would you do?" Dax nodded to the dark structure.

"I don't know. Sell out? Walk away? I couldn't bear to have anything to do with it ever again. People died here." She turned to look toward the ruins, almost invisible now. "I'm glad it's not my decision."

"It could be." Dax stepped closer, almost too close, as he captured her hand in his. "Someone is going to have to make the final decision. If your dad is in jail, what then?" He moved closer, his breath a whisper against her ear. "Your mother is on the verge of a breakdown. Someone needs to be forceful, to decide…"

Rose recoiled, pushing him away. "What are you saying?"

"Maybe what needs to be said."

"I'm not listening to this."

But he caught her arm as she tried to walk by. His grip was iron, and this time he wasn't letting go. "Yes, you are. Rose, your dad is going to do whatever the lawyer tells him to. It's up to you to influence the decisions. Didn't you tell me once he called you his 'Daddy's Girl'?"

"I never should have told you that!" Rose struggled against him, twisting, but he shoved her against the building. There was nowhere to go.

"I'll let you go in a minute, but you need to listen to me. Omni isn't safe. They're going to make an offer, a rather good offer to buy out, to make things right. Money which can pay for your Dad to have the best representation in the world."

"Why would they do that?" Rose cried out, trying to step on his foot to make him let go. "Don't they understand? They can have the place for a song. My mother wants nothing to do with it, and Daddy...Dad doesn't know what he's saying. He's trying to hold on. Just...Let me GO!"

Dax wasn't prepared for a homeschool trained fighter in martial arts. While Rose had never taken to the discipline the way Bethany had, she certainly knew the basics to self-defense. She hooked her leg around Dax's and used her weight to propel him up and over. In seconds he was lying on his back, staring up with such a look of bewildered disbelief that she almost took pity on him.

Almost.

Rose kicked him once, hard, while he was down and again as he scrambled to his feet.

"Will you just STOP?" Dax howled and tried to sidestep her, stumbling on broken pavement. "Listen, Rose, you have to get him to stop. To *not* sell."

Rose stilled. Besides, she'd made her point. "Wait, what?"

"It's what I've been trying to say, but you don't listen. Look, we don't have much time. Promise me you'll keep him from selling. To hold on until I can make some calls. There's got to be someone..."

"Calls? Wait, if we don't sell, then how would he pay for a lawyer? How would he get out of jail?"

"We'd have to find a way. Your friends were hunting for evidence to clear him, weren't they? If they knew where to look—" His gaze went to the street, and he broke off suddenly. "It's too late." His voice was suddenly cold, flat.

"What's too late?"

But he didn't answer. He had her by the hand and was already towing her across the parking lot. It wasn't until the headlights appeared at the gate that she understood. Someone was coming—someone who scared Dax. As one, they ducked down alongside her car so as not to be seen.

Someone in a long, black sedan.

Rose sucked in her breath. If she thought Dax had scared her before, it had nothing on this ominous presence behind her. "Who is it?" she breathed, though deep down, she knew. They'd come for her.

No. Him. They'd come for him. She tried to make out his expression, but the dying light cast deep shadows behind the car. What of his face she could see looked pale.

"Dax?"

"Get in. We've got to get out of here."

"They'll see the light the second I open the door."

"Then we'll just have to move that much faster. On three. One. Two. Three!"

He flung open the door and dove into the car, Rose right behind him. She settled behind the wheel, starting the engine in one smooth action. Behind her, she heard shouts, the revving of an engine.

"They're blocking the exit!" She cried as she twisted to look behind them.

"Is there another way out?"

"A service road. There's a gate. Maybe? It might be open from the emergency vehicles." She spun the wheel and sent the car flying down the length of the building without waiting for a reply. "Why are they after us?" Her arm was still sore where he'd grabbed her. "Who are you, exactly? What's going on?"

"Let's just say I see things in a way I haven't before."

She shook her head. "If you're about to go all romantic on me, forget it, Dax." Headlights lit up the rearview. Rose stifled a shriek. "Tell me what to do!"

"Where's the service entrance?"

"There! And it's open!" She gunned the engine, and the car leaped in response. The rear tires spun a moment in a puddle and caught again.

She sent the car through the gate, just as the downpour started again. For a moment, she was blinded by the spattering of rain on the windshield. She fumbled with the switch. "Dax? They're still behind us!"

"I'd call the cops, but apparently, my phone broke when I landed on it."

"Take mine!" Rose flung her phone at him. He caught it badly, fumbling it between his fingers. He was still juggling with the device when they hit a pothole particularly hard. The phone went flying, landing somewhere in the back seat.

She twisted, trying to grab at it, steering one-handed. The speedometer crept up, reading forty, then fifty. Where was a cop when you needed one? They hit the state road heading toward the river doing sixty, and the car behind them was still there.

A bang told her something had just hit the car.

Dax's hand was on her head. "Rose, get down!"

"I'm DRIVING!"

"They're SHOOTING!"

He was right; she needed both hands. There was no way to get her phone, not when she was struggling to stay on the road. The windshield wipers beat on top speed, and still, she was struggling to make out the road. If she thought the storm earlier was violent, it had nothing on this one.

"Where are we?" she asked as they sailed through an intersection. "I couldn't read the sign!"

"I don't know. We'll get out of here and find your friend. I have evidence that'll keep your father out of jail and from selling out. Just follow the road."

But she couldn't. There was standing water in the road ahead. She had to twist the wheel, take to a side street that she wasn't sure of. Or was it a driveway? Worse, it led down to the park, down to the river.

One of the small windows behind them shattered. Rose screamed and jerked the wheel.

The car left the road. She couldn't control it on the wet grass. Rose hit the brakes, but they slid. Trees loomed up, illuminated specters with clawing branches in her headlights. Rose screamed, twisting the wheel, recognizing too late just how close to the riverbank they were.

"God, help us!" The prayer came out in a long wail, a last-ditch effort at a miracle. The car began to spin.

The last thing Rose saw was water.

CHAPTER 28

RIVERS AND REGRET

Jamie

Jamie liked mornings. He particularly liked mornings with Bethany. Since they'd started dating, going down to the river to fish had become a favorite pastime for both of them. It was less about fishing and more about being together in a quiet place and enjoying each other's company. This morning though, he'd been unsure about going.

Rose hadn't come home.

Of course, she'd probably stayed out at a friend's house. It would be like her to prove a point. Yesterday she'd made a really big deal about wanting to avoid the arraignment. She'd said she wanted nothing to do with their family right now. The way she'd looked at him when she'd said it had quite frankly made him kind of mad, and Jamie wasn't one to get mad easily. Rose was "holding him at arm's length," as his mother would say, and that's what hurt more than anything.

The thing is, they'd been fairly close, even for siblings. Sure, they'd fought before, but nothing like the tension between them now. And her not coming home was just one more annoyance threatening what was shaping up to be the perfect day for fishing.

Really, he needed to focus on the good things in his life. His dad was home. Sure, he was recovering slowly from his injuries and would be expected to stand trial eventually, but right now, he was right back where he belonged.

With his dad home, Dana Wood had blossomed overnight. For the last few weeks, his mother had been looking pale and frail. This morning she'd been up early, with a bright happiness in her eyes he hadn't seen there in a long time. In fact, it was she who suggested Rose had probably stayed out with a friend.

"Give her time," she'd said when she'd handed Jamie the picnic lunch she'd made for them. "She'll come back when she's ready. God will watch over her."

Ready. Jamie snorted. Fine. Whatever. In the meantime. He had a perfect day with blue skies and the hand of the girl he was starting to love, right there in his hand. He looked down at Bethany as she walked next to him and couldn't help but smile. It was hard to believe a girl like that wanted to be with him as much as she did. He felt a surge a pride that he couldn't have hidden if he wanted to, and he didn't particularly want to.

Bethany chanced to look up then, her face blossoming into the most beautiful smile. "What?!"

Jamie ducked his head, hoping like crazy he wouldn't go and blush or something. "Just...You even make that ridiculous hat look good."

She did, too. He knew how she loved that old hat of her dad's. She peered up at her from underneath the brim, and the way she looked at him with her hair in two curly pigtails flipped over her shoulders and the way the sun hit the smattering of freckles across her nose, left him almost breathless with delight and no small pride. Was it any wonder he walked a little straighter, with a more self-assured step when she was by his side? Any man would.

She rolled her eyes at this, and he stopped, needing her to understand what he wasn't putting into words at all well. "Seriously, though, Bethany..." he took a shaky breath, trying to choose his thoughts carefully to get them right. "You know my whole world is falling apart, but...being with you...I feel like the luckiest guy in the world."

He did too. Why else would he be stuck with a smile that wide upon his face at this hour of the day if he wasn't? He found he smiled a great deal when she was with him.

It was Bethany's turn to look away. She was pleased though, he could see it in the smile she tried so hard to hide. But when her eyes met his, it was with a seriousness he hadn't expected.

"Look, Jamie, I know we're going to figure out what really happened at the warehouse and clear your dad's name. Everyone knows he wasn't the one to cause the explosion." She sighed and shrugged. "We just have to keep digging."

This right here was why he loved her. Who wouldn't love a girl like that? She looked tired, though, and it worried him. When he'd called this morning to tell her about Rose, she'd said she'd seen her last night. That they'd had 'words' whatever that meant.

He wanted to ask more about that, but the moment passed. Bethany was smiling again, her tone teasing as she poked him in the chest with one finger. "And I hope you're the luckiest guy in the world because the last time we went fishing, you caught zilch. Zero."

"Oh, really?" He drew himself up, ready to defend himself.

She snickered. "Nada."

"Humph. I guess if it's true, I mean——"

He broke off. Something had Bethany's attention. Something behind him, down toward the river. Still laughing, he half-turned to see what had caused her smile to fade and her skin to go pale beneath her freckles.

He still didn't see it. Not until she asked the question did he even know what she was looking at.

"Is that Rose's car?"

They dropped their poles and ran.

Bethany took the lead as they bolted down the hill to the riverbank. The closer he got, the harder it was to breathe. There was no doubt about the car. Rose's car was so unique; there couldn't be another like it in the entire county.

The vehicle tipped forward into the water. Broken windows exposed the interior to the elements. The door nearest them was open, water flowing through the compartment.

"ROSE!" Bethany's scream pierced the quiet morning. There was no reply.

Whatever had happened, it had been violent. The hood was crumpled, what they could see of it. The front end of the car was deep into the river, the currents pulling at the vehicle as though eager to finish the job, to carry it away.

"Do you see her?"

Jamie reached Bethany's side. She had waded out as far as she dared, but the currents were swift. Jamie pulled her roughly back onto the shore. He could see from there no one was in the car.

"Don't go out there; it's dangerous! No, she's not in there. ROSE! ROSE!"

He turned back toward the woods, back the way they'd come as though they might have missed her somewhere on the path.

Bethany crept down the bank again, testing the ground. "The water was really high last night because of the storm. You don't think…"

"NO!" No, he didn't want to think what he was thinking. The idea that Rose wasn't off pouting at some friend's house, that she might be in danger…Jamie tried to pray but couldn't find the words. He could only clasp one hand to his head to try to still the pounding of his heart in his ears. "What was she *doing* out here?" The question tore from him.

"I…I don't know."

He turned on Bethany. Something in her half-sobbed answer connected something in his mind. What had she said this morning? That they'd had *words*?

He looked at her now, truly looked at her. Bethany was standing as though deep in thought. No. She was doing more than that. She was biting her lip. Looking… guilty?

"You two were together last night. What were you talking about?"

Bethany flinched away from the question, turning the gesture into an awkward shrug. "Nothing. I mean…I asked her to help us with our investigation again."

Jamie drew himself up, lips compressing to a thin line. He stared at Rose's car, trying not to cry, and here this…this girl seemed to think she had all the answers.

As usual.

"…And then she got all irrational…"

Irrational? Jamie jerked around to face her. "Bethany!" he snapped the name, sharper than he intended, for she jumped and if anything looked guiltier than ever. Still, he could not seem to stop himself from speaking further, knowing his words were hurting her. No. Because he knew they would hurt. Because he was hurting, and he couldn't understand anything else but pain. Not just then.

"She didn't want any part of our investigation. We agreed we would leave her out of it."

"I know!" Bethany snapped out the words, looking angry now from the way her fists clenched at her sides. "But she worked at the shipping company part-time before the explosion, and I just thought—"

"So, you tried pushing a little harder?" He gestured to the half-submerged vehicle.

"No, that is not what happened." Bethany's voice was raised, her stance opening, becoming more confrontational. It was one of her stupid karate moves, designed to build confidence, and it made him even angrier that she felt the need to use it on him. As though *he* were the bad guy here.

"As soon as I even brought the subject up, she got all evasive and defensive, like she was hiding something. Then she just stormed off." Bethany flung out her hand to emphasize the point.

He couldn't take any more of this. "So, you just let her go?"

Bethany stared at him a long moment before answering, pulling herself visibly under control. "What was I supposed to do?" she asked, her eyes narrowing on him, staring him down.

"Well, NOT THAT!" he shouted and stalked away, grabbing at his phone because it was high time they called someone. If Rose was out here somewhere, the last thing they needed to be doing was standing around arguing. He needed to get someplace where he'd have a cellphone signal.

Bethany didn't follow. When he looked back, he saw her still standing on the riverbank where he left her. She stood next to Rose's car, a tiny figure in an oversized hat. For the first time since he'd known her, Bethany Shanholtz seemed small and even fragile.

Yet it was his sister who was missing.

Somehow he managed to keep the tears at bay until after he called 9-1-1.

CHAPTER 29

FAITH AND FATALITY

Bethany

Bethany couldn't stop crying. The tears burned on her cheeks, but they kept pouring down in rivulets as though they were some sort of release valve for her emotions. The thing was, she wasn't feeling any relief. Rose hadn't been found. The car had been empty, discarded like so much refuse on the riverbank. Rose's phone had been found in the back seat.

Dax's phone was under the seat, the screen cracked and broken.

None of this was looking good.

"Honey."

Bethany's mom came into the room and settled herself at the foot of Bethany's bed. She reached for her daughter, pulling the girl into her arms the way she'd done when Bethany was young, and her puppy had been hit by a car. Bethany leaned into her mother's caresses gratefully.

"I can't stop crying, Mom. What if something terrible has happened?"

The fact was, something terrible had already happened as far as Bethany was concerned. Rose loved that car. The idea of dumping it deliberately in the river was inconceivable. The tracks from the road down to the riverbank seemed more likely to be attributed to an accident. The crushed vegetation told the story fairly clearly. To all effects, it looked as though she'd lost control of the car somehow, had tried to avoid hitting a tree, and then wasn't able to regain control of the car the rest of the way down to the river.

Which left the question then of where Rose was.

"What if they don't find her?" Bethany asked, swiping at her eyes, surprised to find she still even had tears left.

"Then God still knows where she is, and we'll trust her to him."

She heard a noise at the door. Bethany sat up, still sniffling, to find her sister standing there. Joy had in her arms a fluffy rabbit, which she came and dumped on the bed next to her sister despite her mother's raised eyebrow.

"When I'm sad, I find that Oliver helps." Joy bit her lower lip, looking for all the world like she was desperate to help and hadn't a clue how.

"Oh, Joy!" Bethany gathered her little sister in her arms for a hug, who immediately scrambled to find a way to fit Oliver in there somehow. The angora rabbit seemed somewhat used to such behavior and placidly sat between them, nose twitching until Bethany absolutely had to laugh. Joy was well-named. The ache was still fresh, but the tears finally paused.

Eventually, it was Tina Shanholtz who broke things up. "Okay, troublemaker," she tapped her youngest daughter's nose, "why don't you take your bunny and scoot. I want to have a talk with Bethany."

"Am I in trouble, mom?" Bethany asked after her sister had left the room.

Tina shook her head, thoughtfully. "Not in trouble, but I do think we need a talk. How about some tea?"

"Sure?" Bethany followed her mom downstairs, where she was not surprised to find the water already on, the kettle boiling away merrily. "You plan everything, don't you?" she asked, finding to her surprise she could still be amused by things when her insides were knit together with grief.

"I try to be prepared," she corrected her as she poured hot water into two mugs. "I thought maybe lemon balm might be good."

"I'm not depressed; I'm sad," Bethany muttered, sitting heavily and reaching for a muffin from the basket on the table. Not that she was hungry, but it gave her something to pick apart.

"They're fairly closely related, and right now, you're experiencing a great deal of sorrow and uncertainty. I say let's use what we have at hand to help alleviate the situation. What else do you remember from the psychology class I gave you?"

"Warm beverages help with shock," Bethany recited, cupping her mug in her hands. "A quiet atmosphere helps too. And...prayer?" The last wasn't really a guess. Her mother's well-worn Bible lay between them. "Prepared, huh?"

"I try. I added a hint of ginger to the tea as well. It might help alleviate some of the pain."

How did her mother know how hard it was for Bethany to breathe? His chest had been tight since seeing Rose's car in the river. Unbidden, the image of that car came back to her.

Rose...

"Mom. What if Rose is..."

"I'm not going to sugarcoat it. The fact that her car was found hours ago and there's still no sign isn't good. You're right; the water was much higher last night."

"I should be out looking!" Bethany started to get up, but her mother caught her hand and tugged until Bethany was sitting again, even if it was on the edge of her seat. She didn't know which way to turn.

Tina stirred her tea. "Let the professionals do their job, honey. They don't need a lot of people getting in the way right now."

"But when they do searches for missing people, don't they want a lot of people to show up to mark areas off in quadrants and do a meticulous search of the area? When you came and got me, I expected to change and go back, and you told me to wait, and now..." Bethany's words died in her throat. "They're not searching the woods around the river, are they?" The realization hit her like ice. "They're dragging the river. Oh...oh, Mom!"

Bethany put her head down on the table and sobbed.

"Lord, watch over my child." Bethany could feel her mother's hand on her back. It was oddly soothing, just knowing someone was there. "Watch over all our children today, tonight...we're all hurting so much, Lord, and sometimes we don't see where you are in all of this. But we're thankful you're still here. Be with us as we go through this difficult time. Help us to know you're still in control."

Bethany whispered an "amen" with her mother, but her heart wasn't in it. She lifted her head and swiped at her eyes. This was fast becoming a habit.

"Mom? Can you not be my mom for a minute?"

Tina Shanholtz's mouth quirked up in a sad sort of smile. "Okay…?"

"It's just…I need a friend more than I need my mom right now. I argued with Rose last night, and the last things we said to each other…weren't nice. And then this morning Jamie and I…well that didn't end too well either. I lost one of my dearest friends, and I think I've lost my boyfriend, and since Amy isn't around, I kind of need…well…"

"A woman to woman talk?" Tina picked up her mug of tea and sipped after blowing on it. "I can do that. I think. So, you're feeling kind of abandoned and alone right now?"

Bethany nodded, poking at her teabag with one finger to see if her tea had steeped enough. "I don't have Jamie to talk to, not anymore. I know he's hurting, but I'm afraid that he and I are…and Amy isn't back yet. She went out with her father. She wants to study forensic science, and because she's older, they allowed her to come, and yet…" Bethany's voice trailed away miserably.

"You're feeling left out. I get that. I feel that way sometimes too."

"You do?"

"Sure. We all do. Being grown-up doesn't mean we have all the answers or even know the right questions to ask. The only true certainty we have in life is the constant love of Jesus Christ and the saving work he did on the cross." She reached for Bethany's hand, "but you didn't want me to give you a sermon. You wanted a BFF. Someone you could talk to about all this hurt you're carrying around right now."

Bethany kind of laughed. It was hard when she was still sniffling, but felt good all the same. "Amy is better at the God stuff than I am, Mom. And yeah, I am hurting."

"I'll wager a guess you're feeling a little like you're not supposed to be either, given what Jamie or his parents are going through."

Bethany started. "How did you know?"

"Because I've been there too." Tina settled back in her chair, frowning a little and talking into her teacup. She looked as though she was seeing something a long way off, or maybe just long ago. "There was a time when I was angry and felt so defeated. Only the feeling didn't fade with time, and there were those around me who thought it should."

"When Dad died," Bethany whispered the guess.

Tina nodded, her red curls bobbing around her face. She swept them back with one hand. "I realized then that it's okay to feel whatever I was feeling at the time. You're hurting because you said some harsh things you regret, am I right?"

Bethany winced. "Yeah."

Tina stirred some honey into her tea and thought a minute. "Jamie said some harsh things too, I'm guessing. Hurting people lash out. It's one of the ways they deal with the pain. The best thing we can do with that is to apologize when we hurt those we love and forgive those who hurt us."

"And what if I don't get that chance? To apologize?" It only occurred to her that this might be the end of her relationship with him, that he might never want to talk to her again.

That it might be the end of her relationship with Rose was too painful to even contemplate.

"Hold on tight; this is going to get all religious again." Tina laughed and tapped the Bible sitting between them. "We give it to God. We let Him carry it."

Bethany sipped her tea while considering this. The hot liquid sent tendrils of warmth through her body. "So...what if I can't?" she whispered, peering through the rising steam from her cup. She cradled the mug in her hands, trying to absorb the warmth. "I don't think I'll ever be able to let this go, no matter how long I live. Not if..." She couldn't suppress a shiver that had nothing to do with the tea or temperature.

Her mother reached out to touch her face, cupping Bethany's cheek with a work-worn hand. "I'm afraid I'm not good at being just a friend. Right now, I want to hold you and try to make everything better. I don't want to see you sad or unhappy, Bethany. But I also know I can't protect you from the world, much as I wish I could. All I can do is be here with you as you go through this." She sighed softly. "As *we* go through this," she corrected herself. "No one wants to go through a day like we are now, especially so hard on the heels of the explosion and everything else."

"It hurts. All of it does." Bethany set down her mug and picked up the Bible, shoving aside her muffin to flip through the pages idly. "Where—"

A knock sounded at the kitchen door. The book flipped shut as Bethany stood up, moving so quickly she knocked over the chair behind her. Heart in her throat, she flung the door open and saw Amy there.

One look at her face told her the news was bad.

Amy did not look like herself. Her long brown hair tumbled loose from her ponytail. A smudge of dirt decorated her nose. She slumped as though the mere act of standing was too much for her to bear and, in fact, wavered on her feet as she was ushered into the room. Her eyes looked haunted, as though she had seen a ghost. Or something worse.

Amy's face was streaked with tears.

"Nooooo...." Bethany staggered, grabbing at the kitchen table to hold herself steady.

"They found Dax," Amy said, her voice little more than a hoarse whisper. "He was in the river, not far from the car."

CHAPTER 30

TRACKS AND TRIBULATIONS

Amy

When Amy had decided she'd wanted to study forensic science when she went away to college, she hadn't expected her desired field of study to become so personal.

Because Steven's Mill was so small, they didn't have a forensic investigator. Her father had filled in more than once over the years. Now she was finally able to see him in action as they removed the car from the water and pulled it up onto dry land.

There wasn't much that the water hadn't already washed away. The discovery of the two cell phones had caused a great deal of consternation among local law enforcement and had immediately necessitated a call to the Omni Millennium people. Word came back quickly. One of their delegation, Dax DiMarco, had never returned to the hotel the previous night. Charity Clifton hadn't seem worried by the news. "Young people can be unreliable," was her explanation for why she hadn't sounded any kind of alarm.

Admittedly, even Rose's parents had thought little of her not coming home last night, given her mood of late.

Now, with so much time having passed since their disappearance and the work of the water on the car, there was little to discover in the vehicle at all. And what they did find was certainly not heartening.

"Neither of them were wearing their seatbelts."

Amy felt the bile rise in her throat as her father detailed his reasoning to the sheriff. Given the state of the seatbelts was pristine, with no damage or anything to imply they'd been strained on the impact, accompanied by the circular pattern on the windshield, it certainly didn't look good.

Rose…

Amy swallowed hard and resumed taking notes, the job her father had tasked her with. He hadn't wanted her to come, but how could she stay away knowing Rose was still out there? She'd said she could handle the job; now, she needed to prove her worth. Obediently, she repeated his findings into the recorder. If her voice wavered just a little, maybe she could be forgiven.

It wasn't until the teams came out to drag the river that she lost it.

Amy bit back a sob. Everything seemed so tragic, so very real. This wasn't like it was on TV or in the movies. These were real people missing. One of which was someone she had known and loved her entire life. She swiped at tears and tramped through the mud on the riverbank with her father—hunting clues that were nowhere to be found. The tire tread marks coming down the riverbank told a haunting and tragic story, but there was nothing to indicate it was anything more than an accident.

"Think, Amy," her father said quietly as they stood up by the tree where the tracks were deepest. "What do you see here?"

"She braked, hard, and twisted the wheel." The sudden veering of the tracks down the riverbank started here, at this point. Standing here, between the tire marks, she had a fairly clear idea of what Rose might have seen at this point, the river tumbling past, the sharp bank, muddy and unstable. There would have been no way to stop the car at this point. The physics of the situation had left her with only one clear path to follow, straight down to the water.

"She wouldn't have seen the river," Amy said thoughtfully. "The mud and the sharpness of the tracks would imply it had been raining heavily. The tracks not being more blurred or washed out would imply she hit the slope at the end of the rainstorm, or near it. The way the storm acted last night, it came on hard and fast and was over kind of quickly. So visibility would very likely not have been good."

"Well done!" Martin Bradford's face sagged with tiredness, his complexion somewhat sallow and worn. This couldn't be easy on him either. He was close friends with Harlan Wood. He had to be feeling this tragedy as deeply as she was. It was a surprising thought to Amy. For the first time, she realized that her father was a person outside of herself. Not just her dad, but a man who grieved and somehow still found the strength to go on despite it all.

Amy slipped her hand in her father's and gave it a squeeze before turning away, retreating further up to the road. "So she lost control up here?"

"Back further would be my guess. Look for the spot where the car hit the shoulder. There should be marks there too."

But they didn't find them. Other cars had been along this way; someone else had driven along the shoulder since the storm, obliterating all tracks.

Coincidence?

Amy debated bringing this up to her father, but in all likelihood, he had seen it already. "What do you think, Dad?" she asked, coming to stand next to him at what seemed the likeliest trajectory.

"Look closer," he advised.

Amy lay down on the ground, trying a whole new angle to examine the problem. It felt good, having something to do to take her mind off the noise, the shouts as the crew with the heavy equipment and boats moved farther downstream.

From this angle, the crushed vegetation was easier to see. The car had definitely passed through about a foot to her right. She backtracked and went to stand in the road. There was no need to worry about traffic as they'd cordoned off the entire street. Not that it was a street—really, more an access road down to the river.

Which brought them back to the tracks on the shoulder. "Dad, there isn't anything else down this road, is there?"

Her father thought a moment before answering.

"Just Bill Thompson. He's kind of tucked back up in these hills, but the road dead-ends out at his place. There used to be another couple—rented the house across from them, but as far as I know, it's still empty."

Amy swiped at a bug on her nose and turned to look the other direction. "This wasn't where Jamie parked his truck?"

"No. I noted that. They were farther down by the trailhead. The dirt track meanders down intersecting with Rose's path...there." Martin pointed, and Amy nodded.

"It's an easier walk down. I went fishing down there with them a few times back when it was the...four...of us." Amy bit her lip and turned away.

Rose, where are you?

"Hey...you don't have to do this." Martin put a hand on Amy's shoulder, squeezing gently. "If you want to go back, I can catch a ride from someone else."

"No. I'm good. This is...well, it's harder than I expected. But I want to do this. If it helps us find answers, then you can count me in." Amy tried to smile and found, to her surprise, that she still could.

"Good girl. OK, let's take this apart then. You almost had it. There's no traffic on the road this time of year except fisherman. We'll check with Bill and see if he saw anything. Who knows, maybe he stopped along here to look at the view or something. Or to wait out the storm if he was coming home late last night. You were right; it would have been hard to see in all that rain."

"So you think it's something?"

He was about to answer when his phone rang. In that same instant, shouts erupted from down by the river. Amy looked between the two, unsure. Her father motioned for her to head down. Amy nodded and bolted down the steep bank, careful to avoid the tracks in case there was evidence there they hadn't found yet.

The boats had moved further downriver than she'd expected. Amy was out of breath, her hair down around her face by the time she got there. She'd gotten tangled in some bushes and nearly lost her ponytail holder. She swiped at the hair. Shoving it back out of her eyes as she came through the trees to the bank, in time to see them pull something large from the water.

Not something large. Something human. She caught a glimpse of dark trousered legs, a lax foot and stopped cold.

No.

No. No. NO. NO. NO.

There were no prayers for this.

Amy sank to the ground, her legs unable to support her another minute. Numbly she watched as they heaved the body into the boat. The crew moved in silence, solemn now that they'd found what they were looking for.

How had he gone so far?

The rain. The river would have been higher; she reminded herself. Rose....Rose could still be anywhere.

With a sob, Amy bent her head over her notebook, no longer caring that her tears soaked her notes. Any pretense at being a calm investigator was lost as she cried.

Her father found her there. He helped her to her feet and held her until she had herself under control again. In silence, they watched as Dax was brought back to dry land.

"Omni Millennium called," he said quietly. "They're blaming Dax for the explosion."

Amy's head shot up.

"And?" she prompted when she saw the gray tinge to his face. "Dad, you're scaring me. What else?"

He sucked in a deep breath. "You might as well hear it from me first. They say Rose might have had something to do with it."

CHAPTER 31

INCOMPETENCE AND OTHER IRRITATIONS

Charity Clifton

Charity hung up the phone with a satisfied smile on her face, which faded when she saw Ted hovering outside the door.

"You may as well come in," she called out, setting the phone with great care next to her. Charity was one for deliberate actions, which was why this entire affair annoyed her to no end.

Ted seemed almost hesitant. Where was the confidence he'd exhibited before? Ah yes, shattered by the sheer incompetence required to pull off the previous night's work. He slunk into the room, head down, shoulders rounded as though to ward off a well-deserved blow. That annoyed her even more. *At least stand up to your mistakes.* She motioned impatiently for him to take the seat opposite her. He sat so hastily he nearly missed the chair and had to readjust himself quickly to keep from hitting the floor.

"Would you care to tell me how you and Gustav managed to kill my new protégé? Because I do not recall asking you to deal with her at all."

"You said nothing about the girl one way or another," Ted pointed out, raising his head to look at her with a hint of defiance. Coupled with the obvious irritation in his voice, this was quite a daring display of bravado, especially for one who liked to hide at a safe distance, using timed explosives to make his point. Was he finally growing a spine? She wasn't sure how she felt about that.

"If I recall correctly, I asked you to take care of a problem, not create a new one. I already have to do damage control."

"You've pinned the whole thing on Dax? Isn't that a bit risky?" Ted leaned in, palms flat on the table.

"They were looking at the old man who ran the place, had him secure. We could have gotten the place for a song. Now they're going to be looking at us. How does that affect your *master plan?*"

He sneered the last two words, his lip curling in distaste.

For a moment, she actually thought to justify her actions to this hired creep. Dax was working against her; no doubt turned by a pretty face with a conscience. Dax would have exposed her, all to impress a little hick girl who hadn't been able to shake off her Christian upbringing.

Though she would have, given enough time, of that Charity had no doubt. Of course, now, she'd never get that chance, would she? All because of that idiot Ted and his sidekick Gustav.

"Enough!" Charity's hand came down on the table with a resounding smack, which echoed throughout the room. "What I do with this is none of your concern. My more pressing concern is Gustav. Tell me he's not down at the river, making our interest in the matter obvious."

Ted drew back, crossing his arms over his chest as he settled more comfortably in his chair. "Give us more credit than that. I've got it handled."

"Like you had it handled last night? My dear sir, I will give you exactly as much credit as you deserve. Now, if you will please be so kind as to inform me as to the whereabouts of our associate."

"He's down at the hospital. Establishing an alibi."

"An alibi? Oh, do tell. This ought to be interesting."

"He went in last night after having eaten some bad sushi. Really upset stomach. That way, if anyone thinks something, bam boom, he's been there all night. He should be coming back soon. Every time they think to discharge him, up he comes with something else wrong, so they have to do more tests."

"Huh." Charity sat a moment, her fingernails tapping her phone as she thought this through. "And let me guess, you were the helpful friend who brought him in? Of course, I was here all night, but I had dinner in the dining room and a drink afterward in the bar. You might have done something clever after all."

Ted sat up a little straighter. Gone was the tension from his body. If anything, he seemed a little too relaxed. Self-satisfied. A little too full of himself.

The problem was, both Ted and Gustav were taking far too much initiative. While they'd been somewhat clever in covering their tracks, there were still too many variables in play. She'd cast suspicion on Dax because it suited her needs to do so. Now she needed to know she could count on Gustav and Ted to carry out the rest of her plan.

Right now, she wasn't sure she trusted either.

"Fine." Charity picked up her phone and started scrolling through screens. "Let me know when Gustav is back. Tell him I hope he's feeling better after his... difficult...night. But no more adventures. I ask you to take care of something, and suddenly you're out there acting like the Hardy Boys off on an adventure, sticking your nose in where you're not asked. I need to know what's going on every step of the way. We still have loose ends to clean up."

She glanced up, hoping Ted had gotten the message he'd been dismissed. He was a little slow on the uptake sometimes.

This time though, he'd either figured out he wasn't wanted or knew enough to know he shouldn't tick Charity off further, for he pushed back his chair and stood, even if a bit awkwardly. "Right. I'll do that."

He turned and headed for the door.

"Oh, and Ted?"

He paused, one hand out to push open the door. "Yeah?"

"Don't cross me ever again. You are every bit as expendable as Dax was."

His eyes narrowed. "Understood."

Yes, he most certainly was going to be a problem.

CHAPTER 32

CLUES AND CANINES

Amy

"I can't do this."

Bethany dug her heels at the foot of the driveway. Amy knew that look. She'd known that look since they were five, and Bethany hadn't wanted to go to the dentist because she was afraid he would pull her wiggly tooth out.

Actually, with her hair in pigtails, and with the particular way Bethany was digging in her heels harder, the more Amy tugged on her hand, the similarity was striking.

"You're afraid to talk to him," Amy said, letting go abruptly, not the least bit sorry when Bethany staggered against the mailbox and had to cling to the post just to stay upright. "You're being childish."

Bethany shifted awkwardly, one hand swatting at a mosquito buzzing around her neck. "He made it quite clear he didn't want to talk to me."

"How?" Amy demanded, hands on her hips. At her feet, Mrs. Wilson's cocker spaniel watched the exchange with interest. Amy was supposed to be walking the rather rotund little dog, but so far, they'd spent more time arguing in the Wood's front yard than in actually getting any exercise. The dog began sniffing the post Bethany was leaning on.

"By not answering his phone."

"Bethany, that's only evidence that he's too overwhelmed to deal with stuff. Can you imagine how many people are probably calling him right now? I wouldn't be surprised if he's shut his phone in his closet or something by now. Don't assume the worst."

Bethany eyed the house, her expression wary. "You didn't see how he looked at me when we found Rose's car. I told you what he said!"

"I also told you he was scared and hurting. People say stuff they don't mean when they're upset. You know that."

"He's probably watching us right now. Staring at us from the upstairs window." Bethany tilted her head back, eyes narrowing as she scrutinized each window.

"Like that's going to help?" Amy swatted at Bethany's arm with the end of the leash to get her attention.

"Just go up there and talk to him. You both need to clear the air. Especially with his sister's memorial service coming up."

"Rose," Bethany whispered the word, and the girls stared at each other. Amy swallowed hard, willing herself not to start crying again.

"I can't believe she's gone," Amy said softly, bending to pull the protesting dog into her arms. While Pixie certainly hadn't minded the pause in her daily walk, she wasn't big on cuddles. Besides, there was an entire world of smells to be categorized.

Bethany still hadn't moved. Amy was tempted to give her a shove if dragging her wouldn't work.

"You can do it," Amy said, straightening up and tugging at the leash. "In fact, I'm finishing my walk. You, on the other hand, are going to march up to that door and ask to see Jamie." She tried a more reasonable approach, "I'm sure he'll be glad to see you now that he's had time to think about it." Amy tugged on one of Bethany's braids. "People need their friends more than ever when they're sad."

"It's not just that. We need to clear the air. He said some pretty hurtful things." Bethany sighed, "I might have too." She bit her lip and, with effort, straightened her shoulders. "But I guess I can try all the same." She took all of three steps up the driveway, then spun on her heel and came right back to where she started. "You do it."

"Me?" Amy almost dropped the leash; she was so startled. "You've got to be kidding."

"No. Hear me out. You're better at talking to people than I am. You could be my...my go-between. You tell him that I'm sorry and all that, and then you can come back and tell me what he says. No actual confrontation necessary. I'll even watch the dog for you. I'll even *walk* the dog for you." She made a dive for the leash.

"Oh no, you don't!" Amy held her arm out, away from Bethany's mad grab. "I'm not doing your dirty work for you. The fact that you had a falling out makes it all the more important that *you* talk to him yourself. The Bible even has a verse about this."

Bethany stopped grabbing for the leash and stared hands-on-hips. "Oh yeah?"

Amy wracked her brain, wanting to get this right. "I could check it on my phone, but let me think. It's Matthew 18:15. I memorized this ages ago, but I think this is right. "'If your brother or sister sins, go and point out their fault, just between the two of you.' Basically, what the Bible is saying isn't so much about shoving in someone else's face the fact that they did something wrong, but letting them know you were hurt by their words. The Bible goes on to say that if the other person listens, then you've got a true friend."

"And if they don't listen?" Bethany asked softly, her brow crinkled with worry.

"Then we maybe try to talk to him as a group or with someone else as a mediator to resolve it? The Bible talks about that too."

Bethany scuffed at the ground with her sneaker. "Can you kind of wait here while I go?" she asked softly.

"I can wait." Amy looked down. Pixie had fallen asleep, dozing in the sun. The pudgy puppy was definitely down for the count. "Yeah, I don't think I'm going anywhere."

Bethany almost smiled. "Right." Still frowning a little, she pulled herself up and walked to the door. Amy watched her go, admiring how Bethany just threw herself into things. Once the decision was made, there were no more hesitations. She just strode into the situation, head high, ready to take on the challenge. It was getting her there, which was sometimes so difficult.

Amy settled on the curb next to the slumbering dog, trying not to watch, but paying attention all the same as Bethany rang the doorbell and waited. And waited. Finally, someone came. Amy had to lean to the side to see better, as a tree was blocking her view, but the person Bethany was talking to looked like Jamie's mom. It definitely wasn't Jamie.

A moment later, Bethany came flying back down the driveway. Amy scrambled to her feet, tugging at the leash to wake the dog. "What is it? You look like you've seen a gh—"

The word died on her lips. Amy cringed. How could she be so careless?

"He's not here. Get this: he just now went down to the shipping office. Apparently, the Omni people wanted to get into his dad's office to look for some important papers, and Jamie went down to help them find what they were looking for."

Bethany didn't wait for Amy. She simply started down the sidewalk, half-running back toward Amy's house where she'd left her car.

"Wait! So, he went to get some papers. What's the big deal?" Amy scrambled along behind her, dragging one very unwilling dog.

Bethany skidded to a stop so abruptly that Amy plowed right into her. "Stop and think a moment. Who was it who told the authorities that Dax had something to do with the explosion?"

"You know as well as I do that it was Ms. Clifton. I was right there when my dad got the call." Amy put out a hand and knelt to pet the very confused dog who circled around her feet anxiously.

"But why would she say what she did? About Dax…and Rose?" Bethany paced in short circles, gesturing wildly while she talked. "This whole thing is fishy. She as much as said Dax and Rose together had something to do with the fire, but that makes no sense. Except now everyone is saying Mr. Wood had Rose, and her 'boyfriend' set the fire for him somehow. Which doesn't make any kind of sense at all."

Amy flinched. "Yeah, I've heard that as well. But Bethany, you have to remember what my Dad taught us about the criminal justice system. This is all hearsay evidence, and anything else is circumstantial. It'll all get thrown out in court. Besides, no one would ever believe in a million years that Rose would have anything to do with setting a fire. Especially one where someone got hurt."

Bethany shook her head. "You're also forgetting one other very important lesson your father taught us. Motive. Ask yourself who has the most to gain from any of this. If Mr. Wood is in jail, and his family is completely discredited, couldn't you just see them selling out when this is all over? Forget the merger; they'll practically give the company away."

Amy shifted uneasily. The dog sensed her discomfort and reached up to lick her hand. Amy glanced at the puppy in surprise and slipped her hand into her pocket to fish around for the dog treats she put there earlier. "Bethany, I don't like this. If you're right, then they're after something at the shipping office. Evidence or something which would implicate them perhaps."

"And Jamie is going to lead them right to it!" Bethany was practically shouting in her excitement. "Which is why we have to get over there before Jamie lets them in. Or at the very least before they leave with the very thing which might untangle this whole mess. This is why we haven't found any evidence. We've been looking in all the wrong places. Jamie and I were digging around in the ruins thinking we'd find something unusual."

Now it was Amy who was leading the way, dragging the dog along behind her who scrambled mightily to keep up, especially now that Pixie had discovered her dog-walker had treats. "We need to get over there. The office...papers. We're looking for a document of some kind. Oh wait, there's Dad!"

Amy tossed the dog's leash toward Bethany and dashed into the street, waving down her father's black suburban. Only belatedly did she realize he wasn't alone.

All the same, this was important. When he pulled over, she dashed around to his side of the car, motioning for him to lower the window so they could talk.

"What's wrong, Amy?" he asked, leaning out to look down at her in concern.

"Dad, I'm sorry, but can we get a favor? Can you take Pixie back to Mrs. Wilson for me? She'll keep me there all day talking, and we'll never escape if we do it, and we have kind of an emergency."

That got his attention. "What's going on?"

"I really don't have time, but can you trust me? It's something which might help Mr. Wood and Rose too in a way. But if we don't get there soon, we'll be too late."

Her father looked like he wanted to say something. For that matter, he looked like he wanted to say plenty, but it was the other man in the car who intervened on her behalf.

"Let her go, Martin."

Amy peered past her father in surprise. "Oh, Major Piper. I didn't know that was you. I mean, I saw someone in the car, and I thought…well, never mind. Dad?"

"Sure, honey, hand the dog up, and I'll take care of things."

Amy gestured wildly toward Bethany, who scooped up the dog. Together the girls kind of shoved the puppy through the car window, not even waiting for Dr. Bradford to get the door open. There was a precarious moment involving a lot of scrambling and yips, but in the end, the dog was safely installed in the car, and the girls were free to take off for Amy's house.

They ran all the way there, Amy praying all the while that they wouldn't be too late.

───── CHAPTER 33 ─────

DECISION AND SACRIFICE

Dr. Martin Bradford

Martin Bradford watched his daughter and his daughter's best friend disappear down the street. For just a moment, he saw them as they had been not all that long ago, all arms and legs, gangly and lean. Back when the height of adventure had been found in climbing trees. But this time, the stakes were higher. This particular adventure wouldn't end in skinned elbows and scraped knees. It was all he could do to keep from going after them. For that matter, if he could just keep them as children a little bit longer.

"I don't like it."

Lance looked down at the fluffy puppy in his lap. "The dog? She seems like a cute enough little thing to me. A little overweight, but for a small dog—"

It was not often Dr. Martin Bradford leveled a glare on another individual with so much weight laid into it. He positively seethed as he angled this stare upon his longtime friend and colleague, saying nothing at all even as he set the Suburban back into gear. "You know precisely what I mean."

"Of course, I do. You want to protect your daughter."

"Of course, I want to protect my daughter!" Martin wasn't usually one for shouting, but on this occasion, he was willing to make an exception. "I want *nothing more* than to protect my daughter, and right now, she is most decidedly going into what could be a dangerous situation." Hearing that said out loud, it felt like insanity that he let her go and agreed to take the dog home.

"You don't even know where she's going," Major Piper said softly, holding the dog against him to keep it from wobbling to the floor as the vehicle started down the street again. For a military man, he had a surprisingly soft spot for dogs.

"I know enough that if what they're chasing has anything to do with this entire situation," he waved one hand in a great circle to encompass everything that had been happening, "that it's certainly dangerous."

"Likely, not certain."

"How many people have to die to make it certain enough for you?" Martin snapped, trying to remember just where the Wilson house was. His daughter cared for every critter in the neighborhood, and there was no way he could keep them all straight. He suspected that Amy didn't always remember the people either. But she definitely knew every animal in Steven's Mill. She likely had names for the wild raccoons too.

Finally, he pulled over and hit the brakes. Perhaps he hit them a little harder than necessary as the Major was suddenly struggling to juggle one very rambunctious puppy. "Have you forgotten that two very precious young people *died* this week?" Martin asked, struggling to speak around the lump in his throat. "I did what you asked when it came time to do an arson investigation, at least until the local authorities brought their own teams in. I will have you know there isn't a person in the local police or fire services, which isn't at least a little bit ticked with me. No one likes when a federal agency pulls rank, especially one with no jurisdiction to be there, meaning *we* actually didn't *have* the rank to pull!"

"I did what I needed to." Lance scratched the dog behind her ears. Pixie leaned into the caress.

"And I did what I could to help you because I believed you had a right to be there. But you didn't, and now it's *my* reputation on the line. I have more than one job in Steven's Mill. And you have no idea how long I've worked to build up my reputation, to make a name for myself in this town. Before this incident, I had a name for integrity—"

"Is that what you're worried about? Your reputation?"

"Absolutely not! Oh, give me her! She's shedding on your uniform." The puppy hadn't liked their yelling. Martin took the dog from Lance and cradled it against his chest, fighting for a calmer tone. "I'm only saying that my job has some rather unique…crossovers…and you just made it that much more difficult to do what I was hired to do. Now you're encouraging my daughter to go into *certain*," he paused here to glare at Martin, "danger because you're hoping for clues to something that's gotten completely out of your control."

"And if I have?" Lance gave him the stare that accelerated him in the ranks, the kind of hard look that lets you know not to mess with him. "You know as well as I do that we have to look at the greater good here. Something bad is going on and if they manage to dislodge a piece of evidence, so be it. If those kids had waited around to tell us what they knew, then we'd be forced to follow *procedure*." Lance's lip curled on the last word as though it were something that tasted bad to him. Truth be known, his fast rise to the rank of Major was beginning to show signs of slowing down precisely because of his aversion to procedure.

"Yes, there's procedure. For a reason, Lance, or have you forgotten the point of due process? We have to protect the citizens, and sometimes the only way to do that is to protect their rights first. There's a reason we need warrants, and all those procedures you seem to hate so much."

"But do we have time for that right now? Are you prepared for other people to die because you were following due process?"

"Are you prepared to sacrifice my only child? Or her best friend? We've already lost our Rose…" He could go on no longer. The knot in his throat threatened to choke him. As soon as he said the name, he knew he wouldn't be able to keep talking. Another minute and he'd be in tears, which, while they were nothing for a man to be ashamed of, was not exactly the stuff career advancement was made of. Especially not in the hard face of a military man like Lance.

Though truth be told, there were too many stiff upper lips at Mount Hideaway. Maybe it was time they all stripped away the veneer and allowed themselves to feel once in a while.

"Wait here." The words came out harsh and choked. The blue house halfway up the street looked familiar. Apparently, the pup agreed, for she bolted the moment her paws hit the ground. The leash rattled after her like a steel snake.

Pixie led the way triumphantly to her own home, and Dr. Martin Bradford had a few minutes in the fresh air to compose himself. Mrs. Wilson was indeed chatty, but Martin was more practiced at setting out boundaries than his daughter and made his escape fairly quickly. Lance was still waiting in the car for him when he returned. He didn't know if he should be surprised by that. Lance still carried several spookish tendencies, which meant he could just as likely have made his exit while Martin was gone. He was good at disappearing and reappearing at will.

"You obviously have something more to say," Martin said as he settled himself back in the driver's seat.

"I was perhaps a touch out of line." Lance stared straight ahead, not meeting his friend's eyes.

Martin had been about to pull out into traffic. It was a good thing he hadn't, as this statement was so startling it necessitated a good hard look to see if the other man were joking.

Nope. That solemn mug was about as serious as a graveyard.

"You were," Martin said carefully as he signaled and merged into traffic.

"I obviously haven't been sensitive to your situation, and I'm sorry about that. I've been in the military too long, I suspect. Especially when I start to see people as situations that need to be managed. I deal in numbers, Martin, you know that. I have to do what's for the greater good."

"I'm aware of that, Lance. Just as you are. And much as I hate to agree with you, I don't always like what I have to stand up for. That's my daughter out there."

They were silent a moment as they considered this.

"If she finds something we can use, consider the ramifications," Lance said, his voice quiet.

"If my daughter or anyone else dies, consider the ramifications," Martin countered.

"We're blocked at every turn. Even our own superiors have their hands tied." The frustration and resentment were thick in the Major's voice. It was as close to a genuine emotion as Martin had seen from the man.

Martin took in a deep breath, held it, let it out slowly. His blood pressure didn't like this one bit. Where was God in moments like this? He wanted to pray but no longer had the words. His heart already ached. Some of his dearest friends in the world were burying…not their child, but the *idea* of her in a few days. They hadn't even been able to find the body to give proper closure. They were going to bury an empty box.

What if it was his daughter who never came home?

"I don't like it," he repeated softly, struggling to feel the hand of God even now when his faith seemed so small. "I don't like it…but you're right. If Mount Hideaway falls, then so does Steven's Mill. Who knows how far beyond this community such a thing would reach?"

"Millions of lives, Martin. Millions of lives at stake." Martin shot a glance at the man. Still, Lance was looking through the windshield as though seeing a bleak future only he could see.

Could Martin trade his daughter's life for someone else's? Could he let her die to save others? Maybe millions of others?

Father God, how could you endure this pain? How did you?

Martin shuddered. "God have mercy on us all."

"If he will."

Martin might not have been meant to hear that.

--- CHAPTER 34 ---

SEARCH AND SEIZURE?

Jamie

Ms. Clifton was already waiting for him by the time he got out to the company offices.

Jamie hadn't been out to the warehouse more than a couple of times since it burned. Even after the rain, an acrid smell hung over the parking lot as he got out of his truck. To his surprise, the place was deserted. Hadn't they been tearing down the old structure or something? To his way of thinking, the ruins looked untouched, metal fragments twisted into a forest of bent girders and beams.

He and Bethany had explored out the ruins once, not long before Rose's accident. Now, looking back, it seemed so silly to be playing detective with flashlights, poking through the debris like they'd had any idea what they'd been looking for. It was one thing to play crime scene investigator in a forensic science class, quite another to do so out in the real world where you were surrounded by nothing but destruction.

Why Charity Clifton wanted to be in such a dismal place was beyond him. He hardly thought there would be anything of worth in the offices anymore. The building had been damaged. Whatever his father had been working on had already been taken home. What could possibly remain?

Ms. Clifton hardly looked ready to go wandering about ruins. She stood next to a stretch limousine, incongruous on the cracked pavement, parked in the ruins of what had once been a thriving business. She wore white, a glimmering figure in the shadow of the trees, a scarlet headscarf draped over her head and wrapped around her neck. The wind caught at the filmy fabric, sending it fluttering like a flag as she came to greet him, hand outstretched.

"James Wood? I would have guessed you from anywhere; you look so much like your father. Charity Clifton, though you may call me Charity."

"Ms. Clifton." Jamie fingered the keys to the office building as he led the way over to the building.

He wasn't in the mood for small talk. Truth be told, the last thing he wanted was to be here at all. Ms. Clifton had been Rose's hero. Her assistant Dax had died with her. How could he possibly feel anything for anyone from Omni that wasn't contempt? If they'd never come into his life, none of this would have happened.

The fire? His conscience interceded. Would the fire have happened if they'd never come?

Jamie no longer knew what to think. The authorities seemed so certain it was something his father had done through criminal negligence and then gotten caught into. Bethany had thought it was some kind of frame-up job straight out of a mystery novel. Now people were whispering Rose even had something to do with it, and the word 'arson' was coming up more and more. Why couldn't the fire have just been some terrible accident? What did anyone have to be to blame?

He'd allowed Bethany to talk him into trying to clear his father's name. Now he couldn't help but think they'd made things so terrifyingly worse that he no longer even knew how to live with himself. Rose had been angry because of their investigation. Rose had driven away, upset after talking to Bethany.

Rose was dead now, gone forever because of what they had been doing.

No. Because of what Bethany had wanted him to do.

It was no wonder he had no words for small talk as he trudged over to the office building and unlocked the door. He had to shove at it to get it open. Even this seemed warped now from the fire. The entire place would be better off razed, taken off the map completely. If Omni offered him money for the whole setup, he'd give it to them in a heartbeat. Let them have it. They could rebuild or grind it into the ground for all he cared.

Jamie turned on the lights, frustrated when nothing happened. "The power is off."

It was a dumb thing to say. Of course, the power was off. Everything had been disconnected when the fire had been burning, and there had been little reason to turn anything back on. He glanced out the windows. They had a few hours of daylight left. With lots of windows, wouldn't that be good enough?

"You said on the phone you were looking for some papers?"

"Yes. Your father didn't seem to have them when I got in touch with him earlier. He suggested they might be in the files. Not everything has been pulled out, apparently?" Ms. Clifton glanced back over her shoulder, he noticed. Someone was waiting for her in the car. Well, obviously, the driver was.

"Do you want me to fetch someone for you?" he asked, unsure of the etiquette here. Someone like Charity Clifton was likely to be used to being waited on hand and foot. According to his sister, the sun had risen and set on her orders. He wasn't inclined to be errand boy, but at the same time, the sooner they found what she was looking for, the sooner he could go home and forget this place existed.

"No. Don't be ridiculous. A smart young man such as yourself, should have no trouble at all in finding exactly what I need. Why don't you lead the way, though? This place is so incredibly eerie like this."

The reception area sure was a mess. Apparently, here was where the salvage had been in earnest. Someone had pulled the computers at the reception desk, and most of whatever paperwork was stored in the front office. Drawers in cabinets stood open, some hanging awkwardly. Bits of trash littered the floor alongside paperclips and pencils. A battered houseplant with only the barest vestiges of green struggled vainly to survive on the desk where the secretary used to sit.

Feeling more and more the desolation of the place, Jamie led the way down the corridor to his father's office. He guessed one would more rightly call the set of rooms a suite. The door was already open, the desk just beyond showing a similar dissection. The doors to his father's office stood open, the interior dark. Too many shelves of books, too few windows made the space dim and hard to see.

"We're going to need a flashlight," Jamie murmured, glancing behind the desk but knowing already he wasn't going to find one. "I'll be right back."

Behind him, Ms. Clifton protested. She likely didn't want to be left alone in the dark. Jamie picked up the pace, still intent on getting the job done and over with. The door swung shut behind him, not quite closing as he stepped out alone into the parking lot.

He wasn't sure if he had a flashlight or not. Thinking the limousine was more likely to be prepared with some sort of emergency roadside kit, he started there.

The driver scrambled out to meet him. He was a hulking brute of a man who looked like he could bench press a truck. Jamie quailed as the man unfolded from the seat and stepped out of the car. He met him halfway across the parking lot.

For a moment, Jamie wondered if the man thought he'd done something to Ms. Clifton. This was obviously more than a driver. Bodyguard probably. Jamie raised his hands in the universal sign of surrender and tried to smile, though he'd been having trouble arranging his face into anything other than a scowl for a long time now.

"Hey, easy big guy. We need a flashlight. Got one?"

The man stared at him for a long minute. Jamie wracked his brain, trying to remember whether or not Rose had mentioned the other staff beyond Dax and whether or not anyone even spoke English.

The driver seemed to understand something, though, because he went around to the back of the car. Talking to someone inside, Jamie realized, before going to the trunk and checking there. Sure enough, there was an emergency kit that included a flashlight. As Jamie reached in to get it, he caught a glimpse of a man's face pressed against the back window, trying to see him.

It gave him a jolt. He hadn't expected to see the face there. The glass distorted the image somewhat, bringing to mind something out of a monster movie. Laughing uneasily, he flicked the switch on the flashlight to test it. To his relief, it worked.

"Thanks, this should do the trick. Um…your friend there gave me quite a start. Apologize to him for me, will you? I expect I might have startled him too."

Jamie headed back, turning over the encounter in his mind all the way back to the building. There was something about the man in the car which seemed familiar.

When he got back to the office, he found Ms. Clifton on her cell phone. He waited patiently, the flashlight held awkwardly in his hand, trying hard not to listen to her conversation though it was nearly impossible when they were standing so close together inside the outer office.

"Yes. See that you do."

She pushed the button to end her conversation. Jamie mused that rich and powerful people needed to practice better manners. From what he could tell, all she'd done was snap orders and hadn't even bothered to say goodbye.

"Where should we start?" he asked, holding up the flashlight.

"Thank you. You're a clever young man to think of that. Not everyone would you know." She stepped a little too close to take the flashlight from him. If he'd thought her tone was brisk and even rude on the phone, it was quite the opposite now. Honeyed and warm. She lingered too close, her fingers closing over his as she took the flashlight from his hand.

Jamie jumped backward, away from her. He didn't like that she was making him uncomfortable. Deliberately or so it seemed. Nor did he like the way she laughed as she stepped away from him, clicking the light on and off, playing with it as she crossed the room. She bent over his father's desk in a way that made his throat go dry.

That white pantsuit was very expertly tailored. And in the semidarkness, it certainly drew the eye.

Jamie was definitely not prepared for the strange rush of emotions he felt now. First came embarrassment. This lady was old enough to be his mom, even if she was kind of hot when you looked at her a certain way. But more than that was a feeling of growing unease, that something was off about this whole affair. He went to the wall of filing cabinets, flicking open one drawer after another and peering in. About half of them were still full, dozens of folders filled with endless invoices and paperwork. How many of these had he filled out himself?

He pulled one out at random from a drawer somewhere in the middle. Invoices for repairs. Manifests for loads. Schedules. So much stuff. His father had been old-fashioned to want everything on paper. Sure, he had everything on his computer, but he said he never could find anything unless it was in a file folder neatly labeled. He liked being able to lay hands on what he needed without having to do an extensive directory search.

The computer.

Everything should have been on his father's computer, which had been brought home ages ago. His father could have printed out anything Ms. Clifton wanted.

The man in the car.

Something clicked. He'd seen that man before, all right. But not in the back of the limousine. Behind the wheel of a truck. He'd been at the warehouse—something about a truck needing a repair.

Jamie frowned. That couldn't possibly be right. He was mistaking one man for another. Wasn't he?

He started flipping through folders. There was a name. What was it? Something with an 'M.' McHenry?

No, something else.

Nothing looked right. And in the meantime, Ms. Clifton was digging around in his father's office, something which was feeling more and more like it shouldn't be happening. Jamie wished he'd talked to his father more about this particular errand, but between his injuries, the upcoming trial, and now Rose, Harlan Wood was a man broken. His faith had been shattered, and he barely spoke at all.

But I need him, Jamie thought a little peevishly as he shut the drawer of the filing cabinet and turned around. *This shouldn't be my responsibility.*

Immediately Jamie could see he'd made a grievous mistake in ignoring what had been going on behind him. While he'd been busy wool-gathering and digging around in a bunch of worthless old files, the chauffeur had come in from outside. The hulking giant stood just inside the doorway, regarding him with what could only be called a rather menacing smile.

"You wanted us to go check out the warehouse, Ms. Clifton?"

"The warehouse?" Jamie blinked. Of everything the bodyguard could say, this was nowhere on Jamie's radar. "The warehouse is nothing but ashes."

"Not all of it," Ms. Clifton said, straightening from where she was bending over a pile of papers she'd scattered over his father's desk. "It's actually quite a good idea. From what I understand, there's still a corner of the building which the firefighters managed to save. There could still be important documents in those offices. Jamie, why don't you be a dear and go down and see if there's anything of interest."

It was a pointless errand. They would have cleaned out those areas first. Besides, he really didn't want to leave this woman rummaging around in his father's papers without him there to see what she took.

Not that he'd been paying any attention up until now. But maybe he should have been.

Ms. Clifton must have sensed his hesitation, for she drew nearer, getting into his space again. One well-manicured nail tapped against his chest in an altogether too intimate gesture. "Imagine," she said softly, leaning in close still. "You might find something to help you clear your father's name."

"Is that what you're looking for?" he asked, surprised now because that hadn't even occurred to him. He expected she'd be looking for something to do with the merger. Contracts or something.

Except those things would have been backed up on the computer, right?

He was definitely confused now. Something wasn't right.

"Gustav, take young Mr. Wood down to the warehouse, please. He seems to be confused. Maybe you can help clear a few things up."

"With pleasure, Ms. Clifton."

The giant lumbered toward him. Jamie opened his mouth to protest, then closed it again. Truly, did he want to stay anywhere alone with this woman when she'd already proved to be a little too interested in him?

"Yeah. I'll look in the warehouse."

The hulking giant…what was his name? Gustav? Gustav made a face when Jamie acquiesced. He almost looked disappointed.

He followed too close, getting in Jamie's personal space too. What was with these people?

CHAPTER 35

SECRETS AND STEALTH

Bethany

Bethany stopped the car at the road. They could clearly see Jamie's truck down in the parking lot. Nothing else seemed to be moving, though the view wasn't entirely clear from there because of the trees.

"What I wouldn't give for Mrs. Gunnerson's eagle eyes right now. I'd bet she'd know if anyone else was down there," Bethany muttered half under her breath.

"Mrs. Gunnerson would have the sense to turn tail and go back home." Amy flashed a smile at Bethany, even if it was a weak and rather tremulous one. "In this together?"

"Together."

They'd used those words how many times before departing on their latest adventures. The words rang somewhat hollow, though. There was too much uncertainty about the outcome of this particular outing.

"We don't have to do this. One document can't matter that much," Amy said after a moment.

"But what about Jamie?" Bethany sighed, tapping her fingers on the steering wheel while they thought.

"It wouldn't do harm to just check on him. Make sure everything is okay."

"And maybe discover what it is they're so intent on finding?" Amy teased, then stopped when she realized Bethany wasn't laughing.

No, this wasn't the time for humor. Justification, on the other hand, would be quite helpful. Right now, she was half ready to turn tail and run home. Nothing about this felt right.

"It's broad daylight." Bethany glanced at the clock on the dash. "We have hours before dark. What can happen in broad daylight?" This was rationalization at its finest, but Amy did at least relax somewhat. Her shoulders lost some of the tension she'd been carrying. Her jaw didn't seem quite so set.

Now, if only Bethany could get herself to relax in much the same way. She wondered if prayer should cover a real breaking and entering because, in effect, that's exactly what they were doing. After all, they had no business here and certainly weren't invited guests. Given the crime scene tape still decorating the ruins, it was pretty clear no one was supposed to be here without good reason.

Jamie, being the son of the owner, had every right to be here as Mr. Wood's representative. If Ms. Clifton was still here, she likewise was covered legally, being his guest. And Bethany knew for a fact that if they were caught, Jamie wasn't about to go out of his way to protect her. If he were still mad enough, he could have her arrested for trespassing. Amy too.

But what if they were about to lose the only proof of Harlan Wood's innocence.

"Like at my house a few weeks ago?" Amy asked.

"Yeah, like that." Bethany drove the car forward, tucking it further up the road, on the shoulder under some trees. At first glance, no one was likely to notice it there, or hopefully, even think too much of it. Bethany slipped from the car, acting as team leader like she had last time.

I'm missing two members of my team.

This wasn't the time to be thinking of that. Amy crouched next to her in the bushes along the road. The moment they came down the driveway, they'd be in sight. Bethany hunted for a better way. Amy pointed toward the trees just inside the fence. Bethany liked the suggestion and nodded once to let her know she understood.

It took only a few minutes to reach the parking lot, even taking a circuitous route. The moment they broke from the trees, Bethany saw just how lucky they'd been that they hadn't just driven right down. The limousine was parked alongside the office building, out of sight from the road.

Bethany motioned for Amy to duck back behind the trees. Out of sight from the building, Bethany waited for her heart to resume a normal beat before speaking.

"Did you see anyone?" she asked in a hoarse whisper.

Amy shook her head.

"Me neither. They must be inside."

This made things more complicated. From what Bethany remembered, Ms. Clifton rarely traveled alone. Given the size of the car, a driver was quite likely. Seeing as how one was not behind the wheel, it made sense that he was in the building somewhere. Whether or not someone was in the back of the car was impossible to say, given how dark the tinted windows were. But to Bethany, at least, the car had felt empty.

How many people did that put in the building then?

"Maybe we should go," Amy murmured against her ear.

Bethany immediately shook her head no. Jamie was in there somewhere. Wasn't that reason enough to stay? "We don't have to confront anyone. We just want to see what they're doing. Make sure Jamie's okay. Maybe get a look at whatever papers they're going through."

Said out loud like that, it sounded almost reasonable. It was only a matter of getting in. Bethany wished it were dark. This would be so much easier at night.

"God, I hope you're still in control."

Amy looked at her in surprise. "He is."

Bethany blinked. She hadn't realized she'd spoken out loud. Flushing a little, Bethany pointed toward the ruins. If everyone was in the office building, they should be able to sneak up from that side. The wreckage of the building would provide plenty of cover, and no one was likely to be looking that way.

Amy looked and nodded. Good, she was on board.

They kept low and crept across the parking lot, moving quickly. Bethany felt too exposed, but by using Jamie's truck as cover for the last few feet, she could at least shake the feeling of being watched for a few minutes. Of one accord, they stopped at the front bumper and waited. Bethany held her breath, listening for anything out of the ordinary.

All was quiet.

Too quiet.

There was no birdsong. This place felt devoid of life, despite being at the edge of town and being half surrounded by forest. Something was strange. Off.

Bethany considered pointing this out to Amy and stopped. They were risking discovery every time they talked. This was not a logical feeling she had, but an emotional response to the situation. Too quiet? Bethany shook her head and led the way across the parking lot to the bent and broken girders. There was something chilling in that, like in the movies of a post-apocalyptic world. Her imagination turned to zombies and aliens, as if reality wasn't bad enough. She steeled her thoughts and refused the flights of fancy. They were only distractions, and she needed to focus.

They had to duck under the crime scene tape to stay close to the building. As this was no longer an active crime scene, the tape probably didn't apply anymore anyway. It had been left by the investigators, and no one had thought to take it down in the interim. Most of it had already sagged anyway.

She and Amy waited here too. Still nothing. By now, Bethany was thinking they were skulking around the edges of the building for no reason. This whole thing was starting to seem childish and honestly very silly. She almost said so when she heard it.

A crash followed by a loud bang from the back of the building. She almost yelped in surprise. Amy's hand flew over her mouth. The crash had startled her too, but to give her friend credit, she stayed silent.

Amy grabbed Bethany and pulled her back into the shelter of a burned-out vehicle. They looked at each other wide-eyed and panicking. That was certainly not wildlife. The problem was they had no idea if they were facing friend…or foe?

More banging. A shout. Something was definitely going on. Bethany looked up, seeing sky overhead. This part of the building had experienced the worst of the fire. The ceiling had caved in, taking most of the walls with it. They waited in a grotto of steel girders and aluminum siding. Beyond here, though, the walls rose up in jagged pieces. Toward the back were actual rooms that had survived with walls and ceiling intact. She had been in there once with Jamie and remembered the layout from their explorations.

The sounds seemed to come from back there.

Amy mouthed words at her. Something about going? Bethany's heart pounded in her chest, but she forced herself to remain calm, taking special care with her breathing as she'd been taught. This, too, was not a decision that could be made emotionally. Rationally speaking, they weren't in any danger yet; they were only doing what they came to do – to bear witness. They could still carry out the mission if they were careful. All they needed was a look to see what was going on. Then they could return after calling the authorities if they needed to. Simple.

Bethany peered around the burned-out truck, calculating a pathway that would get her closer to where she wanted to go. Amy saw what she was doing and shook her head, no.

Bethany ignored her. She just wanted a look but had no way to make Amy understand this. She crept forward. Amy followed after a moment's hesitation. She was a good friend. Now, if only Bethany could keep them both from getting hurt.

More clattering. A shout. Someone in pain? That sounded like Jamie!

All bets were off. Bethany forgot her fear; anger and concern took over. It was a purely emotional decision to spring forward and fly over the ruins into the heart of the building. She was no longer interested in stealth.

Not when someone she loved was in danger.

CHAPTER 36

GIANTS AND GUNS

Amy

Apparently, Amy saw him before Bethany did. How anyone could miss an ogre in a storeroom was beyond her.

The giant reared up like something out of a medieval nightmare. This was the Viking pillaging the village, Frankenstein's monster whose only intent was to destroy. No, worse, this was a behemoth of old, a Goliath, and she and Bethany were the nearest thing they had to a David with no sling nor any other means to defend themselves.

And Bethany had just rushed headlong into danger. It was like watching Pixie charge a bull mastiff; it should have been ridiculous if Bethany hadn't been in such extreme danger.

Amy gave a cry and followed her friend. There was little she could do, but if Bethany needed her, she would be there following the fading light into the bowels of the building. She arrived just in time to see Jamie flung into a storage closet as though he were nothing more than a rag doll. His limbs seemed limp, his head lolling to one side. Was he already dead? Amy had no way of knowing. She reached for her phone even as she saw Bethany continue headlong. What was she doing?

The giant hadn't noticed them yet. He was gathering something. Rags and papers. Stuff which had been scattered when they'd been clearing out this building. This he piled now into a heap, pouring something over it.

Gasoline?

Amy could smell it from here. The place had already burned once. Was there enough left to burn it a second time? This section had survived the fire, sure, but hadn't the firehoses soaked it? The papers looked crisp as far as she could see. They'd had weeks to dry out.

The giant wanted to destroy what remained. There was too much of the building still standing. The offices hadn't even been touched. Amy swallowed back bile and ducked behind a cabinet as she saw Bethany finally had the sense to crouch down and wait.

Good girl. We'll wait until the giant goes away and then let Jamie out. Amy eased her phone back into her pocket. She didn't dare make any noise; it was a wonder they hadn't been heard already. So long as they called 9-1-1 after Jamie was safe, they could wait. Right now, it would be better to have her hands free.

Amy kept her eyes on Bethany, who crouched a few feet away. One would go high, the other low. Like they'd practiced. In this case, she supposed that Bethany would go for the closet to let Jamie out. It would be up to Amy to try to stop the fire. She began to plan how.

Something to smother it, perhaps? Amy looked around, hunting a tarp, maybe something the firefighters might have left which would be helpful. Anything. Her back was toward the giant when Bethany screamed. Amy spun so fast, she nearly fell.

Bethany hadn't waited. She hadn't even planned or followed protocol. The giant was bending, trying to light the pile when Bethany came seeming out of nowhere, and threw herself at him. Amy started forward and stopped. She honestly had no idea what to do.

Bethany at least seemed to know exactly what she was doing, at least it looked that way. At first. She had been the martial arts champion in their county many years running. The girl was a dynamo of flips and kicks, and she had the element of surprise.

She flung herself at the giant, flipped him around, and somehow knocked him flat on his back. He fell into a table filled with debris, shattering the table and scattering the detritus. Amy took a step forward before she realized she'd moved, in awe that Bethany had taken him out that easily.

Only it wasn't over. To Amy's horror, the giant rose, not even winded. He reached, impossibly fast, and grabbed Bethany by her arm and flung her against the wall as though she weighed nothing. The entire building shook as Bethany crumpled the drywallned down on Amy, who stepped backward, farther away from the fight. In the meantime, Bethany had, against all odds, hopped back up to her feet and caught the giant's arm. Amy knew this move, having practiced it with Bethany in the past. It might have been a good idea if Bethany's hand had been able to go all the way around the thickness of his forearm.

The giant appeared not to know the move because Bethany's arm hold didn't even faze him. He peeled her off of him like she was nothing more than an annoying mosquito. His hand had no problem wrapping completely around her arm. Bethany didn't try to fight his grasp; she just came in closer, hooking a leg around the back of his, and used her weight to counterbalance the creature. He staggered but didn't fall. He did, however, release his grasp to windmill his arms for balance.

Bethany was right there with a hard blow to his nose with the flat of her hand. Amy could hear the crunch of his cartilage from where she stood. The monster groaned and staggered back. A blow like that would have blinded him with tears, at least in the short run. Bethany was ready. Her leg hooked around his again, she twisted into him with a full-body blow, and this time he went down. Bethany danced backward like a prizefighter, keeping literally on her toes, waiting for the giant to rise again. Her concentration was laser-focused on him. For that matter, so was Amy's.

He sprung to his feet once more, showing that amazing speed that belied his giant frame. Amy took another involuntary step back and started looking for a weapon, something, *anything* to help her friend. She wasn't afraid of Bethany getting hurt now; she was afraid she was going to watch her best friend die at the hands of this monster.

The fight moved away from the closet. Amy saw her chance. She was going low. She stepped forward with the intent of letting Jamie out, thinking to at least take that factor out of the equation while the giant was distracted. Only she was brought up short by something hard and cold pressing against her temple.

"I wouldn't do that if I were you." A hammer cocked. Amy turned just enough to catch a look at the gun from the corner of her eye. She categorized the weapon in her mind. Sig Sauer? No. Glock. At this range, it didn't actually matter which.

Either way, she wasn't going anywhere.

Ms. Clifton, for who else could it be, leaned in so close, Amy could feel her breath against the side of her face. "Bang, you're dead," she whispered in Amy's ear, then laughed.

The sound echoed off the roof and came back at them a hundredfold. Both Bethany and the monster stopped cold to look.

Just like that, the fight was over. Everyone in the room waited in silence. Ms. Clifton had the floor.

CHAPTER 37

VOLUNTEERS

Dr. Martin Bradford

Like Rose, Amy never came home.

As the day waned and the sun slipped down behind the neighbor's house, Martin Bradford did what any parent would do first. He called his child. When that didn't work, he tried calling Bethany. And then Bethany's mother, who hadn't heard from either of them. Now, as he stood debating what to do, all he could think was how the similarities were too close and the grief the Woods were feeling now threatened to engulf him too.

With no answers to a situation that didn't look good, Martin then did what someone with access to a secret government installation would do. He called in a favor or two.

The problem was, he wasn't good at waiting. He paced throughout the house, fingering the cell phone in his pocket, waiting for it to ring. He already had a pretty good idea of where she was. Of course, he knew better than to go in alone.

Now, as he waited for his volunteers, he wished he'd had them meet somewhere closer, like the church. After all, they couldn't exactly assemble for the first time at the shipping company where his phone said Amy was. But meeting in the church parking lot would put them in the public eye. The group would be too noticeable. They needed to plan, and at least out here where the houses had a little distance between them, there was a hint of privacy. Besides, he knew his neighbors. Most of them worked at Mount Hideaway. There wasn't a person there that would so much as say a word regardless of what they saw. They understood the importance of keeping some things to themselves, and Martin was widely respected at the facility. He was hoping to cash in on some of that respect today.

Besides, his crew said they'd be there in four minutes. He'd thought he could wait four minutes. Now he wasn't so sure. A lot could happen in four minutes. He fought against a list of possibilities that could be right now happening to Amy. Four minutes could mean the difference between life and death.

Martin started for the door, thinking maybe he would leave after all. He'd call the guys and tell them to meet him there, or at the church, or something. He made it as far as the driveway before he realized they'd already showed up... and brought some friends.

He'd expected the guys he'd called would be able to pull together a comrade or two at best. The last thing he expected was a veritable army outside his front door. Their cars clogged the street. More than a dozen men with grim expressions and a singular intent ranged in front of him. They must have called in every military individual in the county, with more still arriving. To his surprise, Major Lance Piper stood at the fore. He saluted as Martin approached.

"Maybe I owe you something of an apology after all," he said with an awkward shrug. "Besides, if you're right, there might be a promotion in this somewhere."

Martin couldn't help it. He laughed. "A promotion. The last thing we need is for you to take over the facility."

"Things would be vastly different around here if I did. But for now..." He drew back and gave a sharp salute. "this is your show, Martin. What do you want us to do?"

It was a pretty display, but Martin wasn't born yesterday. Lance had needed Amy to lead them to what they needed to find. Now that she was missing, it seemed fairly obvious she'd found it. Lance was here, as always, for his own self-interest first. However, it was nice to think otherwise, even if for just a few minutes. In the end, it didn't matter. So long as Amy was safe at home, Lance could become General off of her rescue, and Martin would call it fair.

Speaking of which, time was wasting. He motioned for the group to come in close, wondering what the neighbors must think, but at the same time acknowledging there wasn't a space in the house for a meeting this size. Not without rearranging the furniture, something he had no time for.

Martin considered the young men and women lined up in front of them. That they were armed to the teeth was a given. That they knew what they were doing even more so. No one worked at Mount Hideaway unless they were more than qualified.

"You're all off the clock, people," he said to those assembled, his gaze going to Lance and lingering there. "If anything goes south, you were never there, nor were you working in any official capacity. If you're not okay with that, then leave now. No harm, no foul. I just ask that you keep things quiet until we have a chance to resolve this."

No one so much as moved a muscle.

Martin nodded. This was no less than he expected, honestly, though it felt good to see it. He pulled his phone from his pocket. Checking one last time to see if maybe she'd called—if maybe this wasn't his nightmare come to life, but more of forgetfulness on the part of a teenager who'd lost track of time.

Nothing.

Right then. Time to get to work. He would have said time to pray, but so far, he hadn't stopped once since she left.

"Everyone form up into teams and send crew leaders to me. Here's what I want you to do…"

—— CHAPTER 38 ——

WELL, THAT CERTAINLY HADN'T GONE TO PLAN

Bethany

Tired and aching in more places than she cared to count, Bethany slumped against the wall of the closet. At least the space was large enough to hold all three of them. Unfortunately, the room offered no way out other than the door, which the giant she'd been fighting had locked. She knew because she'd tried the knob now, several times.

To add insult to injury, this wasn't even a real closet. It was a storage cabinet built into the wall, a plastic unit that had held shelves at one point. She knew this because they were sitting on the things. They'd likely all fallen down when the explosion had rocked the building. She suspected the building had warped somewhat in the heat of the fire because the shelves didn't lay flat, putting everyone at a slightly tilted angle.

At least they had air. A unit like this would have suffocated long ago if there hadn't been a crack under the door, likely caused by the same warping. It also let in sound, meaning they heard every word of the long and drawn out argument happening on the other side of the door.

"...you think I like cleaning up your messes? If you hadn't run their car off the road in the first place..."

Charity had been ranting along these lines for the last five minutes now. They were all bored with it, sick of last-minute revelations when they all knew very well that they would die in this spot, and whatever they'd learned would die with them.

Made worse by the fact that Jamie still wasn't talking to her.

He sat as far as he could from the others, leaning against the wall. He had a goose egg on his forehead, which looked concussion inducing at the very least. He'd turned down Amy's offer of first aid by putting his back to her, which felt rude and unnecessary. It wasn't like this was Amy's fault. She hadn't exactly enjoyed being held at gunpoint, and she'd certainly never intended to get caught.

He wasn't the only one mad. Amy was sitting opposite her, arms crossed, positively seething, which for Amy was saying something. She was holding her phone in her hands, using it for a flashlight despite the fact it would run the battery down. What was the point when they had absolutely no signal? There was too much metal around them for any of their phones to be any good at all.

"...and how do you expect a second fire to escape the notice of the authorities? Especially with the kids all locked in a closet. This doesn't strike you as something which will draw attention to us? I wanted you to do away with the kid because he recognized Ted, but I thought you would have the brains to make it look like an accident. You know, like he was exploring this giant burned warehouse and something could maybe have *dropped* on him..."

It might have been funny had the situation not been so dire.

Bethany leaned toward Amy, speaking softly so their voices wouldn't carry. "We need to plan what to do when they let us out. We'll do it like we did when we practiced. You go low; I'll go high. There's only two of them, and three of us—"

It was Jamie who spoke up, turning very deliberately toward Amy as he did so, making a huge point of not speaking to Bethany at all. "Amy, can you remind our esteemed colleague that in case she hasn't noticed, they're not going to be letting us out. Any second now, they'll start a second fire to burn this entire place down. Besides, there are three of them, not two. There's another guy. One who's been here before."

Bethany drew herself up. "Really, Jamie? Are we really doing this now? We're about to die, and you're still not going to speak to me? Besides, what makes you think they're not going to let us out? You heard the lady. They want to make our deaths look like an accident. Keeping us in here certainly isn't going to do that."

"Yeah? Well, what do you call that?" Jamie pointed toward the door, where a thin tendril of smoke snaked upwards.

They'd been so busy arguing they hadn't noticed that they hadn't realized the matter of what to do with them had already been resolved.

Bethany stared, realizing two things in the same instant. First, Jamie had spoken directly to her, which was a progress of sorts, and second, that it was quite likely they were going to die after all.

"Amy, you're the genius of the group. What do you think?" she asked, trying not to cough as smoke filled the tiny space.

"Try to block it. There's enough air in here for a few minutes if you can keep the smoke out." Amy started scrambling, looking under the shelves she'd been sitting on. Bethany grabbed a shelf and wedged it against the door at the same instant. Jamie tried to do the same thing. For a moment, their hands touched.

He drew back so fast he almost fell.

"Really, Jamie? You'd rather die than come near me?"

"In case you haven't noticed, we're going to die anyway!" he snapped.

"How about you quit looking at me like this is all my fault. I'm not the one who got captured in the first place. Well, I did get captured, but only after you were. And only because you were."

"Bethany, would you be quiet a moment? I'm trying to think!" Amy had found a pile of cans, which she was turning over, trying to read the labels. "Give me some light?"

Bethany and Jamie both grabbed for their phones. Despite their attempts to block the smoke, it was seeping in anyway. Bethany struggled to catch her breath, trying to wave aside the haze with her hand so they could read what was on the cans.

"Acetone?" Bethany said thoughtfully. "Why is that familiar?"

"Because it's something my dad tried to drum into us not all that long ago."

That Amy would be able to think of such a thing when Bethany was struggling to breathe was nothing short of a miracle. That Amy was even able to stand and apply the acetone to the area around the lock was even more so. By now, the smoke had filled the chamber. Bethany held her breath, wondering how long she could hold it when her lungs ached, and all she wanted to do was cough. Part of her wanted to reach for Jamie, to find the comfort she used to feel when she held his hand, but she knew for certain that was lost to her now.

Besides, it was a distraction when they needed more than anything to get out.

Whatever Amy was doing, it had become impossible to see. Their cell phones lit the smoke weirdly. Outside they could hear the rush of flames, an inferno brewing. If they stayed in here much longer, they wouldn't need to break out; the compartment would finish melting with them in it.

Come on, Amy. Whatever you're doing, do it!

Something happened. It must have for Amy was turning toward them, motioning them to get up. Why were Bethany's legs so weak? She felt light-headed and strange. She wanted…no…needed to cough. Her eyes stung, making it impossible to see. Someone caught her hand. Not Jamie, his fingers were calloused, and these were smooth. Amy.

A rush of air hit her face.

And smoke. And heat.

She'd gotten the door open! Bethany lunged forward, falling on her hands and knees on the floor, trying to suck in great breaths of air in a room where this was fast disappearing. The building was open to the sky on the other end, and here she was suffocating because she couldn't crawl away from a campfire.

Someone hauled on Bethany's arm, trying to get her to move. Bethany nodded sluggishly. What did they say about fires? Stop, drop, and roll? No, she wasn't burning, just dying of smoke inhalation. She needed to crawl. To keep low. Bethany pulled her shirt up over her mouth and nose, wishing she'd thought of that sooner, trying to use the fabric as a mask to filter out the worst of it.

This fire was no mad inferno. It blossomed up the sides of the office area, dancing along the ceiling in front of her. She was trying to crawl through a tunnel of flame. For a moment, Bethany became disoriented. Where was she? What if she was heading deeper into the building, not out? And where were the others?

Part of the ceiling crashed down behind her. Bethany screamed and covered her head, taking in too much smoke. Dizzy, unable to catch her breath, the room seemed to slip away. The world was aflame, and Bethany was part of it.

God, help me!

CHAPTER 39

PRAYERS AND PLANS

Bethany

Air. Sweet air. Bethany rolled over, seeing tendrils of pink and orange chasing the clouds of smoke. Sunset. How long had they been in there? Where was she now? A sudden violent cough made her roll over on her side and pull her knees up to her stomach.

Her lungs hurt. There was still too much smoke in them, too much smoke even here in the parking lot. Surely by now, there would be nothing terrible to burn, no more dangerous chemicals. There was little enough left but drywall and insulation, the last remainders of a building which should have been torn down weeks ago. Only that was burning, nothing more. Beside her, Amy coughed, trying to get her breath. When Bethany sat up, she saw Jamie watching her intently.

There was no kindness in his eyes though undoubtedly it must have been him who brought them out.

"Where are they?" Bethany asked, placing her palms flat on the pavement and pushing herself to a sitting position. The world spun crazily for a moment and settled. To her surprise, the limo was still there.

"They don't know we're out," Jamie said, and she saw him reach for his phone. He wasn't speaking to her exactly, more to both of them, but still, it gave her hope. At least until he looked up and she saw the bleak and defeated look on his face.

She reminded herself that his family had lost everything in the past few weeks. What must it be like to see the building burn, to know the people who were responsible for killing your sister were still in the office?

Yet, he was weirdly calm. His body tense with anger, his expression laced with pain. He was still blaming her, and it wasn't fair. Not to mention the killers were about to get away. She held out a hand to interfere with his phone call. He pulled away as though reluctant to touch her, but he set the phone down.

"Wait. Just wait. We call the cops, and you know they'll run." She pointed a thumb at the office. "They were looking for something here, and they haven't found it, or they would have left by now. We can trap them. Call the cops when we've got them locked in or something. If the cops come, this will turn into a SWAT situation in minutes; you know it will. They might still get away." Bethany scooched over toward Jamie, ignoring the way her body ached as she moved. "Jamie, they have to pay for what they did."

"What about you? Will you pay, Bethany?"

He still blamed her? Even now? There was the confirmation she'd been looking for. It gave her no satisfaction. Bethany drew herself up, scrambling awkwardly to her feet. "It wasn't my fault. You heard them. That giant guy as much as said he'd killed her." She ignored the cough that followed that. Right now, clearing this up was more important than breathing.

He was on his feet now too. Towering over her, his face pale and streaked with soot. "Which they wouldn't have been able to do if you hadn't driven her away. She might have gone home instead. Never been out with that guy."

"That's not fair!"

Amy shoved her way between them. "Guys! Whether or not we call, the smoke will be seen and reported. If we're going to trap them, we do it now or not at all."

"You're in?" Bethany looked at her in surprise.

"We can't let them get away." Amy's face showed a bravado Bethany didn't think the girl felt.

The three of them looked at each other. "I'm in." Jamie was the first to answer; his expression angry and full of disgust. Whether it was her he hated or himself was hard to say. He didn't want to work with her, that much was obvious, but he was still throwing in with them.

Fine. She'd make this easy on him.

"Jamie, they're most likely to come out the main entrance. You lock that door, Amy and I will go around to the side and make sure that they can't get out. We can keep them contained until the police arrive."

Amy shook her head. The building behind them was fast becoming fully involved, even without fuel.

"Look at the way the wind is blowing. The offices are going to go if this keeps up. If we lock them in, *we'll* be murderers."

There was a long silence as they stared at one another. Bethany imagined that she would remember this moment for the rest of her life. Never had she understood the desire to take another life until now, when the lives of Rose's killers lay in her hands. Right or wrong didn't factor into it. That was the thought that stopped her cold.

"We need to pray," she said, choking out the words only with great difficulty, and not entirely due to the cough that followed her pronouncement. Amy nodded, reaching for Bethany's hand and offering the other to Jamie, asking him silently to complete the circle.

He hesitated a long moment, his eyes never leaving the door to the main building. "Do it," he said shortly, standing with them but making no move to hold either of their hands.

Fine. Let him sulk. They needed prayer whether he wanted it or not.

"Father God, we're in a mess. Maybe we should have listened or asked for help. Right now, we're not even sure if we're doing the right thing. But we need to know you're there with us. That you've got this even if we don't." Bethany bit her lip, unsure what else to say. "Just…help us. Please."

"Amen." Amy squeezed Bethany's hand before letting it go. Jamie just stood there, his face reflecting the light from the fire, his head tilted to one side. "I hear sirens. We have about five minutes tops."

"This is it then." Bethany took a shaky breath, trying not to cough when she needed to inspire confidence. "Last time then. Like before. Team, we stick together. Go in and out fast. If they're on their way out, we do what we can to stop them. We're not letting them go without a fight."

"They have at least one gun," Amy reminded her.

"That's why we're just trying to delay them long enough for the authorities to get here—no crazy chances. We stall them, that's it. Use available cover."

It felt like they'd already taken too long to go in, but Bethany couldn't regret the time they'd taken to pray. She felt more centered, more at peace than she'd ever felt before in her life. Jamie might not be ready to forgive her, but for the first time since they'd gotten here, she was able to lay that aside.

Her sneakers slapped the pavement beneath her feet as they ran. There was no pretense at subterfuge this time around. The sun had dipped below the horizon, and with the fire glowing away to their right, they had their choice of shadows to hide in as they moved as low to the ground as they could until they made it to the door.

This was familiar; this dance was theirs. Amy and Bethany stood one on each side of the door. They had no weapons except themselves. Bethany didn't know about Amy, but she ached from the earlier fight and was still out of breath from her time in the fire. Still, she was ready to go in. She looked at Amy and nodded. They would clear the room the way they'd practiced a hundred times before.

The door opened easily, not having been closed fully. As it turned out, they could have made all the noise in the world. They could hear Charity screaming from the reception area. Crashes and bangs interspersed the angry cries. The group looked at each other and kept going.

The hallway was a risky point. Open doors to other offices provided spaces to fall back, to reassess. They moved slowly. As they drew closer, it was easier to hear what was being said.

"Did I or did I not tell you not to start a fire? I distinctly remember saying no. And there you go starting one anyway. You're finished, Gustav, do you hear me? Finished! Because as soon as we find that piece of paper, we're out of here."

"Why don't we just burn this building, and then we have nothing to worry about?"

There came the sound of something heavy hitting the wall. "What is it with you and fire? What guarantee is there that the paper we need would burn? If it's in one of these cabinets, it might well survive, and then where will we be?"

"Boss, I hear sirens." This was the third voice; one Bethany didn't know.

She looked at Jamie, and he motioned for them to fall back to the room with a giant photocopier sitting in the middle of it. "That's the third guy. I recognized him. He brought in a truck a couple of weeks ago for a repair. He seemed awfully interested in the place. Kept nosing about, you know? Instead of waiting like the other drivers do when they have a repair."

Bethany considered this. There were ramifications there she was going to have to think through later. Right now, they had to focus on what was right in front of them. Three bad guys. Three of them. But they still had the element of surprise.

She looked around the room, knowing they had no time at all for a better plan than this. "OK, guys, here's what I want you to grab…"

CHAPTER 40

CONFRONTATIONS AND CASUALTIES

Jamie

The whole plan was stupid, but Bethany had been right. He wasn't about to let these creeps get away for anything. Whatever culpability Bethany might have had for driving Rose away, it was those three that took his sister away from him.

He felt heavy loaded as they slipped into the hallway. Carrying too much stuff, and his arms hurt under the strain of his burden. Bethany had said he could drop what he carried easy enough and run, which made sense much as he hated to admit it. Running away was logical; it was the smart thing to do. Fine. He would do what they came to do.

Which turned out to be sooner than they thought.

Evidently, the searching group found what they were looking for, or the sirens were too close for them to be comfortable because they appeared in the doorway the same instant Jamie and his crew did. For a split second, it was impossible to know who was more startled, them or Jamie and his friends. Now that they engaged the enemy, he wasn't sure how to start.

They were only a foot apart, close enough for him to see just how much makeup it took to create the illusion of 'perfection' in Charity Clifton's face. She wasn't so pretty up close. In truth, she looked like she'd been through it. "Rode hard and put away wet," as his grandmother would say. Her hair was askew, her hairstyle tilting sideways. Her immaculate pantsuit was streaked with mud and soot. And more importantly, the gun was nowhere in sight.

"Fire!"

It was Bethany who gave the order, but it was Amy who delivered the first volley in the form of a stapler which hit Gustav square between the eyes. Goliath didn't exactly keel over dead, but it did distract him pretty well.

It all went downhill from there.

Jamie had a strong arm from playing football. He needed it now as he lobbed reams of printer paper at the villains, smacking Charity Clifton hard enough in the solar plexus that she staggered backward into the others. The giant roared and flung his boss out of the way, intent on getting in their faces, but he ran into the other guy who was of a similar mind, wedging them both in the doorway. The smaller one took the worst of the constriction. He visibly tried to pull back, but the giant would have none of that; he tried to get through the door with a single-mindedness that was like a bull trying to ram everything in sight. It also left them vulnerable to Jamie's best fifty-yard-pass throws.

Reams of paper smacked them both, one after another. The blocks broke on impact, sending clouds of paper into the air, further confusing them even as another stapler, and, of all things, a small printer crashed into someone's shoulder, shattering on impact.

"Okay, that wasn't very effective," Amy allowed as she went back for more.

Jamie was running out of paper, which was just as well, as the sheets scattered over the floor were making footing treacherous as the men in the door shoved free. Rather, the small man was shot from the doorway like stepping on the side of a rubber ball. He flew out, going sideways as the giant won free. The little guy went down in a heap, tripping his partner and setting the big one off-balance. Bethany screamed and dove right for the giant. Where she hit, Jamie never knew. The guy was up one minute, down the next, falling hard, probably aided by the piles of papers on the floor. The little guy was staggering up, reaching for something in his jacket.

Gun! Jamie might have yelled it, maybe it was just in his head, but he knew without a doubt there was a gun in the man's jacket.

This whole idea was stupid. Jamie should have just called the cops and let them handle it in the first place. Now that they were in the thick of it, there was nothing to do but fight. Even if they could retreat, the risk of being shot in the back was too high. Jamie called on his years playing in the Homeschool Football League, took his stance, tucked his head in, and ran.

He hit the little guy square but wound up catapulting both of them into his father's office. Here the debris was not so far removed from the hallway. Papers were everywhere, the filing cabinets in shambles. Whatever they were looking for, they weren't subtle about it; they rifled the room, breaking furniture in their mad frustrations.

Jamie rolled on folders and couldn't regain his footing. To his relief, neither could the other guy. They looked like two men on an ice rink, neither of them able to get his feet under him.

It was Charity who broke the whole thing up.

"Stop!"

The word was accompanied by a loud bang. She had the gun and was shooting. Apparently, the heels on her shoes gave her an advantage, but several sheets were stuck through like the sharp pin restaurants use to skewer receipts.

Not stupid enough to stand around and be shot, Jamie dove for the desk, snagging his ex-girlfriend, who was only just staggering up and dragging her with him. Truth be told, he slipped on the pages and turned the fall into a dive, wrapping one arm around a confused Bethany and dragging her with. They wound up in the cramped space together, too close for comfort.

He couldn't bear it. Despite the smoke, the fight, the panic…she smelled *good*. He couldn't stand to be so close to her.

He didn't have to be. He could run at any time. Maybe try being shot if that was better.

Okay, maybe he could stand it a moment or two longer.

"Now you're going to come out of there like good children and be my hostages," Charity sneered. "But wait, there's only two of you back there. Where's the other one?"

Other one? She hadn't seen Amy? In the hallway, everything had been in darkness and confusion. She might never have noticed Amy at all.

"Dead. She didn't make it out of the fire!" Jamie shouted from behind the desk. It was a bluff, but if he could save Amy…

"I don't believe you!"

Gone was the impeccable businesswoman. The woman screaming invectives at them, each more creative than the last, was beyond any pretense of civility. She sent a bullet into the desk, causing Jamie to flinch involuntarily. When he glanced at Bethany in the fading light from the window behind him, he was surprised to see she wasn't scared so much as angry. In fact, given the set of her jaw, the way she squared her shoulders, she was about to do something incredibly stupid.

"Don't."

He wasn't acting to protect her. He was doing it because he was tired of senseless death. What was it about his father's company which made it so important? Why did so many people have to suffer just so they could take what his father had spent his whole life trying to build? They could have it. Lives were so much more important.

"I'm coming out. Don't shoot."

Standing up seemed foolhardy. Stupid. But it was that or wait to be shot in small increments. He had no doubt they'd blow up the desk to get to them if they had to. Jamie stood on legs, which felt the way they did after running sprints for coach. He raised his hands in the air and stepped out into full view. He expected to be killed on sight.

The office would be dark in a moment. The sun was gone, the only light from the fire, and yes…from headlights. Someone else out there, just now arriving. Emergency vehicles? Did he care? The purpose had been to delay the bad guys until the good guys showed up. Mission accomplished. Current mission? Continue breathing.

Charity drew herself up on seeing him. She even smiled, the look of a woman who was fast regaining control. "Hostages. Both of you. You're our ticket out of here."

"It won't work," Bethany said from behind him. Stepping carefully out, her hands up. On the floor, the little guy still hadn't gotten up. The giant, on the other hand, was furious, and he wasn't trusting that the hallway was empty for anything. He turned to look—

—just as Amy sprang out of nowhere. There came a bright flash of light, blinding if you were looking straight at it as Jamie was. He staggered, putting a hand up to his eyes, feeling more than seeing Bethany rush past.

All was chaos and confusion. Another flash followed by another. Bethany was everywhere at once, her training in the martial arts being more than adequate to take down the stunned giant. Gustav roared and went down fighting. Someone, he thought Charity, screamed. There came the sound of flesh hitting flesh—a bang. The gun going off so close he could smell the gunpowder.

Something heavy fell—a body.

Jamie scrambled for his phone, hitting the flashlight and turning it on, seeing to his surprise it was the little guy who lay without moving. He must have tried to get up and help, for he was twisted in an impossible position.

Amy had Gustav hogtied, using zip ties meant for making computer cables neat and tidy behind desks while Bethany...

Bethany was holding the gun on one very chastened Omni executive.

"Amy, what in the world did you do?"

She flushed. "Toner is flammable. If you throw the powder over an open flame, it kind of reacts like a flashbulb. Don't ask how I know that." She sheepishly held up a lighter. "I found the lighter stashed with a pack of cigarettes in the copy room."

Bethany shook her head and handed the gun to Amy. "You take this. I'm feeling a little light-headed, and I might shoot this woman's head off by accident."

"Gladly." Amy handed her zip ties to Bethany, who took over the job of tying Charity's hands in front of her. The woman tried to kick out at Bethany, but Jamie woke from his stupor enough to haul the woman to her feet and keep her out of the way once she was safely tied.

"Check him, Jamie. Please," Amy said, motioning to the still figure in the middle of the room.

His mystery truck driver was dead. Shot through the head.

Jamie's hands shook as he eased his hand away from the man's neck, where he'd been looking uselessly for a pulse. It was only just sinking in that this might have been him.

The big guy writhed on the floor. He opened his mouth, spewing expletives. Amy gave him a look and stuffed some wadded-up paper in his mouth to silence him.

"Thou shalt not take the name of the Lord, thy God in vain!" she recited primly.

It was over—time to go home.

CHAPTER 41

RELIEF AND RUINATION

Dr. Martin Bradford

When he saw the flames outlined against the sky, Dr. Martin Bradford questioned his faith. Where was God when the world was an inferno, and your only child was out there in it somewhere?

His foot hit the accelerator. He took the turn on two wheels, tires squealing, almost rolling the Suburban in his haste to reach the parking lot. He had to hit the brakes hard to keep from hitting Jamie's truck.

Beside him, Lance was shouting something. He couldn't hear past the blood rushing through his ears. The roar coupled with the squeal of brakes, the slamming of doors, the shouts of men, it was the noise of a war zone. The only thing missing was the sound of artillery.

A single shot rang out.

"Who's shooting already?" Martin roared, turning on Lance, but he was looking past him, toward the building which housed the offices.

"It came from in there."

In. There.

The words rang through Martin's mind. He started forward; then training kicked in—the plan. Lance was already on it, organizing the units. Men deployed, at a dead run, building a perimeter. Nothing would get past them.

His daughter. His precious daughter Amy was in there.

Lance had his arm, holding him back. Martin hadn't even been aware of starting for the door. He fought him, trying to get free. "I need to get in there!"

"And get yourself killed?"

It would be a fair exchange—a life for a life. Martin shook him off, running now only to be brought up short by the figures which stepped through the falling ash and billowing smoke. Several figures, actually.

Five of them.

Thank God.

They strode out of the building like a scene from an action movie. Ms. Clifton in the lead, propelled by none other than Bethany Shanholtz. A giant of a man with the build of a quarterback, in the capable hands of James Wood. And his daughter Amy. His precious Amy.

Holding a gun on the lot of them.

Martin blinked. Looked again. Then again.

Yep, that was his baby girl, managing a Glock like she'd handled one her entire life.

Okay, to be fair, he might have given her some training in firearms as part of her phys-ed requirement.

It was all he could do to manage some sort of decorum. Especially given that right now, he wanted nothing more than to hold his daughter in his arms and make sure she still had all ten fingers and toes she came into the world with. Or do something else horrifyingly embarrassing. Instead, he stepped forward and held out his hand to her. "I can take it from here, soldier."

"Thank you, Sir!"

Then beaming mightily, Amy saluted, handed over the gun, and became his little girl all over again by flinging herself into her father's arms as around him as an entire army descended on the group.

"There's another one inside. He's dead, Dad."

She looked up at him, her glasses askew from having her face pressed into his shirt. The eyes behind them were somber. Barely holding on after what had certainly been an ordeal. Martin's throat tightened. His little girl had grown up over these past weeks in ways he wished she hadn't had to.

"We'll take care of it," he assured her and turned as the parking lot filled up with more vehicles, these the entirety of the Steven's Mill Police Department. In minutes, the place would be full of authorities wanting to interrogate anything that moved. Beside him, Lance cleared his throat. Martin nodded. Let the troops disperse. There would be fewer questions asked the fewer people stayed on at this point.

In the meantime, he buried his face in his daughter's hair, holding her so tight she began to struggle. "Dad, I can't breathe."

"Then maybe you should check your phone now and again," he informed her as he let her go. He stepped back, watching as Lance made the suspects kneel on the grass. Waiting for pickup from the local police.

"Forty-seven new messages? Dad! I thought you trusted me."

Behind them, firefighters scrambled to salvage what was left of the warehouse and keep the fire from spreading.

"You clearly had the matter entirely under control," he observed with a wry shake of his head.

Something collapsed in a cascade of sparks.

"Obviously," she responded and rolled her eyes, as behind her, Bethany laughed.

— CHAPTER 42 —

CHARITY AND RESOLUTION

Amy

"I would have gotten away with it too if it hadn't been for you meddling kids."

Amy stared at the TV screen and laughed. "Well, it was kinda like that. Maybe."

"Not funny, Ames." Her father took the remote from her and switched the channel from Scooby-doo over to the local news. "Now hush, it looks like we're right on time."

Amy settled on the couch next to her dad. She had a ridiculous urge to grab some popcorn. It was like watching the end of a movie, where everything was finally wrapped up. Or it would be if they would ever start. What her dad thought was a news report was actually only a teaser. There were several stories they had to sit through before the one they wanted came up.

Amy tapped a foot impatiently against the coffee table until her father nudged her with his foot to make her stop. Restless, she got up and wandered around the room, tidying up, though there was nothing to do while the newscaster talked his way through several stories of national importance and the local weather.

"She confessed to everything, though, didn't she, Dad?" Amy asked again, half dreading seeing Charity Clifton again, even from the safety of a news broadcast.

"Everything. Including ordering the murders of Dax and Rose."

Amy nodded, her desire for popcorn gone. She sat and leaned against her Dad's shoulder instead, drawing her feet up under her. In times like this, she didn't mind being a little kid still.

Her father dropped a colorful afghan over her as the story on the screen shifted over to some sort of protest. Amy sat up, knocking the blanket to the floor as she recognized the dark-haired woman holding a sign front and center.

"Elena's mom is back at it again!" she said in wonder, wondering how Elena felt about that. Amy had actually felt kind of sorry for her that day at church, but with everything going on hadn't taken the time to reach out to the teen again.

"She's been about causes ever since I've known her," Martin said thoughtfully. "Looks like she moved on to bigger goals."

"Do you think they'll fight the sale of Steven's Mill Shipping to Omni Millennium then?"

"What makes you think they're selling?" Martin asked in surprise.

"The scrawl at the bottom of the screen?" Amy pointed. Sure enough, the newscaster was talking about their town.

"...and in Steven's Mill, Virginia, we bring you a complicated story of murder, betrayal, and double-dealing. Charity Clifton, a former executive for Omni Millennium, an international concern looking to invest locally, was indicted today on several charges of first- and second-degree murder."

Amy listened wide-eyed as the story unfolded. They closed on a statement from the new CEO of the company.

The screen shifted to show a man with dark hair, expertly styled. His tailored suit screamed money. When he put his hands up to still the crowd of reporters peppering him with questions, several heavy gold rings glinted on his hands. This was a man who exuded money and power. Amy frowned.

"Yes, we have been absolved of all responsibility. Ms. Clifton, by her own admission, very regrettably acted entirely in her own interests rather than that of the company. That she chose such nefarious means to achieve her goals is both horrifying and repugnant to myself and the Omni Millennium family."

A reporter shouted from the crowd, "What about Steven's Mill Shipping? Why would you say she so unfairly targeted one particular business in such a way?"

"Truly, I cannot answer as to someone else's state of mind. You would have to ask her."

"What about the merger with Steven's Mill Shipping?" someone else called out.

"Our desire has always been to put money into the community of Steven's Mill. We feel this particular location holds a lot of untapped potential for a company such as ourselves and that we are in a unique position where we can do something positive to impact the community. Together we can make Steven's Mill a better place. To this end, we not only were willing to go through with the merger but have, after some deliberation, made a very generous offer to the owner to buy the company outright. Only this hour have we gotten word that he has accepted our offer."

Amy snorted. "I'm starting to see what Elena's mom gets so uptight about. If they own the company outright, won't that mean a lot of change for the community?"

Martin turned off the TV and got up to stretch. "Well, change of that nature takes time, though I expect you're right to a certain extent. If they rebuild the company and decide to expand it, there will be more traffic through Steven's Mill." He shook his head. "I don't know about you, but I could do with a scoop of ice cream. You?"

"You can eat at a time like this?"

"I can when there's fudge ripple in the freezer."

Amy laughed and followed him to the kitchen. She got out bowls and spoons while her dad found the ice cream and dished them each up a bowl.

"It doesn't make sense, though, does it? That CEO, he said they'd made a 'very generous offer' to the Wood family. Is that just media speak?" Amy tapped her spoon against the side of her bowl thoughtfully. "At church, I heard that Mr. and Mrs. Wood are moving away, so they got something out of this."

"What are you getting at?"

"Well, Mr. Wood taught me basic economics. To my way of thinking, couldn't Omni get the shipping company for a song? There are no vehicles, the warehouse is destroyed, the offices not in the greatest shape. It's hardly a viable business, nor is it likely to be anytime soon. Yet at church, they were talking like the Wood's just came into a lot of money. I mean a LOT."

"Gossip, Amy," Martin waved his spoon at her in warning, "you can't believe gossip."

"Do you have any idea how hard it is to get reliable information around here without talking to Mrs. Gunderson first? Seriously, Dad, you should employ her out at Mount Hideaway."

"Who says we don't?" he countered, digging contentedly into his ice cream.

Amy stared at him. "I'm going to pretend I didn't hear that. Anyway, I'm just saying it doesn't look right. I thought they were investors, not owners. People who put the money in and let others do the work."

"That's a somewhat simplistic view of things…"

"Hear me out, Dad. They've just lost a key executive to some very shady dealings. Now they're all about building the community and going so far as to buy a company that barely exists on paper. They must want that company an awful lot, Dad, and it's just a shipping company. Out of how many other shipping companies on the east coast?"

Martin set down his spoon. "Amy, I need you to let this go."

"As a father, or as an employee of Mount Hideaway?" she asked, her tone perhaps a little more challenging than she meant it to be for her Dad looked her a very long time without answering. She was afraid for a moment that she'd said something to upset him.

When he did speak, his tone was carefully neutral. "Just let it go. Don't get caught up in conspiracies."

"Ha!" Amy shoved her bowl away, really not interested in ice cream anymore. "Listen to me, Dad. The whole thing was one big conspiracy after another. The whole reason Charity went back into the office was to find the paperwork from when Ted brought that truck into the company on a dry run to get an idea of the layout and how the setup worked so he could bring in the next truck and leave it right where it would do the most damage when it blew. If that's not a carefully planned out conspiracy, then I don't know what is."

"Which we would never have found the proof of if you kids hadn't intervened. I know, I know. You did good. Now I'm asking you to back down. You're still a student. You're leaving for college soon. Let it be, Amy. Concentrate on moving forward. You're going to Tech to study veterinary medicine. This is a noble goal."

Amy bit her lip. "So, you're saying to live my life and not look back?"

"Yes. Exactly. Let me deal with this."

His eyes were somber. There was so much he was trying to tell her in that look. She might have missed it if she hadn't been looking. He was trying to reassure her. To let her know that he was being vigilant. That maybe she didn't have to be the hero after all. At least not yet.

"Okay, Dad." Amy pulled her bowl close and used her spoon to stir her ice cream until the chocolate was evenly distributed. "Just don't get into trouble without me around to bail you out."

He laughed at that, in a welcome explosion of sound.

Right now, that was more healing than any amount of ice cream.

CHAPTER 43

MEMORIES AND MOVING ON

Jamie

He couldn't believe they were leaving. He'd spent his whole life in Steven's Mill, and now they would be…gone.

Jamie stood for a long time outside Rose's bedroom door, empty boxes in his hands. He couldn't ask this of his mother. With Harlan still so sick, and the loss of Rose, she seemed to be made of spun glass anymore. To pack these things up would surely cause her to shatter.

He stepped into the bedroom and stood a long moment with a quiet reverence. No, he hadn't gotten along well with Rose this last year. She'd gone all prickly and strange as she'd struggled to find who she was. He wondered if he could have been more supportive. Done something more.

He sighed. Looking around and trying to determine what to pack. What to throw away. What to donate to the church. His mother hadn't been able to answer these questions. Maybe it was easier to take everything and let her sort through it later, when she felt stronger.

Unsure where else to begin, Jamie set the boxes down on the bed and moved toward the dresser. Clearing the surfaces seemed the most sensible. Then he would have places to set the packed boxes until the movers could deal with them.

He glanced through the items on the top of the dresser. Makeup could probably be tossed. Jewelry he tucked inside the open lacquer box. He pulled up a bracelet. She'd gotten that for Christmas from Bethany one year. He remembered how she'd squealed over it, saying the Chinese design had been just perfect though really it was more Bethany's thing than Rose's.

But then Bethany had never been good at giving gifts. She tended to think that just because she liked something, someone else would too.

No. He wasn't going to think about her. Not now. This was about Rose, not him.

He grabbed a sheet of bubble wrap and wrapped it around the jewelry box. It didn't weigh much, so he set it aside, thinking to put some books in the bottom of the box first, to balance things out. He sighed again as his thumbs got caught in the wrapping on the next knick-knack, and he was sure the porcelain cat figurine would probably break in transit. He really didn't know what he was doing.

Jamie supposed the movers could pack this up for them. They certainly had enough money with what Omni paid them for the remains of the shipping company. But somehow, having strangers being the last people to paw over his sister's belongings felt wrong. The ladies from church might have helped, but did his family need the invasion of a well-meaning stranger? No. They didn't.

So, he worked quietly. Trying to pretend he was just packing up Rose's things to send to her at college or something, but the game waned quickly. He could not be deceived. Rose was gone forever. End of story.

Funny though. He couldn't find certain things. He supposed the earrings he gave her for Christmas were the ones she was wearing...that night. She'd probably tossed out that little blue stuffed elephant he gave her when they were kids. She used to carry that everywhere. But where was Rose's favorite sweatshirt? The one she'd stolen from him last winter when she was cold, that she'd never given back. She certainly hadn't been wearing it when she'd...

His mind shied away from the thought. Maybe it had been in the car. He flinched away from the thought. He didn't like to think about the accident. If the sweatshirt was gone, it was gone.

He wondered if his mother had it. Or if it was in the laundry room. Suddenly that stupid sweatshirt became the most important thing in the world to him. It had been his sweatshirt first. He wanted it back. No. He wanted it because Rose had loved it.

Jamie left the boxes and went in search of the sweatshirt. But while he found other items belonging to Rose in the laundry room, it wasn't there. Nor could he find it anywhere else in the house. The rooms were half-packed, though. His parents were heading to South Carolina to retire near his father's brother. They thought it might help in his recovery to start over somewhere new. Somewhere they were loved and would have someone to watch over them while Jamie went away to college.

Fine. It was just a sweatshirt. Not important.

But it was. He returned to Rose's room, angry and put out. He hated this job. He hated that he had been the one to be tasked with doing it. No, that wasn't right. He'd volunteered because it needed to be done. He was getting muddled. Upset.

Crying.

He swiped angrily at tears, hated himself for crying when he'd already cried at Rose's funeral. When would there be enough tears? When would he be done? Ever?

He picked up one of the pillows on the bed, flinging it toward the dresser, sending makeup clattering against the wall. Bottles fell and hit the carpet. The destruction felt good. He threw the next pillow and the next. When he ran out, stuffed animals rained down in the room, knocking books and mementos from the shelves.

He threw things until there was nothing left to throw. He was fighting Rose, angry at her for leaving him. Fighting himself, recognizing that he had a part to play in this as well. It wasn't entirely Bethany's fault what had happened. He'd pushed Rose, too, back that first day when they'd created the plan to save his father.

And they had too. Bethany had stuck through this, and in the end, his father's name was cleared. He'd gotten what he wanted, even if the cost had been too high.

He bent to pick up the books, noting the blank covers, the leather bindings. Still wiping at the tears he'd never meant to shed in the first place, he flipped through one and found, to his surprise, that it was a journal. Jamie's heart clenched painfully as he stared at her familiar writing. He couldn't bear to read it, and yet he strangely needed to.

He grabbed the entire stack of books and took them to his room. Reading them there seemed liked sacrilege.

Reading them here just felt…odd. Like maybe he shouldn't be reading these at all. At the same time, he craved the ability to be near her, at least this way. To hear her voice in his head as she talked about her day.

There were eleven journals. They started back when she started homeschooling. Jamie kind of recalled a time when journaling had been part of their daily lessons. Their mom had made a big deal about how they needed to write down their thoughts. She'd given them prompts sometimes when they didn't know what to write about.

Most of these early entries used those prompts. Comments about the weather, bits of poetry. Talking about him.

Jamie laughed as she described their first dog. Jamie had been afraid of dogs when he was small. She'd made a big deal out of that, turning the story into a comic strip.

He was about to set them aside, wanting to pack them with his own things that he might look at them later, when he realized something strange. What he'd thought was the last volume was her leatherbound Bible. Not a journal.

Going back over the books, he put them in order by date, stacking them with the oldest on the bottom, the newest on the top. Yes, there was no doubt about it. The journal which was meant to start in January of this year, was gone.

Had it been in her car, too, along with the sweatshirt? It bothered him to no end that the book wasn't there. He would have wanted to read the end of the story.

He wanted to know if she blamed him—if she was angry with him still when she died.

He flipped through the last one he had, seeing she'd stuck photographs between the pages. She'd taken up photography as a hobby last year as part of her homeschool curriculum. He paused on a picture of himself, laughing, looking so much younger than the man who looked back at him in the mirror these days. In the picture, Bethany stood next to him, laughing at something he'd said.

Jamie's face hardened. He slammed the book shut and dropped it in a box with the rest, hesitating because he didn't know if he wanted Rose's Bible or not. Where had God been in all this?

He didn't know. He wasn't ready for that question just yet. In the end, he added it to the journals and closed the box, putting the name of his college on the outside, and setting it aside with the rest of the stuff intended for his dorm. It was like putting away his childhood forever.

He didn't have time to be mooning about. He had a job to do.

─── CHAPTER 44 ───

DRAMA AND DAISIES

Bethany

Ever since the accident, Bethany had found a strange sort of solace in going to the river. For months now, it had become her place to walk or sit and talk to God.

Sometimes she talked to Rose as well. There was a peacefulness here, despite the turmoil that had taken place.

Everything had been so different since then. With Jamie going to South Carolina with his parents, and Rose gone, the co-op hadn't been the same. In the end, Amy and Bethany had both pushed hard, concentrating on their studies that they might go away to college sooner rather than later. Maybe they, too, were trying to escape from Steven's Mill. Maybe it was just the pain they were trying to run away from. Losing Rose was going to hurt for a very long time.

Bethany never did find the faith Amy had. Where Amy never swerved, Bethany still questioned. She was doing that now, sitting on a rock on the riverbank near where Rose's car had gone into the water. She sat with her finger in her Bible, marking her place, and talked out loud to God, watching for Him in the sunlight shining off the water. She wasn't sure, but she thought she saw him sometimes in the way the trees bent to the breezes as if the wind were passing secrets from one tree to another.

"I don't understand any of this, Father. Amy says that you're in control. Pastor Hemi tells me to have faith and to believe." She took a breath but couldn't help the thin wail that threatened to burst out. "But Rose is still, gone, and Jamie…

he hasn't spoken to me *yet*. I've tried everything, Lord. You know I have. But he won't forgive me." She lay her free hand on her chest, over where her heart hurt.

As usual, there was no answer. Bethany was growing used to that. This silence on the part of the Almighty was becoming something she'd learned to live with. Maybe someday, she'd be more like her mom or Dr. Bradford to understand better what that kind of silence meant. Amy said she felt that way too sometimes, and always took it an opportunity to share the silence with God, figuring maybe He was asking her to figure something out in those moments where He wasn't forthcoming with the answers.

Bethany sighed. Whatever she was supposed to figure out, she wasn't getting it.

"What do you think, Rose?" She asked this question in a whisper, as if afraid of the answer. This, too, brought only silence, one with an aching hurt to it. Rose wouldn't have been interested in helping Bethany sort out things with Jamie. Rose hadn't ever wanted her to date Jamie in the first place.

The air was chilly. Bethany sighed and gathered her things. The Bible she tucked into a backpack, which she slung over her shoulder. She had homework to do if she were going to be ready for classes in a few weeks. She'd been studying advanced psychology with her mom to get a head start on the semester.

She left behind the river with regret. There would always be sadness here in this place. In her psychology textbook, there were probably all kinds of explanations as to why she felt the need to return again and again to a place where one of the greatest tragedies of her life had been enacted. Self-punishment? Or nothing more than a way to be close to a friend she dearly missed? Maybe it was because she felt closest to Rose here.

So deep in thought was she, that she didn't notice the young man walking down the trail toward her until they were almost on top of one another.

"Jamie!"

He was the last person she had expected to see. He carried in his hand a bouquet of flowers—daisies, which Rose loved because they were so much simpler than the flower she was named after. Rose had only ever wanted to be an uncomplicated girl, down to earth and real.

Jamie must have been just as distracted as Bethany was, for it took him a minute. When he looked up, she saw the recognition on his face. A whole slew of emotions washed over his face. For a moment, she saw naked vulnerability. Longing.

He stepped toward her and stopped. For a precious, fleeting moment, he looked as though he was glad to see her.

She felt it too. Her whole being trembled with the need to speak to him.

But Bethany couldn't seem to make herself move. Her feet stayed stubbornly glued to the trail while she waited for him to speak.

Only he didn't. In fact, whatever movement he'd made in her direction, he retreated now. Deliberately leaving the trail to walk around her. Going down to the water as though she wasn't even there at all.

Bethany blinked back tears. She hadn't spoken to him, not truly spoken since their argument right here in this very place. Any words spoken in the confrontation in the shipping offices didn't count. Those had only been a smattering of orders, a handful of nasty remarks designed to hurt and not clear the air at all.

For a moment, Bethany recalled the feel of his hand in hers so long ago, the way he'd smiled when they'd gone down, fishing poles in hand—what she would give to go back to that moment and freeze her life there before everything had changed so terribly much.

"So now what do I do?" she asked, not sure if she were addressing Rose or God. Probably God since He was actually there listening, and Rose was not. "Do I follow? Make him talk to me?"

Where before there had been no answer, this time she heard it. God's voice in the stillness of the morning, as clear to her as the sound of rushing water or trucks on the highway a quarter-mile away.

Let him go.

Bethany swallowed hard. It wasn't the answer she'd wanted.

Yet in the end, wasn't that what trusting God to be in control was all about? That meant He had the steering wheel even when you didn't like the destination. Because sometimes you had to believe that there was something bigger and better that He was taking you to than you might ever have imagined otherwise.

To do what *she* wanted, to follow Jamie now would only be damaging to both of them. They both needed time away from one another to heal. They each had their own roads to follow, and whether or not that meant they would cross paths again was entirely up to God. Not her.

She wouldn't want it any other way.

Still, she couldn't help but look back anyway. Jamie had thrown the daisies into the water, letting the current take them where they would go. Her heart throbbed with a longing to go to him. In part because she understood. She wanted to share the grief with him, maybe that they both might be cleansed of it once and for all. Not that this kind of deep sorrow worked that way. She would always carry Rose with her, she knew. And Jamie too.

Maybe that's what God had intended all along. Both Jamie and Rose would be instrumental in making her the person she would become.

Jamie stood, watching the water. For all she knew, he was standing down there, waiting for her to go so he wouldn't have to talk to her. If that were the case, she could give him that, even if she couldn't give him anything else.

Bethany turned her back on him and walked away.

No, he'd walked away first, she reminded herself. This distinction was important. Or maybe it wasn't. Maybe that was another question she'd just have to lay at the feet of the Almighty another day. Not that any of this made the pain any less.

It was a good thing she'd walked down to the river today. She could never have seen through her tears well enough to be able to drive home.

CHAPTER 45

GOOD-BYE AND MOVING ON

Bethany

How did you possibly figure out what you needed in a new life when all you had to carry you there was one suitcase and one carry-on? Bethany stood in the middle of her bedroom, hands on hips, and tried to decide just what was important enough to include in the space which remained. It looked like such a small corner of her suitcase that still had room for anything, and there was still so much left in her room. If she could only shrink the dresser down…

Her eyes were immediately drawn to the pictures over her desk. The bulletin board had become a place to hold her favorite memories over the years. She let her fingers slide over the ribbons she'd earned showing animals in 4-H, the satin cool and slippery in her hands. Next to them were ticket stubs for concerts. The program from a play they'd gone to see in D.C., signed by the entire crew. She traced the name of the players but left it alone.

It was the pictures that drew her attention.

There was, of course, her favorite picture with Amy. That was definitely coming. Then Rose. She'd caught Rose with her nose in a book, her hair in a messy topknot, so absorbed she hadn't noticed the butterfly which had landed on the top of her head. It was a beautiful picture, somewhat silly, which had juxtaposed beautifully with Rose's serious nature. This was the Rose she wanted to remember, the one who had always been so complicated, so undeniably Rose.

Below that was the picture she hadn't been able to put away, though maybe she should have. It was from a selfie she'd taken the night they'd broken into Amy's house to 'steal' the goblet. How perfectly the camera had caught each of them. Bethany smiled too big, gung-ho for the adventure. Amy had practically been bouncing; she'd had so much enthusiasm for the night's work, tempered by the slight frown which told clearly of a hint of worry. She hadn't wanted to let down her dad. As if she ever could.

Rose had been frowning, arms crossed, not quite one of the group. Bethany lingered over this image, wondering just how much Rose had resented her even then. Jamie had been looking not at the camera but at her. Had that been part of Rose's dissatisfaction? Whatever Rose felt, Bethany never had anything but love for her; she proudly numbered Rose as one of her best and closest friends. It still hurt that she'd died before they could clear the air between them.

Bethany bit her lip but added the picture to those she wanted to take. Maybe she wouldn't put it up right away, but someday she would. Someday when she was ready to remember. Someday when the memory brought less pain than it did joy. She prayed for that day, though she couldn't conceive of it. Not now, anyway.

The last picture was of Jamie by himself. Bethany pulled this one from the board, wondering how long it would be before this particular ache left her. To her surprise, the sting had gone out of it already, leaving behind a dull soreness in her chest. Maybe time healed all wounds after all? Maybe it was a promise of healing, a preview when the hurt would be less.

"I'm not taking you with me," she said softly to the picture as she set it in the top drawer of her dresser.

"Jamie, I can't move forward if you're going to always be holding me back." She glanced at the second picture, one of all of them together. Bethany set this one in the drawer on top of the first.

Bethany was tucking away the pictures she'd chosen to take in her bag, secure between the pages of her Bible when her mom came in. Tina Shanholtz set down a pile of clean laundry on the bed and looked around the room in surprise.

"I didn't expect you to clean the place out. It's still your room, Bethany."

True, the room seemed somewhat impersonal with the pictures gone, the other trinkets either packed or put away. On the other hand, she liked the way the room had become clean and new, especially with the way the sun streamed through the window. "I think when I come home next," she considered her words as she spoke, "I'm going to be a different person. I thought maybe it would be best to give myself a blank slate."

"So long as there's still a little of you in there somewhere, I'm good what that," Tina said with a laugh. "Don't lose the best parts."

"You mean like how I feel about my family?" She sat on the edge of the bed next to her Mom.

"And your faith in God."

Bethany smiled. "You prepared me for that, Mom. You've been teaching me about God from the time I could walk."

"From before that! I used to read the Bible to you when you were tucked safely in the womb." Her mother smiled and wrapped an arm around her. Bethany leaned into the hug, content to be her mother's little girl just once more. "Your father and I wanted you to have a firm foundation to build on, wherever you wound up in life. Don't lose that."

"I don't think I could." Bethany grabbed her mom in a long hug. "Can you believe it? Tomorrow I leave for Madison. Political Science!" It sounded real when she said it out loud, as though everything so far had been preparation for "someday," but someday had come.

Tina chuckled. "I'm not sure I've ever heard anyone cheer quite so loudly for political science before. Got everything you need?" Her mother released her and turned her attention to the bag. If Bethany noticed a particular watering in her mother's eye, she didn't mention it.

"Kind of lacking one thing." She thought of the pictures in her dresser drawer. "I never talked to Jamie." She sighed and dropped her head into her chest. "I guess I'm going to have to let him go."

"By looking forward," her mother agreed. "You can start with finishing packing." She stood and gave her daughter another hug, a long one. It startled Bethany that they were of a similar height. When had that happened? "Then I believe," her mother spoke briskly as she let Bethany go, "your sister has something special planned for tonight. As a heads up, you might never think of either rabbits or ballet in quite the same way again." She laid a finger on her nose and gave Bethany a wink.

Bethany's eyes grew wide. "Tell me you're kidding."

Her mother only laughed. "Come downstairs and see for yourself."

Bethany let her go on ahead without her. She just needed a minute. She picked up the clothes her mother had just brought up and tucked them in her bag. Then, with everything securely zipped and locked, tagged, and ready for travel, she paused to take one last look around the room. *Goodbye? Goodbye. It won't be the same me when I come back.*

Who will I be the next time I come to stay in this room? What will me of the future be like?

Of course, God didn't tell her. She didn't expect Him to. She supposed she would have to wait and find out, like everyone else. It was up to her. And Him. She trailed her fingers over the dresser as she walked out, closing the door behind her quietly with a soft snick.

TRAINS AND TRANSITIONS

Dr. Martin Bradford

This was it.

Were goodbyes supposed to be this hard? Amy looked so young, still a child in his heart, though he knew her to be a beautiful young woman, ready to take on the world.

He wasn't supposed to call her back to him. This was the part of parenting where you were supposed to let them go, eager to see them spread their wings and fly. But he'd almost lost her not that long ago, and the world was a big and terrifying place sometimes.

Amy stood somewhat apart from him on the train platform. She talked with a great deal of enthusiasm to Bethany Shanholtz. The two girls had grown up a lot in the last year. That they could talk with such joy and animation was a testament to their friendship and their faith. He watched them hug as though it was for the last time. Here's where he was supposed to step in with the corny dad joke, to make things better. So that he could send them off laughing. That, too, was part of the duty of being a father.

What could he say, though? There should have been three girls on this platform, not two. How was he supposed to forget that?

The way they haven't. He knew for a fact his own daughter carried Rose with her every day of her life. He had no doubt Bethany did as well. That they were able to keep going after such a horrifying experience spoke volumes of their faith, not to mention their ability to keep looking forward.

May they always have that, Lord. Keep their eyes always on You.

Smiling now, he started toward them, hesitating when he heard his daughter speak.

"Wouldn't Rose have loved that movie last night? Oh, I'm glad we had a night out."

"I picked the movie with Rose in mind," Bethany said, laughing. "She loved that actor. The blond one. You know who I mean."

It stunned him that they were able to include their third even without her here. Then he saw the shadow of pain in both of their eyes. Oh, they were trying so hard. Rose would never be forgotten; he knew that with certainty now. Maybe including her was healthy, but they needed to let her go too, for Rose's sake as well as theirs. She was in God's hands now, and there was nothing better than that.

Move on, girls. Move on.

It was definitely past time for some Dad jokes. Martin rubbed his hands together, took a deep breath, and searched his mind for a good one. By "good," of course, he meant bad, something to make them groan. It was the duty of Dad, after all. He stepped into their conversation. "Hey, I was thinking of buying a new TV, but the ones I saw had 'Built-In Antenna' written on the box. Either of you know where Antenna is? It didn't come up in Google maps."

Amy stared at him in perfect silence.

"They must have a big export business; they seem to make most of the TVs these days."

"Dad, you have got to be kidding."

Bethany shoved at her friend playfully. "Well, of course, he's kidding. He's being a Dad. That's what Dads do." With that, she put her arms around him and gave him a kiss, smack in the middle of his cheek. "Thanks for being my Dad too, when I needed one," she said softly. Martin held her tightly, realizing that it hurt twice as much to lose them both. Yeah, Bethany was a good kid.

"Hey, if we're kissing Dad goodbye, I've got dibs. I saw him first!" Amy piped up, diving in to wrap her arms securely around Martin's middle. Martin let out with an "oof" but held his little girl against him.

For some reason, her comment struck everyone as hilarious, and they laughed about it until they saw the train coming in the distance. It was cathartic, a way to get the energy out between them, a way to handle not being able to say enough to each other. It was time for goodbye. It was too soon, but it always would be. Martin shifted, looking between them and the train.

"Maybe you should have taken a car," Martin said, worrying now that the inevitable was upon them. He hated the train just then. Irrational, but it was his little girl that the train was taking from him.

"Are you kidding? The campus is centrally located, and you know it's horrible to drive out there." Amy reached for her backpack and adjusted the straps. "I'll be just fine, Dad."

She was going away to college, not to the ends of the earth. But Rose had walked out of the life of Harlan Wood one day and never come back. He thought about that now, as he prayed over and over in the back of his mind a simple litany of, *Keep her safe, Lord. Please keep her safe.*

Yet she looked so radiantly happy, how could he do anything but let her go? He'd prepared her to go out into the world with every lesson. He'd given her the knowledge to succeed and the ability to discern the truth. Her incredible compassion was the gift of her mother, as was her ability with animals. When Amy returned home next, she would be a different person, one ready to take these gifts and find a way to make the world a better place because of it.

The train came screaming to a halt. Doors opened. Announcers went through a list of instructions. Amy hugged him one last time and was gone.

It all happened too fast. He stared after the train, watching it as it moved out of sight.

I should have gone with her.

He could have. He could have escorted her personally into her new dorm, helped her unpack.

Treated her like a child.

Martin winced. No. He'd done the right thing.

"Are you okay, Dr. Bradford?" Bethany asked concern etched on her face.

"Fine. Just fine."

She hugged him one last time. Maybe not as fiercely as Amy had, but it was nice all the same. Kind of like he had two daughters, not just one. Ha. Who was he kidding? Bethany had always been a second daughter to him. He couldn't have been prouder of either of them.

"You have a safe trip now, you hear?" he called after her and waved as she disappeared in the general direction of the parking lot. Dr. Martin Bradford was left alone standing on an empty train platform on a Sunday afternoon.

What was he supposed to do now?

When his phone rang, he grabbed at it as though it were a lifeline. Lance was there on the other end. A very upset Lance who was talking so fast it was nearly impossible to make out his words.

"Slow down, Lance. Tell me, what's going on?"

Martin's eyes widened as the story became clear. Suddenly the train platform seemed sinister, the world a darker place. The game was afoot, and it was Martin's turn to go.

You and me, Lord, he prayed as he bolted for his car. *We've got this.*